CLASSIFIED
OFFICE OF STRATEGIC SERVICES
WASHINGTON, D.C.

FBI WASHINGTON
7-81-47
URGENT

AT APPROXIMATELY 16:00, THIS OFFICE RECEIVED A TELEPHONIC COMMUNICATION THAT TWO JOURNALS WERE RE COVERED NEAR JOHNSON VILLAGE, COLORADO FOLLOWING INCIDENT ▮▮▮▮▮▮.

JOURNAL NO. 1 CONTAINS APPROXIMATELY TWO-HUNDRED PAGES AND IS LEATHER-BOUND. SOURCE IS A CAUCASIAN MALE: JACK REYNOLDS, AUTOMOTIVE MECHANIC, THIRTY-FOUR YEARS OF AGE.

JOURNAL NO. 2 CONTAINS APPROXIMATELY TWO-HUNDRED PAGES AND IS HARD-BOUND IN RED. SOURCE IS A CAUCASIAN FEMALE: LISA JAMES, DOCTOR OF MEDICINE, THIRTY-TWO YEARS OF AGE; OFFSPRING: REX JAMES, FOUR YEARS OF AGE, DIAGNOSED AUTISTIC.

JOURNALS BEING TRANSPORTED TO ▮▮▮▮▮▮ FOR EXAMINATION. ATTACHED DOCUMENTS ARE CLASSIFIED SECRET. NO FURTHER INVESTIGATION BEING CONDUCTED.

END

ASSOCIATED DOCUMENTS
-TWO (2) JOURNALS, APPROXIMATELY 77,000 TOTAL WORDS IN LENGTH
-INVESTIGATIVE ELEMENTS OF WORLDWIDE RHABDOVIRUS EPIDEMIC
-POSSIBLE WHEREABOUTS OF J. REYNOLDS AND L. JAMES

DEPARTMENT OF DEFENSE

Narrative Summaries of Incident 10052042
Ongoing

Attached are unclassified summaries describing the circumstances surrounding 5.5 billion incidents involving a medical emergency or epidemic.

These summaries have been released to the public and were prepared as journal entries following the ███████ outbreak. These journals were found near ███████ where patient zero was held (see figure "1.2"). Summaries include excerpts of the ███████ outbreak from two survivors whose whereabouts remain unknown.

The Department of Defense urges the public to complete the report for the purpose of safety precautions in lieu of a second medical epidemic.

ACKNOWLEDGEMENT

The Department of Defense would like to acknowledge the following individuals for their support in creating and funding this report.

Mr. Matthew ▮▮▮▮ – Supervising Editor

Mrs. Mary ▮▮▮ – Secretary of Readers

Mr. Jimmy ▮▮▮ – Singer and Songwriter for *The Bloodhound Gang*

In memoriam of Miss Alexandra (Lexi) ▮▮▮ for her continued dedication and support of this and many other projects.

This page intentionally left blank.

[Begin summary]

October 16

My son was too busy looking out the car window and watching the fiery-colored trees sweep by to notice anything was wrong.

I looked at the blood stain on my blue scrubs. I needed a distraction, so I turned my attention back to the road. I'd left the hospital immediately after an infected patient had bitten the surgeon. They were moving closer and closer.

I hit the *Seek* button on my radio again, watching it fly through the channels, trying to find a station broadcasting *anything*. But all I got was static and one classical music station. Up until about an hour prior, there were still a few news DJ's talking about the outbreak.

Just last week, Rex's father had been bitten when he was trying to get to my house. He came to the door, scratching the bite wound on his forearm. It was already starting to become red and swollen. After two days, he became extremely thirsty, but the muscle spasms in his throat caused him to fear any water I offered. The day before, he'd turned.

I winced at the sudden twinge of pain that tore through my ribs. My body had been slammed into the dresser when I'd tried to save my son from his rabid father. I'd fought him a little, but he was stronger. So, I did the only thing I could think of doing; I grabbed a nearby vase and smashed it over his head. He was dead.

But I didn't murder the father of my child. I killed one of *them*.

On the right, a McDonald's was coming up fast. I was feeling hungry, but I knew there'd be no one there. I'd probably never eat a Big Mac again. The golden arches swept by and Rex started to whine.

"Hungry!" he said, pointing out the window.

"I'm sorry, Rex, we can't stop. Not now."

He sniffed and whined louder. "Please, momma?"

"No. I told you we can't stop until we get to Aunt Sylvia's."

"But, momma! Hungry!" I could hear the tears in his voice and adrenaline pumped into my veins. I'd never be able to offer him his favorite fast food again. His childhood was taken away from him and he didn't understand why.

"I'm sorry, Rex, I'm sorry." I felt tears threatening to escape my own eyes. "But we can have ice cream when we get to Aunt Sylvia's, okay? Would you like some ice cream?"

His little round face scrunched, trying to decipher my tone. "Okay, momma."

At least I'd diffused one stressful situation. I turned back around to face the road just as another presented itself. The silhouette of a male was lumbering across the asphalt about a mile in front of us. I pressed down on the gas, watching the speedometer crawl up past seventy. The car's engine whined. Rex began to fidget.

"Momma? Fast!"

"Everything will be okay, Rex. Just close your eyes."

"No, momma! Slow!"

The infected victim was inching closer. I could see it turn to look at the car. It started to lumber toward us, dragging its feet and pulling at its hair. The speedometer went up to eighty. It was closer.

"Slow down, momma!"

I sniffed. The infected were *not* going to ruin my son's life. They were *not* going to steal his childhood away. Eighty-five miles an hour. I could see the foam dripping from its chin.

"Momma! Don't hit!"

Instinctively, my foot slammed down hard on the brake. The car swerved onto the opposite side of the empty road, narrowly missing the diseased thing that was once a human being. It dragged itself near the car. I could hear it gurgle and groan. When it started hitting its fists against Rex's window, my son scooted away, but didn't look up.

"What's wrong with him, momma?"

"That man is very sick."

"Help?"

"No, Rex," I said. "There's no helping him."

The thing was sliding its way toward the passenger window now. It clawed at the glass, trying to get inside. I turned the key in the ignition; my car had stalled when we'd skidded. It clicked, but the engine didn't turn over. I'd been meaning to take it into the shop to get it looked at, but things were crazy at work, and I'd never had a chance. I'd never have a chance again, either. And it was just too coincidental that it decided to die on me then.

"Start!" I slammed my fists into the wheel. The thing pounded harder at the window. If only I were a doctor of cars and not medicine.

"Momma."

I'm sure Rex felt my fear and frustration. He was succumbing to sensory overload and I couldn't do a damn thing to help him.

As he started to whine, the thing outside slipped back to his window, scratching at the rubber frame and tearing the nails from its fingers. Blood streaked across the glass. Rex's face was turning purple. The engine still wouldn't start. My heart pumped harder.

"Stop it now, Rex. Be quiet, please."

"Start the car, momma! Go!"

"I'm trying."

"Please, momma! Go fast. No slow!"

"I'm trying, Rex."

The key turned and the engine roared to life. I stepped hard on the gas, nearly fish-tailing. The back end of the car hit the thing as we started to drive, knocking him onto the road where he howled. That was the first time I'd ever heard one of them howl. It was such a sad sound.

Rex tried to stop crying. He tried so hard to be quiet and still the rest of the trip. He was so well-behaved. My chest grew tight. I hadn't meant to scare him.

After only thirty more minutes, we pulled off the highway and into my best friend's hometown. She lived in a town called Soledad right off the 101. Her street was entirely deserted. There weren't even any of those things around. I was certain the outbreak had reached her.

I pulled into Sylvia's driveway. After I'd shut the engine off, I sat there and realized I had no plan. What was I going to do if I got out and one of those things came out of nowhere? The car was enveloped in silence.

"Momma...?"

I jumped. Looking in the review mirror, I smiled weakly at my son. He looked so frail and small with his hands tucked under his chin.

"Lisa!"

When I heard my name, I snapped my gaze around. Sylvia was standing on her front porch, waving for me to come inside. Without another minute's hesitation, I jumped out, rounding the back and unbuckling my son from his seat.

"Lisa, hurry!" Sylvia called.

I hefted Rex into my arms. He begged me to let him down so he could walk on his own, but I refused. I wasn't going to let him run off. I reached Sylvia and she ushered us quickly into the house. Then, she spun around to bolt the door shut.

Leaning down, she patted Rex's head. "Hey, Kid. How about some ice cream, yeah?"

He bobbed his head.

"Lexi's having some right now. Go get her; she's in the kitchen."

Rex hobbled off toward where Sylvia had pointed. I started to go after him, but she put a hand on my arm.

"Where's Chase?" she asked, referring to his father.

I swallowed. "He's dead."

At first, her eyes welled with an emotion I couldn't recognize. It looked like guilt, but felt like panic. But then, she nodded. "I'm sorry, Lisa."

"It's fine."

The panic subsided into a look I knew well. She was frustrated at my lack of empathy. She sighed. "Did you hear any news?"

"Not a thing." I shook my head. "All the radio stations are down as of an hour ago."

"That's what I thought. Last I heard it had spread as far as you guys. I was so scared that you'd been...infected."

"Why aren't there any here?" I allowed her to lead me into the kitchen. Rex was already munching on some vanilla ice cream with Sylvia's twelve-year-old, Alex. I ran my fingers through his fine, dark hair.

"Dunno. They said it hasn't come this far yet. But I saw some people heading down the street this morning. They told me they were moving out of the apartments downtown because they were afraid it was coming. I don't know what they thought they were gonna do this way."

I stayed silent. It was all I could do.

"Momma, guess what?"

Surprised, I looked down at my son, ice-cream dripping from his chin and covering his hands. Sylvia moved away to get me a damp cloth. "Yes?"

"Lex got a new doll for her birthday and I gonna play with it!"

"Oh?" I glanced over at Alex. He still wasn't able to say her name right.

"Yeah. It's just a teddy bear, but some of its stuffing is coming out of its head," Alex said.

"I think it reminds her of one of them." Sylvia swept over to wipe the ice-cream from Rex's mouth and hands. I took it from her. It was my job to take care of him.

"Can I have now, momma? I want play." He watched me with dark eyes. Those were the eyes of his father. I ruffled his hair as I stood.

11

"Yes." I handed the towel back to Sylvia.

The two of them ran off up the stairs while my best friend and I stayed behind in the kitchen. Tiny footsteps echoed from the hallway until they could be heard overhead before coming to a silent stop.

"So, you haven't seen *any* of them?"

Sylvia shook her head. "Only on the news reports. But they stopped broadcasting yesterday. It's still spreading, isn't it, Lisa?"

I nodded. "Yes."

She looked me up and down. "You need to change out of those scrubs."

"I agree."

"What are we gonna do?"

"Before the broadcasts went down, did you hear something about a place called Braycart City?"

She shook her head.

"It's supposedly a sanctuary for people who aren't infected. There is a doctor there who's trying to develop a vaccine. We can go there."

"Where is it?" Sylvia wondered.

"It's in a town called Johnson Village, Colorado."

"Jesus." She hugged her arms around herself.

"We should get going pretty soon, Sylvia. Who knows how long it'll be before they come here."

October 16

Red.

All I saw was red as I tried hard to move my weakened legs. I could barely push myself forward and those things were gaining on me. Damn Biters. If I'd had a gun...

Wait...I *did* have a gun. My boss Silas had given me his sawed-off shotgun so I could protect the house.

I had the gun somewhere... But I wasn't able to find it in time. A Biter lunged at me with a bitter howl. I dodged it, slamming into a wall. My shoulder ached. I didn't even know where I was.

Another Biter was hot on my trail. It could smell me. As soon as it was aware of my presence, it came toward me. Of course I was frozen with fear. Fantastic. I was going to die and I hadn't been laid in six years...

A hollow bang bit into my eardrum. Someone had fired a shot straight through the Biter's head. It went down in a convulsion of blood and foam. And at the sound of the second bang, I was startled awake. I'd been asleep on my boss's couch the entire time.

Thank God. Or whatever.

I slowly rolled to sit upright. The pain in my shoulder was almost knocking me out again. I felt like I'd been hit by a bus, so I rubbed my hands over my face.

Heavy footsteps echoed down the hallway. Those were the angry Silas footsteps. He was steamed. I couldn't blame him. I'd fallen asleep on watch again.

As I stood – my bones creaking the whole way – I yawned and grabbed the shotgun from the side table.

"Yeah, I know. I know." The kitchen was still dark. I rolled my shoulders to ease some of the tension in my neck. "I fell asleep again. I told you I couldn't—"

My sentence stopped dead – no pun intended. My best friend was stomping down the hallway. Only he wasn't my best friend anymore. He was a Biter. Thick foam dripped from his mouth. His steps were heavy and uneven. He looked like a ghost.

"Balls."

Silas stretched out his arms. He was inches from me. I could almost feel the cold grip of his fingers. And that's when I pulled the trigger.

The blast almost turned me deaf. It was the loudest thing I'd ever heard. But my aim was on point, because there was now a decent-sized hole in my best friend's chest.

But that wasn't the shitty part. Nope. The shitty part was when he started to die. Because he grabbed his chest, stared at his bloody hand for a second, then fell against the wall. He looked up at me with eyes that were still alive.

"Why...?" His voice came with a few of those "death gurgles."

"What...?"

"It was...a prank...bro..."

"The fuck?" I knelt beside him. For some reason, I thought trying to push the blood back into his chest with both

15

hands would do something. But before I could even figure out another course of action, the life drained from his eyes. For a moment, I just sat there and stared at him, trying to comprehend what had just happened. Then I got mad.

"What the *fuck*, Silas? You think this is a motherfucking game? You can't play pranks on me you...! Jesus fucking Christ, man!" I could feel the burn of tears behind my eyes, but they wouldn't come.

No ideas of a next step came to me. My thoughts were racing at a thousand miles an hour. Should I call the police? Hospital? What was the emergency number again? Jesus Christ. Should I bury him?

Feeling around in my pockets, I found my cell phone. Then I punched in the numbers 9-1-1. A beep rang in my ear.

"We're sorry, the number you have called cannot be completed as dialed. Please hang up and try your call again."

I pulled the phone away, hung up and tried again. But again, I received the same message.

"We're sorry, the number you have called cannot be completed as dialed. Please hang up and try your call again."

The phone lines were down. All of them. Not even the landline worked. Well... At least I wouldn't go to jail.

I was just about to sit down and think about putting the shotgun in my mouth when I heard something outside. Out the window, I could see across the street to the neighbor's house. There was an old car in the driveway and a woman was hunched over the open hood. That ass, man. Damn.

"Well, since I'm a mechanic...I might as well help some booty. Body! Somebody." Gutter mind could never be cured.

I took one last look at my poor friend and headed for the door. But when I passed the giant mirror, I noticed blood all over me. There were droplets on my shirt and even my face. If I went out like that, she would have run off scared.

I turned and went to the bathroom where I hastily wiped all the blood off my face and changed into a dirty t-shirt. When I was half-way satisfied with the way I looked, I headed back toward the door.

I held the sawed-off shotgun close to my chest and stepped off the curb to the house across the street. But I realized having a huge gun in my hands would probably scare her, so I tucked it into the seat of my jeans. As I neared the house, the woman cursed and pounded her hands on the bumper of the old Honda.

"Something wrong?"

I must have startled her because she spun around to face me with lightning speed. "Jesus! I'm sorry. My car won't start," she said. "It's been doing this forever. I just haven't had a chance to take it in."

Her eyes were dark blue, almost black. I found myself mesmerized by them and her heart-shaped face. I shook myself back into reality.

"You may not get a chance again."

"I know." She sighed.

I peered into the engine, fiddling with a couple wires. I noticed the problem right away, but my mechanic's training kicked in without hesitation.

"What's it doin'?"

"Unfortunately I'm a doctor of medicine, not a doctor of cars."

That was funny. I chuckled. "Try me."

"All right. Every time I try to start it, it clicks. It takes a couple of times to start." She leaned against the hood. I caught a quick glimpse of her cleavage.

"'Kay, well, your battery's corroded, here. See the buildup around the wires?"

"Okay."

"You need a new one."

"Well, there isn't a way for me to get a new battery now."

I shrugged, wiping my hands on my jeans. "Five finger discount?"

She looked at me like I was crazy. "I've never stolen anything in my life, and I'm not about to start now."

I put my hands up in defense mode. "Got it. Sorry. Where you headed? I can let you borrow my buddy's car... He won't be using it."

She hesitated, avoiding my gaze for a moment. "We're going to Colorado."

We? "Land of legal dope, huh?" I kicked a loose pebble into the road. It skittered halfway across and stopped. She

watched it with brows knitted together. I had that effect on a lot of women.

"There may be a sanctuary there."

"Sanctu-wha?"

"A safe place to stay. What about you?"

I looked up. "Huh?"

"Don't you have someone you need to protect? It's not a good idea to stay here." There was a mother's care in her voice.

"I don't have anyone," I said. "My boss was the only one and he..." I trailed off, but she seemed to understand right away.

"He's infected." Her monotone statement caught me off guard. She must have had a killer intuition. I stayed silent.

"You should use your friend's car to get to Colorado," she said.

"Nah... You need it more than I do. Besides, I can fix yours and use it if need be. I'll just go grab the keys and be back in a sec."

"Okay."

I ran back into Silas's house, thinking about how much of an idiot I looked in front of a pretty girl. Of course, she'd never go for a guy like me, anyway. Aside from that, she seemed way serious.

I stepped over Silas's corpse. A line of sticky red stood out behind him on the wall where he'd fallen. I felt a hiccup in my chest, but I had to keep going. Silas was gone now, and it

wasn't my fault! I grabbed the keys to his SUV off the counter. And when I turned to go back out the door, I heard a woman scream.

I rushed out into the street just in time to see one of those things trying to bite the girl across the way. It was backing her up against the door to the house. She kept crying out someone's name and slamming her first against the jamb, but no one was coming to her rescue.

I sprinted across the street, trying not to listen to the thing howl and snarl. It was a terrible sound. The girl spotted me and her eyes widened.

"Help!"

It lunged for her.

But I was faster. "Bad touch!" I hit it with the butt of my rifle right in the temple. There was a loud crack, and it went down, writhing on the concrete porch. We watched the thing squirm and cry for a while. Finally, it went still.

The front door of the house flew open and a tall, dark woman looked at us in surprise.

"Lisa?!" she cried.

"Sylvia!" She went to her friend. "Where were you? Didn't you hear me?"

Sylvia looked down at the dead thing and yelped. She pulled her friend into the house, but didn't shut the door. "I was upstairs with the kids. I...I'm sorry..." She looked at me. "Did you save her?"

"Yes." Lisa answered before I could. "He saved my life."

20

"I was just in the right place at the right time." I ran a hand through my hair.

"No." She shook her head. "You saved me." Carefully avoiding the bleeding thing on the porch, she took a step toward me. Then, she looked into my eyes and asked the question. "What's your name?"

"Jack. Jack Reynolds."

"I'm Lisa James and this is Sylvia Hargrave. Why don't you come inside?"

I hesitated, clearing my throat. "I don't think—"

"Listen, Mr. Reynolds—"

"Whoa, there. Mr. Reynolds is an actor. You can call me Jack. I haven't done anything in my life to get the mister title."

There was a brief pause where they both looked at me blankly. "Okay. Jack." It was as if she tasted my name. I kind of liked the way it sounded coming from her. "Neither of us would be able to fight something like that off." She gestured toward the thing on the porch. "And neither of us know anything about cars. But you seem to. If you'd be willing to accompany us to Colorado, we'd be grateful to have your skills."

Sylvia snorted behind her. "Way to lay it on thick, Lisa."

Lisa put her hands out. "It's better to be up front and honest than dancing around the issue."

"No." I stopped them. "I appreciate it, Lisa. Can I call you Lisa?"

"'May' you call me Lisa. And yes."

"I'll go with you."

"Should we get going, then?" I followed Jack and Sylvia into the kitchen. I could already tell she was trying to make him more than her friend.

Sylvia waved a hand at me. "That was the only one of those things for miles. Quit worrying." Turning back to Jack, she put on one of her seductive smiles while batting her eyelashes. "I'm sure our new friend would like some coffee before the world runs out of it. How do you like it?"

"Like prisoners."

"What?"

He shook his head. "Never mind. Bad joke. However you're taking it."

I noticed he seemed a bit preoccupied, but I put it off as we were all preoccupied. Specifically Sylvia, but her preoccupation was with something else. When we got to the kitchen, Alex and Rex were packing a few snacks into a bag. Except Rex had gotten a hold of one of his toy cars and was driving it around the floor. Its wheels scraped the tiles.

"Who are you?" Alex was the first to speak.

"Lexi!" Sylvia scolded her daughter.

Jack bent down. "I'm Jack. I hear your name is...Lexi? Is that right?"

"Alex." She still seemed a bit guarded.

"Ah. You know what that name means?"

"No..."

"Means you're the defender of all mankind."

Alex tilted her head to one side. "That's a lot of pressure."

A smile spread across Jack's face. "You know what Lexi means?"

Sylvia's daughter perked a bit more. "What?"

"It means you have to protect all of Greece."

Alex's nose crinkled. "That's not a very good job."

"Ooh." Jack took a quick look around. "Don't tell a Greek person that."

She giggled.

"And who's this?" He turned toward Rex, but all my son did was chomp at the air as if he were vicious. "Let me guess... Jaws?"

Alex giggled again. "That's Rex. Aunt Lisa's son."

"Rex." Jack mused for a moment. "Good name. Nice to meet you, Rex."

"Rex." My son repeated his name. Sylvia turned to make coffee.

"Rex suffers from autism." I moved closer to my son as Jack stood.

"I noticed." He shrugged. "I just wasn't sure how sensitive of an issue it was."

"You noticed?"

"Yeah." He looked at me. "I had a cousin who had Asperger's. Where is he on the spectrum?"

The question put me back for a moment. No one had ever asked except doctors. "Well, he sees patterns in everything, but has trouble learning. We think he's somewhere in the middle with a mild learning disorder."

Jack nodded. "Has it been difficult?"

"Oh, hell yeah." Sylvia handed Jack a cup of coffee, but offered none to me. "That kid gives Lisa a run for her money all the time. Sometimes she can handle it, but most of the time it's a struggle."

Jack glanced at me. Presumably because he thought I'd want to start a fight, but I was accustomed to Sylvia's odd need to compete with me. I paid no mind to it any longer.

A thump on the sliding glass door caused Sylvia to yelp. She let go of her coffee mug where it shattered to pieces on the floor. Startled, Rex began to sniffle. I bent forward to pick him up. He struggled with me at first.

"Get the bags." We all looked at Jack whose focus was on the door. When we all switched our gazes, understanding flooded through everyone.

A woman with a large bite out of her shoulder was shuffling along outside. We knew she'd seen us as she'd turned and banged on the glass again. Rex whimpered. After the second attempt to break the glass, the woman began clawing at it, chomping at the air as Rex had done a few moments earlier. Foam collected at the sides of her mouth.

"Get the bags." Jack's voice once again destroyed the haze of stunned silence and booted us into action. I lurched forward with my son still in my arms and grabbed his bag. The woman pounded on the glass, causing me to jump. When Alex went to snatch her duffle, the woman threw her entire body into the door, causing it to shudder in its frame. Alex squealed.

"Let's go, guys." Jack's voice was low and calm. We turned to follow him out the front door. But as soon as we got there, an infected male popped up in the side window, howling at us. Sylvia screamed as a few more victims began rapping on the door.

"You got a fire extinguisher?" Jack asked Sylvia. When she didn't answer, he shook her shoulder gently. "Hey! You got a fire extinguisher?"

Sylvia shook her head. "Y-yeah. In the garage."

He squinted at her. "Why in the...? Forget it. Let's go."

We followed him down the hall and through the doorway to the garage. Jack began to sorting through piles of junk my friend had collected because she was too petrified to remember where the thing was. I set Rex down and joined in.

"Thanks." Jack tossed some old clothes away. They still had tags.

"We need to get out of here."

"Yeah, no shit."

We tossed boxes of crap aside until those things started running into the garage door, causing the metal bangs to reverberate off the dry wall. That only made us search faster. I was the one who found the fire extinguisher beneath a pile of discarded perfume bottles. I tossed it to Jack then ran to grab Rex.

Jack positioned himself by the door opener. "Okay, on my signal, you run across the street to my buddy's car."

I nodded. After a deep breath, Jack hit the button and the door to the garage began to slowly open. Before the damn thing was even halfway open, infected people began clawing their way underneath. Jack sprayed each one right in the face with CO_2 until they howled, clawing at their faces while running backward.

"Go!" He shouted when the door was open. We all took off running. Occasionally, he'd turn around and fire the extinguisher at them, laying them out as if he had a flamethrower. And when the thing was spent, we were only halfway there. Jack looked at it for a second, then flung the empty container into the mob of infected victims. Then, he turned and ran after us, keys in hand.

We piled into the car and immediately buckled our seatbelts. A few diseased pounded their flat palms against the windows, but Jack had already started the car and was backing out. Rex squealed as we ran over one of them. I think I heard the crack of a skull, but it happened too fast to even give it a thought.

From the Desk of Dr. Lisa James

October 17

"I just want to know how you knew there were none of the infected people here." Sylvia eyed Jack over the light of our fire while taking another swig of her beer.

Jack shrugged. "I know it doesn't look like I listen to the news, but I do." He gave her a crooked smile. She returned the gesture. I could already see the lust blossoming inside her. "They say the Biters are scared of water."

I looked behind him to the subtle waves crashing on the shore of a random beach we'd driven to.

"Hydrophobia is one of the most common symptoms in rabies," I said.

"So what did you do before this?" Sylvia ignored me. All of her attention was on him. I resisted shaking my head.

"I was a mechanic."

Sylvia sat up straight, pretending to be flabbergasted. I knew her too well. "A mechanic? With a face like that?"

Jack grinned. "Yeah, I know. People tell me that all the time. But it's another story when I'm covered in grease and you ask me who's running for president next year or what political party I belong to."

"Why would I ask you any of that?" Sylvia's tone bordered on airy ignorance.

"You got that right." Jack held out his beer and Sylvia clinked it with the neck of hers.

"What about you, Lisa?" Jack took a drink. "You said you were a doctor, right?"

"Yes. I'm a doctor."

Even in the dim firelight I could see Jack's eyes widen. "Is...there more to it than that?"

"Just don't ask her about that rash on your ass. She's not that kind of doctor." Sylvia giggled.

"I take it there's an inside joke in there." Jack took turns looking between us.

"Most everyone wants to know about a rash they have in some inadvertent part of their body I don't want to see whenever it's mentioned that I'm a medical professional. Where are the kids?"

"Relax. Lexi is watching over Rex in the SUV. They're a holler away." Sylvia brought the attention back to her. "Maybe you can show *me* your ass."

A chuckled escaped our companion. "Are you the ass doctor here?"

"Nope. I'm just the one who's focused on the right things."

"Sylvia." My tone was warning. "Please."

"Hey, you had your chance. It's mine now."

"And...exactly what have I stumbled into the middle of?" Jack's voice began at a normal tone, but collected in a crescendo at the end of his sentence.

"Sylvia is a serial dater." I glared at her, but she ignored me.

Jack raised an eyebrow directed at her. Her face remained smug.

"Oh, yeah. See, I just like to have sex. Sex is great and everyone involved benefits from it. It's not my fault you didn't marry Chase when you had the chance."

"Can we please stay off that topic?" I wasn't in the mood to discuss Rex's father.

"Okay, now I really need to know what's going on." Jack had placed his beer in the sand to lean back on his hands.

"No, you don't."

"Yes! He does." Sylvia was beginning to act air-headed — a sure sign she was smitten. "See...Rex's dad, Chase, had asked Lisa to marry him when she got pregnant."

"Sylvia."

Jack held up a hand. "No, it's ok. I'm intrigued."

"Yes, but I'm not. I've heard this story a thousand times. I've lived it."

"Then you can hear it one more time!" Sylvia laughed and leaned forward to put a hand on Jack's knee. Then, she scooted closer to him. "So, they were engaged, right? And everything seemed okay until Lisa did this ultrasonic test or something—"

"Prenatal test." If I was going to hear the story again, I was going to hear it correctly.

"Whatever. Prenatal test. And it turned out the baby had a seventy-five percent chance of having some sort of defect. Which...well...you can see... Anyway, Chase up and bailed. Couldn't deal with it. I told Lisa she should try and go after him, but she's too damn stubborn. Has too much pride."

"Yikes." Jack said the word as if he'd been holding his breath the entire time. "Chivalry really is dead, isn't it?"

"Not entirely, right Jack?" Sylvia's hand lingered too long on Jack's thigh. When he didn't respond within her time table, she pretended to lose balance and flop into his lap laughing.

"Okay, sweetheart, I think you've had enough." There was reluctant laughter in his voice as he sat her back up.

"Momma, momma!"

We all turned as Alex sauntered into the firelight.

"What is it, kiddo?" Sylvia's voice sounded bored.

"I found this, see? What is it?" She held out a gold object with what looked like a button on the end. Sylvia studied it for about half a second.

"I don't know. Go back to bed."

"Let me see." Jack held out his hand. Alex turned and gave him her new toy. He looked it over carefully, inspecting every angle. "Where did you get it?"

"In the glove compartment."

"Huh...wonder why Silas put it there. It's a straight key."

"Does it unlock a door?"

He laughed. Sylvia announced she was getting another drink and stood to leave. "Nope. This was used to communicate across big distances way back when. It's used for Morse code."

"Oh, cool! I learned about that in school. Do you know Morse code?"

"Sure do."

"Can you teach me?"

"Maybe one night I'll show you, ok, honey?" He handed it back to her.

"Okay! Goodnight, Auntie Lisa."

"Goodnight, sweetie."

"Goodnight, Jack."

Jack smiled. "'Night, honey."

She took a moment to study him before running back to the SUV to sleep. Jack and I were alone. The story Sylvia always told to male guests about my relationship with Chase was inappropriate. Every time, I would tell her to stop, but she'd keep going. It was almost as if she wanted men to steer clear of me. It didn't faze me too badly, however. I had Rex to look after. There wasn't much time for dating.

"So what did you specialize in?"

Jack's voice tore me out of my thoughts. "Oh. When I started the program, I wasn't sure what I wanted out of it. All I knew is that I wanted to be in medicine. I spent a semester attending a surgeon, but it didn't quite challenge me enough. I followed a podiatrist, but I didn't learn anything. Then there was private practice. That was where I met Chase."

"Oh, was he a doctor, too?"

"No, he was a patient. He'd come in for a domestic abuse case." I paused, lost in my own thoughts. "But it was her who'd hit him."

Jack nodded while watching the fire.

"I actually ended up attending at a hospital. I liked that work much better. Several new cases daily and I had to learn a blanket of things. I was able to assess and recommend treatments. I worked right up my delivery day."

"Wow. Tough gal."

I shrugged. "It was what I felt I was meant to do. I'd still be at that hospital if the doctors hadn't all been infected."

"How did you get away?" Jack asked.

I looked at him. His attention seemed genuine. "I ran." It was a simple answer, but the truth.

He nodded again. "So, you didn't study rashes, huh?"

"I studied dermatology for a semester, yes, but that morphed into oncology due to so many skin cancer patients."

He paused. "That...was a joke."

I cleared my throat. He was decent at making humorous comments. One could hardly tell when he was serious. He reminded me of my father.

"California and their skin cancer..." Jack mused.

"Indeed. It was just very easy work. No challenges. Psychology was entertaining for a bit, but it's difficult listening to other people's issues all day."

"Oh, so you were a shrink?"

"Yes."

"Are you going to try and diagnose my problems?" There was amusement in his voice, but I didn't find the sentence funny.

"I already have."

He gave me somewhat of a skeptical smirk. "Oh, really? Then what's wrong with me?"

"Nothing."

There was another pause. "I don't think I've ever heard a shrink say that to anyone."

I shifted my weight to the right. Sand was beginning to build up on the tops of my feet. "Well, I'm not after your money, so I can tell the truth."

Jack laughed out loud.

"That wasn't a joke. It was an assessment."

"Still funny. So... What's my deal?"

I straightened up with a sigh. He wasn't a very complicated person, so it wouldn't take long. "Aside from deflecting your fear with humor, you're a very mentally healthy person overall. You kept a stable job that you enjoyed and were able to live by yourself without requiring companionship. But, there's something missing. There's someone you feel the need to protect but for some reason, you won't."

Jack gave a nervous shift of his weight. "Where'd you get that?"

"When I asked you if you had anyone to look after, there was a bit of a wistful pause."

He hummed to himself. "Uh-huh... What about you? Do you ever assess yourself?"

"Daily."

"Oh." There was a hint of upward lift at the end of his word. As if he'd discovered something interesting.

"Yes. I'm very aware of my idiosyncrasies. But I've made those personality decisions on my own. With Rex, I have absolutely no time for fun or games. My life is dedicated to him and that's how things are going to be for a while."

He pursed his lips, but nodded. "I like it when someone sticks to their guns. No pun intended."

I allowed myself a thin smile. He was quite well-timed as far as jokes went. Sylvia finally returned, but without a drink.

"All out?" Jack stood and brushed sand from his jeans.

"All out." Sylvia grinned wide at him, then threaded her arm through his. "I suppose it's time for bed now, huh?"

I could hardly hold in my groan.

October 17

"Huh...I could have sworn I brought a twelve pack." Sylvia and I rounded the front of the SUV where I'd set the beer. Lisa jumped in the back after saying a quick goodnight. Although I would have preferred to keep talking to her, I let it go. She was so damn serious and I'd almost gotten her to laugh.

"Oh..." Sylvia came around to my front and lowered her voice. "There are still four in there, but I thought we could keep them to ourselves." Her smile was just far too lopsided to be accidental. Although the sentiment was odd, I smiled.

"Ok..."

Without another word of warning, she grabbed my hand and yanked me to the front of the car. Then we sat in the sand and opened another bottle each. Clinking the neck of her bottle with mine, Sylvia crossed her legs, purposely letting her knee touch mine.

"I just *had* to get you away from her." She took a long swig of beer.

"Is there something I'm missing here?" I set my bottle down. I wasn't in the mood for alcohol anymore.

Sylvia tossed her head back and sighed. "Lisa is the most boring human being I know." She sent me a glance. "I can't imagine what she was regaling you with, but it must have sucked."

Sheesh. *She* was Lisa's best friend? "Maybe I like boring."

Sylvia scoffed. "You're just being nice."

"I thought you guys were like...good friends."

A laugh escaped her. "Oh, yeah, we are. I just like to speak my mind. I'm probably the most offensive person you'll ever meet. Just an F-Y-I."

That one statement told me all I needed to know about the woman.

"And in that same light, I'll get right down to the point. Jack, let's fuck."

The sentence was so sudden I almost laughed. On instinct, my eyes widened as she leaned toward me. In response, I leaned away.

"Hold on, there." After putting a protective hand out, I scooted backward in the sand. "I don't think that's the best idea."

She cocked her head to the left. "And why not?" Her hand slowly slid up my leg toward my crotch, but I caught it.

"You're not my type. I'm sorry."

In an instant, she snatched her hand away and put it on her hip. "Oh, what? I'm not your type 'cause I'm Latina?" She said the last word with tilt of her head and a thick accent.

"Oh, come on. Don't play that card."

"Excuse me?" She stood up, kicking a bit of sand my direction. "I'm not playing a card, man. You're the one who's a racist!"

"Hey, hey." I mirrored her stance. "I enjoy a politically incorrect joke every now and then, but come on. We're fucking

adults, here. There's no need to treat this like a middle school playground."

The sassy look remained on Sylvia's face. Her lips were pursed tightly together as if she'd spew forth volcanic lava if she opened her mouth.

"Lo que sea, culo. Chico blanco estúpido. You'll come crawling back, because you know I'll blow your mind." With that, she turned on her heel, put up her hand and sashayed away like a model.

I closed my eyes and let out a long breath. "Thank God I don't speak Spanish."

*　　*　　*

The crashing of the waves lulled me to sleep, but something else woke me hours later. It was a sort of shuffling sighing noise. I was halfway awake when a thump got my ass up.

I sat up in the sand. The fire had died down, but I could still see. A soft white light from the moon washed over the beach. Its reflection swayed in the waves as they jumped onto the shore. I swallowed hard.

I heard the sigh again. As I turned, that's when I saw it. A Biter was making its way toward the car. The fire tossed orange shadows across its weathered face, highlighting the foam dripping from its mouth in a surreal way.

My thoughts shifted toward an indifferent "oh well." I'd slept out in the sand because I could protect my new friends if

one them of happened by. But also because Sylvia was one of those women who no doubt would make sure I'd get no sleep.

I shook the rest of my sleepy thoughts out of my head and reached for my gun. Except it wasn't there. There was only empty sand. Panic set in. My heart began to thump against my ribcage. As quietly as I could, I searched the beach in a few inch radiuses around me, but found nothing. I must have left it on the seat in the SUV. Fuck.

And as I looked back toward the Biter, my stomach fell to my knees. Silas was sitting quietly at the fire, grinning at me.

"You're in trouble now, ain't ya?"

I swallowed hard, trying to blink. Only I was frozen. My muscles refused to move. There was my old friend – just sitting there like nothing had ever happened.

"Hey!" Silas turned and waved to the Biter. "Over here! Dude! Raw meat! Over here!" When the thing didn't respond, he turned back and rolled his eyes. "The thing's deaf."

Finally, I shut my eyes. And when I opened them again, Silas was gone. But the Biter wasn't. It was fumbling closer and closer to the vehicle. It hadn't seen me yet, so I scrambled around the front of the car and quietly opened the driver's side door. After a brief search of the seats and glove compartment, I realized my gun was still missing.

Behind me, someone stirred in their sleep. I did the first thing that came to mind and flung myself into the backseat on top of whoever had moved. All it would take was one sound to make that thing come closer.

Fortunately, I hadn't landed on top of Sylvia. Instead it was Lisa. As soon as she opened her eyes, our gazes met. I probably looked pretty weird since I was scared shitless. But her almost immediate response surprised me.

She twisted her face into a grimace. "Oh, really? Seriously? So, you're going to rape me? If you don't get off right now, your testicles will be in your throat."

Under any other circumstances, her statement would have made me chuckle, but instead, I put a finger to my lips and cocked my head toward the Biter outside. After one glance, she shut up.

"Stay here," I whispered as I eased up.

She nodded.

"What the fuck am I gonna kill it with?"

"They're sensitive to light."

I looked back at Lisa. She was clutching the blankets to her chest. Her eyes were wide with what I could only assume was panic.

"Kill it with fire?" My question was more of a silly statement, but she nodded again.

I took a deep breath and exited as swiftly as I could. The Biter had drifted off toward a sand dune, but was still too close for comfort. None of us would sleep with it so close. And since the car was parked in sand, it was going to take a good shove to get it going.

I crept toward it. When I was close to the fire, I bent down and grabbed one of the logs that was still flaming. The

Two Men and a Lift Auto Garage

"We Auto Know"

Biter was facing away from me and had stopped walking. It was just standing there growling and grumbling. I was feet away when I decided to take a swing. Holding the log like a baseball bat, I brought it down on the Biter's head. There was a sickening crack, but the thing didn't go down. Instead, it turned and screeched at me. In one swift movement, it knocked the log out of my grip. The fire fizzled out in the sand.

"Well, fuck."

The Biter took a step toward me, reaching its arms out and gnashing its teeth. I was pretty fucked.

"Jack!"

I turned to see Lisa with my gun in her hand. She tossed it toward me. It sailed through the air and I caught it, only to turn around and face the creature again.

"Bye bye, fucker." With one squeeze of the trigger, the thing's head exploded into a thousand bloody bits. I had to admit it was mildly satisfying. I turned back to the SUV to see everyone standing outside with horrified expressions. My legs felt like gelatin, but I kept my cool as I approached them.

"Whew! We're all safe thanks to Lisa Croft here." I tucked my gun into the seat of my jeans and smiled at her.

Her eyebrows knitted together. "My last name is James."

"Are you serious?"

"He's talking about Lara Croft, Lisa. Tomb Raider?" Sylvia rolled her eyes.

"I see."

"So...where the hell did my gun end up?"

Lisa glanced at Sylvia whose face remained blank. "It was in the backseat."

I studied the two of them for a moment. "She took it, didn't she?" I gestured toward Sylvia.

"Why the hell would I do that?" She raised her voice.

"You did, momma. I saw you put it under you before you went to sleep." Alex stared up at her mother.

Sylvia looked down at her with fire in her eyes. "*Mocosa! Has olvidado quién soy?* Go to bed!"

"But momma!"

Sylvia grabbed the little girl's upper arm and dragged her back inside the car. Even though the two were out of sight, we could still hear Sylvia berating her daughter in Spanish.

"Lovely."

"For the record, I never saw her take it."

I looked back at Lisa. Her face was completely blank. I couldn't read it. "You know in some other countries people get stoned to death for lying."

"I'm not. I'm just a terrible truth-teller."

I let out an amused chuckle. "Haven't heard that one before."

After a moment of silence where we stared into each other's eyes, she said, "You saved our lives again."

I shrugged. "I didn't do anything I wouldn't have done otherwise."

"Well, regardless of that...thank you."

There was a strange electricity humming through my body. I recognized it as a kindergarten crush-like feeling. I was into her, but there was no way she'd ever go for me. And if I didn't say anything in the proceeding seconds, she'd probably think I was a pervert, too.

"Don't mention it, pal."

Well that was stupid. But what was stupider was making my hand into a fist and nudging her shoulder with it like she was my bro. I even nudged too hard, because she winced.

"Ouch."

"Shit. Sorry." I pasted a stupid grin on my face.

Jesus Christ. What the fuck?

"Where are we going?" Sylvia asked as I took an exit into Bakersfield. I'd already had more of her than I wanted to deal with, so my answer was short.

"I need ammo."

"Oh-kay." There was an upward lilt to her statement as if she were talking to her scolding father. I imaged her rolling her eyes along with it.

"Perhaps we should search for food, while we're at it." Lisa leaned forward in her seat like she was looking at something. I saw it too. A car was coming toward us on the opposite side of the street. It was a minivan packed with household items and luggage. We slowed at the same time. The man inside prompted me to roll the window down.

"Rabies in town. Everyone got the hell outta dodge this mornin'," he said.

"Mr. Avery?" Lisa leaned over me. I could smell her sweet scent.

"Dr. James! I thought you'd left. What're you doin' back out here?"

"We're headed to Colorado. Is your family safe? Anyone hurt?"

Avery tilted his head. "We're okay. But I'd turn tail if I was you."

"I need ammo." I cut in, wanting to get out of the town myself.

Avery scratched his partially bald head. "Wal-Mart's been cleared out since a month. You won't find nothin' there."

"Damn." Lisa sat back in her seat.

"But Andy's probably got somethin'. He was hanging around until this morning. Didn't bring nothin' with him other than a duffel."

"Oh, that's right!" Lisa moved closer, putting her palms against the driver side window frame. She was so close. "Mr. Avery, thank you. Please be safe. Take care of your family."

He nodded. "I will, Dr. James. You do the same."

She returned with a bob of her head as I rolled the window back up. "Let's head over to Andy's bait shop. It's just a few blocks away."

I began to drive again. "How do you know that?"

"Bakersfield is relatively close to my home. I come here often when I need to get away."

"Does everyone have a southern accent here?"

"Something like that," she said. "Turn here."

I did as I was told and took a right down a street with a few small shops and a McDonald's. When I parked, I paused to make sure there were no Biters around.

"Okay, guys. Let's be careful." I helped everyone out of the car before taking another look around.

But just as we were about to head into the ammo shop, a scream erupted from behind the closed doors of the dark McDonald's. We all stopped and looked at each other. While I knew ammo was important, I also knew saving a life could possibly be done without it. So, I turned the other direction while everyone else followed.

A warped handprint in blood streaked across the outside of the glass. There was no movement inside. I looked back to my partners and gave them a tilt of my head before moving forward. We pressed ourselves against the side of the building in case any Biters inside saw us. And that was the moment I realized what we were doing was a pretty fucking bad idea.

"Holy... What the shit?"

"What is it?" Lisa's harsh whisper almost scared me.

"When the balls did they start serving breakfast all day? What did I miss?"

There was a silence as I stared at the faded poster in the window.

"Are you fucking serious right now?" Sylvia's whisper was angry.

"Your damn right I'm serious. Who knew about this? I've been—" Another scream cut off my sentence. Slightly frustrated, I decided then was the time to burst through the door and try to save whoever might have still been alive. Even though all I was armed with was an empty shotgun.

"All right, you overgrown teether, drop the dentures and step away from the warm blood."

The scene in front of me froze. A pimply-faced teenager stood, soaked in blood, above a dead Biter. How do I know the thing was dead? Well, there was half a sharpened broom stick embedded in its skull.

"Are you serious right now?" It was Sylvia who broke the silence.

"Answer the lady's question, pizza-face."

"I was talking to you."

I turned my head. "Huh?"

"Don't shoot!"

"What?" I turned back to the kid who had his hands high in the air. Then I looked at my gun. "Oh." Shoving it back in the waist band of my jeans, I stepped forward. "Sorry. It's not loaded. You all right, kid?"

The teen dropped the other half of his broomstick.

Ha. Broomstick. Like Boomstick. That's funny.

"I...think so?"

"Did you get bitten?" Lisa walked around me and approached him.

"Yeah...he got my shoulder."

My lovely companion introduced herself and told the kid – whose name was Kevin – they were going to go wash the wound with hot soapy water. Once they disappeared, I drug the other body into the maintenance closet where no one had to sit and look at it.

Blood soaked into the uniform the Biter was wearing. The only thing shittier about working at McDonald's was dying while you worked at McDonald's. I wiped blood from the former kid's nametag. Red collected in the black lettering, giving his name a morbid outline. ANDY.

"Too bad. Kid died a virgin."

I knew that voice. But I was too scared to face it. There was no way in hell Silas was behind me. So I ignored him, hoping he'd go away.

"Ignoring me is only going to make me louder."

He was bluffing.

"You can't have no fun with an unloaded gun!"

Okay. He wasn't bluffing. He was singing.

"My dad says that's for pus—"

"Shhhhut it!" I hissed the words through my teeth while standing to face him. It was him all right. Except he was white as a ghost. A smile stretched across his face.

"Atta boy."

I looked down at the bloody hole still in his chest. With each breath, a bit of lung came into view. I swallowed hard.

"You look like Rob Zombie threw up on you."

Silas laughed. "And you look just like Ryan Reynolds fucked a dragon."

"That...that is amazing. I'm not even mad."

Silas shrugged. "Uh-oh. Here comes mommy."

"Everything okay?" Lisa emerged from the bathroom with Kevin in tow.

I swung around to look at her. And when I turned back, Silas was gone. "Uh... Yeah. Just gonna grab a weapon." I stooped down to the body again. "Sorry, Andy. Life sucks sometimes." I grabbed the end of the stick jutting out of his head. Then, I pulled with all the strength I had. With a sickening

gush, the wood worked free and I had a new weapon in hand. Just in case.

"What's the 4-1-1?" I asked, heading back out into the lobby.

"There's really no way to tell. We got here just in time. I might have been able to wash the infected saliva out of the wound. Only time will tell."

"Who's hungry?" The statement was more of a joke, but nobody was in the mood for any jokes. I couldn't win. Lisa's response surprised me.

"I could use something. We should all eat, really."

"There are still some patties and stuff in the kitchen," Kevin said, wincing as he sat.

"Yummy." Alex looked up at her mother. Sylvia just rolled her eyes. No doubt wondering what kind of chemicals were in each and every bun.

"Can't be that hard." I went into the back and searched for any kind of food. Luckily, I found about ten burger patties, a bunch of buns and even some French fries. It wasn't until Alex, Rex and Sylvia had already eaten that Lisa approached me in the back.

"What's up, doc?" I sat on the front counter in between two blank registers.

Lisa took a deep breath. "It doesn't look good."

"No?" I turned to look at the poor bitten kid. Sylvia and the kids were sitting around him completely clueless to his pale sweating face. "No shit."

Two Men and a Lift Auto Garage

"We Auto Know"

"It's really only a matter of time."

I grimaced. "Yikes." After jumping off the counter and side-stepping the blood, I got their attention. "I think everybody but Kevin should head to the back office and lock the door."

That's when they all noticed his face and listened to me without a fight. But Lisa didn't immediately follow. I gestured her inside, but she stayed put.

"I'd rather stay out here with you. I'm a doctor."

"You don't say." It was meant to be a light-hearted joke, but the look on her face made me think I'd gone too far. I instructed Sylvia to lock the door behind her and joined Lisa in the lobby, making sure I had my sharpened stick. We were silent for a few moments while Kevin's breathing became heavier. He didn't even seem to be aware of what was happening.

"Sorry if that was a bit harsh. I didn't mean anything by it."

Lisa shrugged without taking her eyes off the teen. "I'm used to snarky people. I can't tell you how many patients think the Internet is a good place to get medical advice."

I looked at her, widening my eyes in the most cartoonish way I could. "It's not?"

She arched an eyebrow at me, but I could see the hint of a smile on her pretty lips. "It's not."

We remained in a staring contest for a few seconds. I was able to see that she was, indeed, super cute. While pretty petite and thin, I had no doubt she could kick a set of testicles

52

Two Men and a Lift Auto Garage

"We Auto Know"

hard enough to rupture them. Why had that thought entered my head? What the fuck?

A groan interrupted our unique moment. We turned to look at poor Kevin who had knocked over a cup of water and was freaking the fuck out. As soon as the water touched his arm, he stood and screeched like a toddler.

"Oh boy..."

Lisa and I were already backed into the counter, so when Kevin saw us and began lumbering forward with an odd hunger in his eyes, I decided to push the wooden stick out in front of me and see if any of the kid's brain hadn't melted yet.

"Stay back!" I shoved my weapon toward him. He stopped in his tracks, but didn't retreat. "I mean it, kid!"

He took another step forward.

"I'll fucking rip you open and spill your guts on the floor."

"You do know that's not possible, right?"

"Huh?" I lashed out with the stick again, nearly hitting him.

"There's connective tissue and muscle holding our organs together. Cutting someone open doesn't automatically spill their guts."

"The more you know." I thrust the stick at the monster formerly known as Kevin once more, but that seemed to piss him off. He lunged forward and I did the only thing I could think of doing – I swept the broom stick in an arch, catching the side of his stomach and ripping a nasty hole in him.

53

Dark red blood and a string of intestines spilled down his legs and across the floor, splashing onto our shoes. Lisa didn't even hop back. Not even when Kevin let out his last breath and crumpled to the floor.

"I stand corrected," Lisa said after a moment's silence.

"No." We looked at each other. "You stand in guts."

October 17

I decided I needed to clean the blood and tissue off my clothes after we left the bait shop, so we stopped by the first house we saw. Because there was really no one left in the town the family who lived there wouldn't mind if we let ourselves in to shower and change.

The house was a two-story on the corner of a quiet neighborhood. It was painted yellow with white shutters. It was cute. And the door was unlocked. Jack put a hand on my arm as I opened it.

"I'll go first."

I nodded, allowing him ahead of me. After a few moments, he motioned the rest of us inside. He then stood just inside the door, humming a song to himself that I didn't recognize. The house was quiet, but everything was in its place. It was such a difference from everywhere else we'd been. It was a home stuck in time.

I walked slowly through the hallway, feeling like an intruder in someone else's domain. My fingertips brushed a stack of books. The covers were worn, scratching against my skin.

"Anybody breathing in here?" Jack's voice made me look back for a moment. His eyebrows shot up as if he were giving me a flirty look. Upon returning to my walkthrough, I noticed the door to what seemed like a dining room ajar. I could see a corner of an oak table peeking through. On top of that was someone's hand.

"In here." Without waiting for everyone else, I pushed through. The table was set with an elegant looking meal. A large turkey sat in the middle surrounded by several sides. The candles were unlit. Plates were clean.

A family of four was seated around the food. They looked as if they were in the middle of a prayer – heads down and eyes closed. But none of them seemed to notice our presence.

"Well, hello."

I turned to find Jack, Sylvia, Alex and Rex standing at the entrance to the dining room. I sighed while placing two fingers against the father of the family's neck. There was no pulse. I shook my head.

"You know, I always found it funny," Jack said, picking up a half full wine glass. "In every movie or TV show where a doctor looks for a pulse and there isn't one, they always look up and shake their head." He sniffed the wine and made a face. "Whew! I think this has gone bad."

I approached him and put my hand on his forearm to lower it to my height. Then I took the glass from his hand. Our fingers touched briefly. The glass made a subtle swoosh sound against his skin. I took a whiff. There was a strong garlicky odor.

"Arsenic. They poisoned themselves."

"Why would they do that?" Sylvia took a step back.

"They probably didn't think they'd survive. It's rather poetic."

"Can't say I blame them." Jack tucked his shotgun back in the waist of his jeans and sighed. "You know some guys just can't hold their arsenic."

I heard Sylvia make the noise she usually made when someone offended her. "That's disgusting! Why would you say that?"

In my peripheral vision, I saw Jack shrug.

"Lisa! Tell him that's gross. It's in poor taste!"

I echoed his movement. "I didn't think it was disingenuous. It's actually very true. Some people can't."

"Boo-yah! Up high, bro!"

I reluctantly patted the palm of his hand with mine while checking the pulses of the rest of the family. When I got to the young boy at the table, I felt the faint thump of a heartbeat. Immediately, I instructed Jack to help me bring the boy to the floor.

"We need to induce vomiting. Push him on his side."

Jack did as I asked and turned the child on his side. I reach my index finger inside his mouth, causing his body to push bile into his throat. Once the airway was clear, I began chest compressions. He needed CPR right away if we were going to save him.

After a few seconds, the boy's color began to resurface and he coughed a few times. When his eyes opened, I could see confusion in them.

"Woo!" Jack stood up, throwing his hands in the air. "Shit yeah!"

"Where am I?" The child asked.

"Shh. Just relax." I sat him up and held his shoulders in place while he regained composure. However, once he noticed his family sitting around the table motionless, he stood on shaky legs and began to get upset.

"Daddy! Mommy! No! I shouldn't be here!" He ran to his father to shake him awake, but the only thing that accomplished was causing the body to slump over onto the table. Tears streamed down the child's face. I tried to stand to comfort him, but he saw the serrated knife before I could get to him. In a movement so quick no one could react, he grabbed the knife, plunged it into his throat and drew a dark line across his neck.

Sylvia put a hand over Alex's eyes as blood began to pour down his clothes and onto the white tablecloth. I ran to the child, placing both hands over the wound. But his heartbeat was strong from my resuscitations, and blood bubbled through my closed fingers. He gasped his last breaths while clinging to his father's body.

"Jesus Christ on a cream cheese and smoked salmon crudités." Jack's words were softly spoken, but full of a sadness that was difficult to hear.

Once again, my clothes were soaked in someone else's blood. After a heavy sigh, I stood to collect my thoughts.

"How in shit's sake are you used to this?" Jack rounded the table, placing a hand on my shoulder.

I motioned Rex to come to me. He did so, hugging my legs. "I once lanced a palm-sized fistula in the anus of a three-hundred pound woman."

"Forget I asked."

*   *   *

We'd been on the road for an entire day in the SUV Jack had allowed us to borrow. It was difficult to shake off the scene at the house we'd been to earlier, but the car was comfortable and made everyone somewhat happy. It was a sixteen hour drive, and a trip like that was nearly impossible to make in one go with Rex. Even after spending the night somewhere, we still had to constantly make stops because he was tired, carsick or hungry.

From the Desk of Dr. Lisa James

We were on highway 15, just an hour past the Nevada State Line. Las Vegas loomed in front of us. I'd only been there once about five years prior. Sylvia had taken me as a bachelorette present after I'd said yes to Chase's proposal. Of course, he and I didn't even make it to the florist.

Even so, I remembered the city being vibrant—full of color, lights, and life. Now, as we drove past the main strip, it looked dirty and deserted. The electronic Mandalay Bay sign was blank, the large 'M' hanging at an awkward angle, threatening to fall at any moment. Every once and a while, I'd see a spark shoot out of the giant screen.

"Stop!" Sylvia suddenly shouted from the backseat.

The car screeched to a halt, almost fishtailing into the Mercedes parked in the dirt. The vehicle's two occupants dove out of the way in a flash. I stared at Jack in the driver's seat.

"What are you doing?"

"Those people aren't infected. We should help them." He looked at me with hope in his eyes.

"Momma?"

I turned to give Rex my attention. "Everything's fine, Rex. We're just going to give the nice couple a ride."

He sniffed. "'Kay, Momma."

"Stay here." Jack unbuckled his seat belt and opened the door to step out onto the empty freeway. I did as I was told.

"Such a man." Sylvia huffed. "Always thinkin' he's in charge."

"He saved our lives and he doesn't seem to have a problem getting rid of those things." I watched him walk in front of the car and toward the people. "Don't be upset just because he hasn't agreed to sleep with you."

60

Sylvia leaned back in the seat and scowled, absently stroking Alex's hair as she watched out the window. "Whatever you say, Lisa."

I watched Jack talk with the couple. They spoke for a few moments, but his face remained blank. I'd talked to him quite a bit over the last two days, so I knew he felt like an education was what made a person smart. But he wasn't stupid. He was brandishing a pretty good poker face.

The woman gestured behind her, then off down the highway, then brought her hands to her face. Her shoulders started to shake with sobs. The man put his arm around her and said something to Jack who nodded.

I rolled down my window as he approached, his face too serious for my comfort. "What's going on?"

"They said they hit some spikes on the road a ways back." He looked down the highway from the direction we'd come.

"I didn't see anything."

"I didn't either. But their tires are shot and they're not going anywhere. Lady says while her husband was trying to put a spare on—wouldn't have done any good, anyway." He lowered his voice. "Lady says some...people came out of nowhere and held 'em up at gunpoint. Says they took their daughter."

"Their daughter?" I sat up.

"Mm..."

"What do you make of it?" Sylvia poked her head between the seats.

"Dunno... Way I see it, we can do one of two things. We can help these nice folks find their daughter, or leave 'em stranded here. I doubt another car's gonna come down this road for a while."

"We can't leave them here."

"We can't just go off on a wild goose chase, either, Lisa!" Sylvia said. "We've got our kids to think about!"

I spun around to face her. She was holding Alex close for the first time since she'd been born. "What if Alex had been kidnapped? If something were to happen to Rex, I'd do anything to get him back."

"Nothing happened, Momma. I right here." My son looked at me.

"I know, Rex." I leaned forward and patted his fine dark hair.

Jack cleared his throat. "I don't think they're lying."

"How can you be so sure?" Sylvia's question sounded more like a demand.

He glanced back at the couple who were now locked in an embrace. "Because their car is full of food and clothes. The guy's packing, too. He doesn't look like the type to use it, though. They drive a Mercedes, nice clothes, and his wife's got enough ice to stop global warming."

"Cute..." Sylvia snorted.

"What I'm saying is...they have no reason to lie. All they want is for us to help them find their little girl."

"What do you think we should do, Jack?" I leaned both hands on the windowsill.

He paused, lost in a moment of thought. Whatever he said next, I would do without hesitation. It felt very strange giving my unconditional trust to someone I barely knew. But there was something about him that made me feel safe.

"We should help them," he said.

"Then that's what we're going to do." I pulled my door handle to exit the car. He stepped back so I could get out as Sylvia voiced her disapproval.

"You're gonna put us all in danger, Lisa."

"Then stay in the car." I slammed the passenger door.

Luckily, I didn't hear another protest out of my best friend. I followed Jack toward the couple. The woman was now wiping her eyes with a neatly folded handkerchief. My companion was right; she did have a lot of jewelry. It sparkled in the harsh sunlight.

"Hi, I'm Dr. Lisa James." I extended my hand out to the man. He looked at it for a moment, the beginnings of a sneer pulling on one corner of his mouth. But then, he ripped his arm away from his wife and shook my hand.

"Rupert Meyers. This is my wife Cynthia."

"We'd like to help." I nodded at the woman.

"You...you'd help us?" She sniffed.

"You should come with us," Jack broke in. "You won't get anywhere in that car of yours."

Rupert Meyers eyed the Jeep we'd been driving as if it were less precious than his opulent Mercedes. I had to remind myself to let the rich have their money. I'd grown up comfortably with the trust fund left to me by my late parents, but it wasn't enough to buy a mansion and a Mercedes. I would have opted for something more reliable and fuel-efficient, but I was far too busy with work and Rex to even shop for shoes.

"Very well." Rupert Meyers eyed us. "But we should go on foot to cover more ground. Just let us collect a few things before we leave it."

"Right." Jack nodded his approval. I followed him back to the car, biting my tongue at the acidic remarks I would have loved to toss the couples' way. "Didn't have the heart to tell the man he may never see his precious $80,000 car again." Jack had muttered so far under his breath that I almost hadn't heard him.

"Eighty-thousand?" I kept my voice at a harsh whisper.

"Yup, all the bells and whistles. I'm sure he doesn't even know how to use the climate control to its full potential, either. And he has the nerve to look down at Silas's car." He shook his head. "That Jeep has a state of the art sound system *and* a GPS I built myself. He's gonna have a real hard time when someone sticks it to him. He's not rich anymore."

For the first time since the whole mess had started, I felt a twinge of humor run through me. What he'd said was utterly true as well as amusing. This man had yet to have a wake-up call, and it was going to be awfully rude.

"Upper class no longer exists."

Jack tossed me a sideways smile. He was actually not a terrible looking man. I found myself wondering what he looked like with grease and sweat covering his body after working on a vehicle. But I stopped myself before the thought was completed.

I opened the door to let Sylvia and Alex out before getting to Rex. He welcomed me with a tilt of his head.

When Rupert and Cynthia Meyers were finished collecting their things, they approached us, staring with blank, skeptical gazes at my best friend and the two children. Sylvia motioned gave them a smile.

"I'm Sylvia Hargrave. This is my daughter, Alex, and this little youngster is Rex, Lisa's son."

My son immediately turned red, buried his face in his hands, and whined. The rich couple gave reluctant hellos, encouraging us to begin our search. Within moments, we were off on what may have been a wild goose chase.

October 17

There was no reason not to trust the couple. I'd fixed a lot of expensive cars in my day, and rich idiots like them always made my skin crawl. They always, *always* argued about the amount of money they owed—like they couldn't spare it.

But in dire times, everybody had to help everybody else. Karma. If I helped them now and got in trouble later, they might be there to help *me* out. I didn't really have anyone else to count on. Except Lisa James. Her friend, Sylvia was just too much trouble.

As we walked past the Mandalay Bay hotel and casino, I instructed everyone to keep their eyes peeled for any signs of life. Fortunately, it didn't look like there were any Biters around.

The streets were deserted of all life, much like the highway. It was kind of weird, too, because I knew there were people still uninfected. They must have just shut themselves in or gotten the hell out of dodge.

"Where *is* everyone?" Lisa asked amid the silence.

"Dead..." Sylvia's voice sounded weak.

"No." Lisa continued in a whisper. "No. There aren't any bodies. It's as if everyone just picked up and left."

"My thoughts, too." I stared at the road ahead.

"Where should go toward the Eiffel Tower," the rich lady said for some reason.

So, we took a left down South Las Vegas Boulevard.

"You sure about that? How do you—"

I stopped short, causing everyone to walk right into me. I heard Lisa's son calling out to her, but I could only focus on what I'd just seen.

It couldn't have been. Absolutely not. Silas was dead. I had not just seen him smirking at me from an alleyway. He wasn't standing there with a huge hole in his chest, blood draining onto his white wife beater.

I looked back at the alleyway; it was dark. Silas was dead. I'd made sure. So, I was either going crazy or death wasn't what it used to be.

"What's the matter?" Lisa coddled her little boy who was trying not to cry.

"I... Sorry, I thought I saw something."

"Jesus!" Sylvia gasped. "Warn a girl before you stop!"

I was breathing too hard to even acknowledge Lisa's friend. When I felt a hand on my arm, I jumped. Lisa was looking up at me with mother written all over her face. It was that or shrink.

"What did you see?"

I looked into the depths of the dark alley. Nothing was there. Inhaling a deep breath, I shook my head. "Apparently nothing."

"We should keep going." Rupert was the one who spoke in a hurried tone. I wasn't going to argue. We came across the foot bridge that butted up against the Bellagio's enormous pool. I stopped at the edge.

"The water looks so gross." Sylvia stopped to watch the gondolas bump together in the murky water.

"It's safest here – around water." Lisa offered an explanation of how the rabies virus turned its victims into hydrophobics.

"Yeah, yeah." As I began drumming my fingers against the concrete, I could feel the sweat begin to squeeze from my pores as my heartbeat quickened.

They were halfway across when Lisa turned back. "Are you all right?"

"I, uh...I hate water."

She tilted her head to the side, broke away from the group and came to me. "You were all right at the beach."

"That's different." I felt like I was talking too fast. "That's shallow. I can see the fucking bottom. This..." I took my shaky hand off the concrete to gesture toward the pool. "This is... No."

"You have thalassophobia."

I didn't have the focus to joke. "What now?"

"Fear of open bodies of water."

"Yeah, okay."

She put a gentle hand on my arm. "Don't worry. There are none of those things around, so we won't even need to think about water."

She was right. I could feel my heart slow, but not all the way. I drummed my fingers against the concrete one more time

before sucking in a breath and taking the first step. But she wasn't right. Oh no. she was dead wrong – forgive the pun.

Because as soon as my foot made contact on the bridge, an ear-splitting scream came out of nowhere. Well, not nowhere. It came from behind Paris Paris. And the other thing that came from behind Paris Paris was a swarm of howling spitting Biters. The weirdest part about the whole ordeal was that I swore the front doors of that chained up casino opened a crack.

"Run!" Rupert grabbed his wife's arm and tugged. Sylvia grabbed Alex and Lisa grabbed Rex. But there was no one to grab me.

"For the love of..." I choked on my own inhalation and just pushed my feet forward. Ignoring a fear was not easy. With every step, it felt like the water was flowing over me. I was closed in. My steps felt too slow. I couldn't breathe. My airway was constricted.

"Jack!"

I don't know who called my name because the swarm of Biters was taking all my attention. Their howls were getting closer. One of them even leapt at me, just missing the heel of my shoe. The snarling became almost deafening. But I was almost across the bridge. I could see beyond. I could see...

I could see the gondolas floating in the water.

"Jesus Chri—"

My sentenced petered out because a Biter had grabbed the back of my shirt and yanked hard. Getting angry wasn't an

option. Logic was no longer a thought process in my mind. I was terrified of having to get in the water. All I could think was...

"Shoot now. Ask questions never." My hero's quote seemed to knock me partially back into reality. I spun around and aimed the shotgun right at the Biter's head and pulled the trigger. No thoughts. Just nothing. Pure fight or flight.

A few more Biters ambushed me, pushing me back into the concrete ledge. The black water loomed below me, taunting me. Each lap of a wave against the wall sounded like laughter.

I held up my shotgun for protection as one Biter chomped at me. Its teeth smashed together, inches from my face. Blood dripped from a wound on its head, flowing down over its eyes. It reminded me of Gene Simmons from KISS.

"Holy shit! Were you born that ugly?" The toe of my shoe made contact with the Biter's gut, sending it doubling back enough for me to run the rest of the way across the bridge to the...boats. The Biters were on my heels. Lisa was calling out to me.

I was in a hurry. I wasn't thinking. All my body was telling me to do was jump in the boat and paddle as far out as I could. By the time we made it to a safe distance, I was breathing hard; my pulse had skyrocketed. The howls of those diseased things reverberated off the water. Then they started jumping in.

One after the other, they jumped over the bridge and into the water. When they made contact with it, they began to scream and flail until they went under for good. We were safe.

But as Cynthia breathed a sigh of relief, panic was squeezing into a ball inside my chest.

The bridge seemed to stretch out infinitely in front of me. It zoomed out until the Biters were tiny little things splashing around. I could see oncoming ripples in the dark water. When the first one hit the boat, it jarred us. And there was nothing to grab onto. I made the mistake of peering into the water. I couldn't see the bottom. The long oar plunged down, but the water was so deep that I couldn't even see the end of it.

My hands flew to cover my face and I fell backward, rocking the boat even more. "Jesus Christ. Holy shit. I can't do this."

"What's your problem?" Sylvia spoke up.

"He has thalassophobia. Jack." Lisa put a hand on my back as another Biter jumped into the water. More waves hit the boat until I curled into a ball.

"Jack."

"No! I can't do it! We have to get out of here. We're going to die!"

"Jack." Her tone never faltered from calm.

Another Biter jumped in. Another waves crashed into us.

I growled deep in my chest. "Make it stop!"

"Jack. Tell me about your family."

Water splashed onto my bare arms, causing me to retract. "What?"

72

"What was your father like?" Lisa reached for the oar to paddle toward the bridge. I grabbed her wrist.

"Don't."

She tensed, but remained calm. "All right. Just focus on you. Tell me about your father."

I put my hands back over my eyes and tried to focus my thoughts. "Um...he was a...an alcoholic. A real fucking douchebag."

"Go on."

More water splashed into the boat. "Jesus... Uh... He beat my mom a lot."

"When's the last time you saw him?"

"Uh...years ago. My sister was on his side. She was young. Went with him. Thought he was innocent. I went with my mom."

"What was your mother like?"

"She was sweet. Um...nice to everyone. Big heart. Stupidly naïve, though."

"How long ago did she die?"

I jerked my head up to look at Lisa. Her features seemed pretty sincere. "How did you...?" The boat bumped into something hard. I almost fell over again. "Fuck!"

"It's okay." Lisa's hand was on my arm again. "We're back on dry land."

"What?" I took a look around. Sure enough, we were back at the front of the pool. All the Biters were floating face down in the water. One was still splashing around but would

soon quiet. I couldn't scramble out fast enough. When I was clear of the water, I pushed my back against a stone wall, then I looked toward Lisa.

"How did you do that?"

Her eyes widened. "It's my job. I have to keep the patient focused on giving answers to keep the panic at bay."

I ran a hand over my face. "So I'm just a patient?"

"Nice to see your jokes are back." Sylvia huffed.

Taking a moment to shake the panic off, I feigned a grin. "Oh, they're back, baby. With a vengeance."

"The people who kidnapped your daughter could be anywhere," Lisa said to Rupert and Cynthia. "I'm not even sure—"

Something hurtled at us, slamming into the concrete with a metallic thud. Lisa jumped so far I thought her head would hit the tree branch above her. The rich woman screamed. "What the hell was that?!"

"Momma!" Lisa's kid called.

"It's all right, Rex."

"Was it a bird?" Sylvia wondered aloud.

I started up the stairs toward the sound.

"Wait." Lisa stopped me as I was about to set a foot on the dry road. "Is it safe?"

I looked around, not seeing any more Biters. Just the same, I tightened my grip on the shotgun. I wasn't going to take any chances. Lisa seemed to think my intuition was spot on, because she followed me, along with the rest of them.

Two Men and a Lift Auto Garage

"We Auto Know"

When I reached the cause of the sound, I stooped to pick up a metal bar between my feet. I inspected it against the hard sunlight streaming through a thick set of fall rainclouds.

"What is it?"

"A wrench." The crow-bar shaped wrench was long and heavy with a black body that curved at the star-shaped head.

"A wrench?" Sylvia twisted her face up.

"Yup. It's a Torx Wrench. Pretty standard," I said. "You use it to—"

"I've seen that before!" Mrs. Meyers cried all of a sudden. "One of those hoodlums was brandishing it at us when they took Rosalie!"

I opened my mouth to say something, but she tore it out of my hand, waving it in her husband's face.

"Don't you remember this, Rupert?!"

"I...suppose..." Her husband took a step back.

Mrs. Meyers stopped, turning her head to the right and left. She settled on the direction the wrench had come flying from. In front of us, a replica of the Eiffel Tower jutted up into the sky. I'd seen it before in a magazine, but I never understood why they'd recreate something that already existed. It just gave lazy people an excuse not to travel.

"That's where they took her! That's where they took Rosalie!" Without warning, she took off toward the entrance.

"Cynthia!" Her husband yelled after her, frustration in his face.

Two Men and a Lift Auto Garage

"We Auto Know"

Me? I didn't even hesitate. I shoved my rifle at her husband, ignored his questioning look, and dove after her. She didn't even make it to the door. I caught her around the waist, almost tackling her. Then, I picked her up, dragging her back kicking and screaming. Her foot made contact with my shin. I winced.

"Let me go, you brute! Rosalie needs me!!"

"Sorry, Mrs. Meyers." I set her down. "I can't let you go off by yourself. That's how you get killed."

"Momma, what's wrong with lady?" Lisa's son was cowering behind her, hugging her knees. She reached down and rubbed her fingers through his hair. My mom used to do that to me when I was little.

"Don't worry, Rex."

"Cynthia, please." Rupert coaxed his wife while grabbing a hold of her upper arm before she could get away. Even though the coax sounded more like a scolding, I abandoned her and took my shotgun back from him. I marched over to Lisa, lowering my voice so only she could hear.

"I think I'm gonna go scout out the place," I said. "Someone threw that wrench, and if I can find them, maybe I can get some answers."

"Be careful please." She nodded. I agreed, cocking my gun. When I passed by Mr. Meyers, I looked him straight in the eye.

"You prepared to use that handgun?"

76

"What are you talking about?" He tried to pretend like he didn't know what I was talking about, but he didn't fool me.

"The Ruger you got stashed away in your belt." I didn't bat an eye. "Are you prepared to use it if one of those things comes out while I'm gone?"

"How did you...?"

I inhaled a sharp breath through my nose.

He swallowed, but nodded. "I...I've practiced on the range a few times. I can use it if the need arises."

"Good. I'll be back in a minute."

I stalked off toward the entrance of the tower. The glass doors were dirty; handprints in grease, blood, and something else I didn't care to know were smeared across the surface. There was a chain and huge padlock wound through the brass handles. I nudged it with the barrel of my shotgun. None of those things were going to get through those doors. There must have been people in there. And there must have been another way in.

Other entrances under one of the tower's enormous legs were also bolted shut with padlocks. There was a side street just beyond the building, so I headed for it. There really wasn't anyone around for miles. There had to be someone inside the tower; why would the doors be locked from the outside?

As I rounded the corner, the Paris Casino and Resort came into view. It was a huge, x-shaped building with a white exterior and windows that reflected the setting sun. I looked

back from where I'd come, but I couldn't see Lisa and the others anymore.

Ah, Lisa…

I couldn't stop thinking about her for some reason. Yeah, she was gorgeous—a great body, young, vibrant. But she was so serious. And she had a kid which meant baggage, but he was pretty well-behaved. The night before when we'd camped out in the Jeep, I'd offered to stay watch in case anything happened. It was harder than ever to stop looking at her. I wanted to grab her; kiss her; do other things to her…

A metal clang echoed to my left. I spun around, bringing my shotgun in front of my chest. How could I let my guard down so easily? *No more thinking about the hot little piece traveling with you, Jack; you have to focus!*

In front of me, a huge, green overhang curved around the sidewalk. Underneath, dark shop windows stared at me. The wind blew an empty recycle bin into the glass window of a store. It thumped, but it wasn't the same sound I'd heard.

"Somebody there?" I swung my shotgun around in all directions.

"Yeah, somebody's here, man."

I passed by my old best friend as he leaned against a post. "You're not here, Silas." Out of nowhere, my head started to throb. Silas chuckled, the hole is his chest stretching and releasing more red goo.

"If I 'ain't here', then why are you talking to me?" He fell into step beside me, mimicking my movements with a pretend gun. "Scared yet, Jack?"

"I'm not scared. Go away." I kicked a piece of trash out of my way, sending it skittering into the street. The sound was deafening.

"Nope." Silas had always been stubborn like that. "I'm not going away until you tell me why you did it."

"Did what?" I kept my voice low.

"Killed me and just left me there."

I spun around, lowering my gun so I could see his face. It was still Silas's face all right—all gaunt and chiseled. But he was real pale, like a ghost. I could see blue veins making a map across his skin. He crossed his arms over his bleeding chest, waiting for an answer.

"You shouldn't have been joking like you were, Silas. It was stupid. It got you killed." I felt bad for talking to him that way, but he needed to know the truth.

A frown broke his face in half. "Listen to you, tryin' to justify your actions and shit. Don't gimme that. You're a murderer."

"I am not."

"Yes, you are. And you shouldn't keep it a secret. Why didn't you tell that hot little piece of ass about me, huh? Why didn't you tell her what you did?"

"Don't talk about her that way."

79

"What are you gonna do, Jack?" He smiled like a jester. "Kill me again?"

"Shut up!"

The metal clang filled my ears again. I spun around with shotgun aimed, and came end to end with a stranger doing the same. He held a mean looking pistol at arm's length, aimed straight at my chest. He was wearing all kinds of leather and was decorated in piercings from head to toe.

"Who are you, man?" He pulled the hammer back.

"I don't wanna hurt you," I said. "I'm looking for a little girl."

The punk narrowed his eyes at me. I stood my ground, forgetting all about old Silas.

"Look…" I lowered my shotgun. "I'm on your side." I put both hands up in a defensive pose. "I'm just looking for a little girl."

The punk stood his ground. "You and me both." He was still pointing the gun at me.

I paused for a moment. "We met a couple on the side of the highway. They said some guys came out and kidnapped their daughter. Know anything about it? She's about eight years old, blond, blue eyes, goes by Rosalie."

It was his turn to pause. "That's exactly who I'm looking for."

"What do you mean?"

"Those morons she calls mom and dad are fucked."

"Keep talking."

He finally lowered the gun. "I stopped to help them, too. I'm guessing they gave you that song and dance about some freaks bringin' her here."

I gave him a skeptical look. "Yeah. They mean you? Did you take her here?" I nodded in the direction of the fake Eiffel Tower.

"No," he said. "*They* did."

I sighed. "Who?"

"Those idiots you picked up on the side of the road, man!"

"Wait...What?" My head was beginning to spin.

"They fuckin' jacked you, man! They live in there, man." The punk pointed his gun at the tower.

"You mean they— "

"*Jack!*"

The two of us jolted at the scream. It sounded like Lisa. I turned in the direction it had come from and found myself face to face with Rupert.

"I see you've found Connor." The man's face had completely changed from one of distress to smug satisfaction.

"Oh, shit!" The punk named Connor turned tail and started running, the chains on his jackets clinking together.

"Oh, no you don't." Without a second's hesitation, Rupert pulled out the Ruger and shot the guy square in the back.

I ducked at the sound and found myself horrified at the site of the poor kid's body bleeding out in the sand. But I

81

regained my composure quickly enough to twist around and point my gun in Rupert's face.

"Drop it." I leveled my voice as best I could.

"I don't think so."

"Why did Lisa scream?"

A twisted smile came across Rupert's face. "You want the truth?"

Without realizing what I was doing, I pulled the hammer back on my shotgun. I wasn't even going to count to three.

But even before I could pull the trigger, Rupert pointed his gun at my leg and fired one shot right into my knee.

"Fuck!" I went down. Blood poured between my fingers.

"Bye bye!" Rupert waved the pistol, turned and hightailed it out of there before I could blink.

"God fucking damn it! I need this knee! Of all the fucking places to shoot me!" I rocked back and forth in the sand. My head throbbed from the noise and dust.

"I need a vacation."

"*Jack!*"

Lisa screamed my name again. Her yell pushed adrenaline into my veins. I had to get to her before something bad happened. Rupert had shot me with a .22, so it was likely – albeit painful – to walk, but it definitely needed to be treated right away.

"Here goes nothing..." I gritted my teeth and stood straight. Bones scraped together. Pain shot into my thigh and all the way up my back.

"Fuck it." I inhaled deeply and started running.

When I turned the corner, I couldn't believe what I saw. Lisa was covered in blood. Her clothes were stained red and there were little droplets on her face. She was trying to hold Rex, but he was squirming and on the verge of what looked like a mental breakdown. Alex, Sylvia, Rupert and his wife were nowhere to be found.

"What the hell happened?" I went from looking at Lisa's stoic face to the trail of blood that led to the door of the casino. When I looked back at her, I noticed her eyes were fixated ahead.

"Lisa?"

"I don't want to talk about it."

For a second, words refused to come to me. "Wha...but...you're covered in blood! Whose blood is that? How did this happen?"

"We should leave."

I felt my brow lower and my heartbeat quicken, causing my knee to throb. It wasn't the time for her to be stubborn and emotionless.

"Well, yeah... Rupert and his wife are not good people. But we need to find Alex and Sylvia."

Rex's face was turning violet.

"It's dangerous here. We should go."

"But, I—"

I wasn't able to finish my sentence because a half roar, half squeal erupted from Lisa's son. His color turned from

purple to red as tears streamed down his cheeks. On instinct, I covered my ears and shut my eyes. Sheesh the kid was loud.

His wailing seemed to snap Lisa out of her daydream. "Alex's in there."

"What?!"

"One moment." Lisa knelt down to her panicking son and placed a hand on his head. Ever so gently, she stroked his hair. "Shhh... It's ok, Rex. Nothing is going to hurt you. It's just you and me here. Just you and me."

I watched in awe as Rex slowly broke from screaming, to just crying and finally to sniffles.

"Would you like the glasses?" She continued to pet his head as he nodded. She fished around in her pockets for a moment. From the back of her jeans she uncovered a pair of dark sunglasses and placed them gently on his nose. The affect was immediate. He calmed.

"The sunglasses are his own world. He prefers darkness, so it blocks out everything else."

"Oh..."

She glanced at my leg. "What happened?"

"I got shot."

"By who?"

"Rupert."

"I should look at it, but Alex is in that tower. I don't know if she's alive or dead."

The word "dead" came from her mouth in monotone. It almost sounded like she didn't care about her friends.

Two Men and a Lift Auto Garage

"We Auto Know"

"Ok, well...I found a way in, but the door is probably rusted shut."

"Where?"

She began walking around the side of the casino before I could even point in the general direction.

"This way..." I said under my breath, limping behind her heels. "What happened back there, Lisa?" I watched her wipe blood from her face and shake it off her hand.

"I'm not going to discuss it now."

What the hell? "Why not?"

"Because."

I tilted my eyes toward the sky. "Okay, mom."

She ignored me as a set of stairs came into view. The rusty door looked the same as I'd left it. Silas was at least gone. There was a large pool of red on the sand a few yards ahead, but Connor's body was gone. As Lisa rounded the corner to descend the concrete structure with little Rex in tow, I leaned against the shoddy railing.

"You owe me an explanation, though. I expect it later."

"I don't owe you anything." She inspected the door carefully, letting go of Rex's hand and pulling on the handle. But it didn't budge.

"I think I deserve to know what happened. I'm not trying to pry. I'm only concerned."

"I appreciate the concern, but it isn't necessary." She began looking around on the ground for something.

85

I heaved a loud sigh. "You know...I'm not a creep. At least I don't think so."

"Okay." She found a discarded metal pipe and picked it up.

"Okay, so...I want to get to know you. I want to make sure you're safe. I want to make sure the kid is safe. If you tell me what happened, I can help."

"No, you can't. I'm perfectly capable of handling whatever emotions come out of that situation. I don't need any help. I don't need protection, but, again, I appreciate the concern for our safety."

"The lock is the weakest part." I watched her try and insert the pipe between the door and the jamb.

"Thank you."

"Don't mention it. But now you owe me."

She took a deep breath and pushed against the pipe in the opposite direction the door would open. "Why do you have so much insistence on needing affirmation that I trust you?"

I pulled back a little. "Is that what I'm doing?"

"Yes."

"Oh."

The pipe broke free of the door and clambered to the ground. Rex squeaked but Lisa reassured him by saying his name softly.

"Here. Gimme." I held out my hand for her to give me the pipe. She looked up at me. I couldn't explain what kind of look she gave me or what she was thinking. She looked angry,

but a subdued angry. Her brows were low, but she did pick up the pipe and hand it to me.

"Sorry if I pried too much." I rounded the corner toward her.

"It's fine."

"You can tell me what happened whenever you're ready." I threw her a smile and a wink, but there was virtually no reaction.

"I don't need a therapist, but thank you. I can handle my own thoughts."

"You're sexy when you're stubborn," I joked.

"Thank you."

There was an awkward moment where we looked at each other. "Okay."

"Okay."

I shook off the weird thoughts in my head and rolled my shoulders. Bracing myself with one foot securely planted on the concrete and the other against the wall, I wedged the pipe between the door and its jamb.

"Here goes something." I pushed hard against the pipe with as much force as I could. The door wasn't budging, but I had to keep going. A little girl's life was at stake and I couldn't take a risk that big.

My head was only swimming with thoughts of a gruesome scene to come. Whose blood was on Lisa? Was it Alex's or Sylvia's? Were they both dead? Were those idiots torturing them?

There was a loud clang to bring me out of my thoughts. The pipe broke and took me down with it. I hit my bad knee and could feel the pull of ligaments. Pain shot through my hip into my upper back.

"Fuck!"

"Are you all right?"

There was an emotion in Lisa's voice. It was concern. My heart almost skipped a beat, but I decided that wouldn't be a good idea.

"Yeah." I put one hand on my good leg and wobbled to a standing position. My knee throbbed, but I could walk at least. Lisa's face held what looked like fear for a split second. But it quickly returned to stoic.

"The door's open."

I looked. Sure enough, there was a sliver of blackness meeting us from the cracked open door. We were in. Taking one last look at each other in the light, we gave a simultaneous nod of agreement and stepped into the darkness.

October 17

It was a terrible idea. Pushing the metal door open to the inside of the casino, I took a quick glance at Jack while squeezing Rex's hand.

What happened to Sylvia outside the casino was utterly incomprehensible. But I knew I'd deal with that later. Because Jack was right; Alex might have still been alive and if I didn't make sure then my decision would forever weigh in the back of my mind. I couldn't have that.

So, we made the journey through the door into the dark casino. I wasn't expecting much, because I never gambled. Gambling was a waste of a life and became an addiction for many people before the outbreak.

Surprisingly, the inside was lit enough so we could see. Most of the slot machines were dark. Some were smashed in – I'd assumed for the money. A few remaining were actually lit and spinning through nonsensical imagery unrelated whatsoever to gambling.

A large metal structure was in the direct center of the casino. I assumed it was representative of the Eiffel Tower's interior in Paris. But I'd never been to Paris.

"Wait." Jack's voice almost startled me. He spoke in a harsh whisper while holding an arm in front of me. I looked sideways at him. I didn't understand why he felt the need to protect us.

"Do you think they can hear us?"

"They already know we're inside." He was looking all around – at each wall, stairway and corner.

"How do you—"

I was cut off by a loud screech. It sounded like nails on a chalkboard. Jack instinctively pushed Rex and me behind him. The, just as suddenly as it had started, the noise stopped. I looked around for the source.

"Machines are malfunctioning." Jack used his normal tone.

"Why aren't you whispering anymore?"

"Because."

I straightened out and planted my feet squarely. He was in my way. Rex was also beginning to fidget.

"Because why?"

My sentence trailed into oblivion when I saw Rupert standing in the center of the casino. He'd changed – now wearing a black trench coat with a purple shirt and leather pants.

"Welcome, welcome!" He raised his arms above his head. There was a full twenty seconds of complete silence before someone spoke.

"Uh..." It was Jack.

Rupert lowered his arms. For the first time, I could see movement. There were men all over. They were hiding in dark corners and behind the slot machines. Some were on their hands and knees.

"We're here for the little girl." Jack didn't shift at all. He was still.

Rupert laughed. "Rosalie? Rosalie is just a stuffed doll on the fifth floor the men use to...pleasure themselves."

I made a face.

"Good to know... What about the woman and her daughter?"

"Do you really believe we'd let her go without...compensation?" Rupert's smile made my stomach churn.

"Look, Rupert," Jack began with a sigh. "These ladies didn't do anything to you. They belong with us and if you just give them back, we'll mosey on out of here without a peep."

Rupert laughed again. It was a throaty almost satanic sound. "I don't think so. You see, we are a community here. We have rules to abide by. Sometimes when we catch someone, we recruit them."

There was a rustle from the hidden men – a sort of murmur of agreement.

"And sometimes we eat them."

It was the final statement that set me on edge once again. My stomach began to roil while my palms were beginning to moisten.

"Any questions?"

"Yeah, one." Jack raised his hand as if we were in school. Rupert paused, his face stoic. "Where do babies come from?"

You could have heard a pin drop, I swear.

He looked at me and shrugged. "What? My dad was never around and my mom was too embarrassed to start the conversation." He turned back to Rupert. "All right, I get it. We all have to live somehow. You...guys chose this way. But women gotta be stringy, man. Just let them go."

Rupert reached behind his back. "Or what?" He brought out what looked like a high-powered pistol plated with gold and pointed it at us.

Jack did the same, positioning the sawed-off shotgun right at Rupert's head. "Or I'll kill you."

"I'd like to see you try. My men here will tear you apart if your trigger finger so much as twitches."

"Yeah, well right now it's plenty itchy."

They played a game of stand and stare for a solid two minutes. It was almost as if no one else were there. As if it were just the two of them aiming at each other. Both wanting the same thing and willing to fight for it. My understanding and appreciation of Jack tilted upward a bit. He was willing to risk his life for two people he barely knew.

It was Jack who finally broke the staring contest. "What do you want?"

A smile spread across Rupert's face. "I'm so glad you decided to comply." With a single nod of his head I felt Rex's hand slip out of mine. I spun around to see a sunken looking man pulling him away. The sunglasses fell off his nose and dropped on the carper with a soft plop.

"Hey!" I ran after the man only to be grabbed by another one. I struggled. I kicked him hard. I tried to remember some defense training, but my mind wasn't working properly. The only thing on it was getting Rex back safely. The other man was able to subdue me as he carried me into the darkness. I stretched a hand out.

"Jack!"

October 17

"Son of a bitch!" I watched helplessly as two of Rupert's henchmen took Rex and Lisa away from me. When I turned back toward him, he had lowered his gun. "Give them back!"

"Tis a fair trade."

"Since when?"

Two other men came out of the shadows. Alex was between them, but there was no sign of Sylvia. She was kicking and screaming. She was a fighter. Luckily, she seemed unharmed. When she saw me, she struggled free.

"Jack!" She ran to me, throwing both arms around my waist. "Mom's dead!"

"Jesus Christ..." I knelt down and let my gun fall to my side, but I kept a firm grip on it. "Are you okay, honey?"

Her face was streaked with dirt and tears. In her eyes was fear, sorrow and a little anger. I could see it all in the way she looked at me. It just about broke my heart.

"They said they were gonna eat me."

I took a deep breath. "Everything's okay, now, honey. I've got you." I stood back up while keeping a protective arm around Alex. "Bring them back and you can have me."

Rupert laughed. The sound was beginning to hurt. "I'm afraid not. Woman on the menu tonight, boys!"

There was a collective rush of what sounded like rejoiced whispers.

"Bring...them...*back*." I pulled the hammer back on Silas's gun. Rupert's smile faded fast. The room erupted in clicks

from hammers. It was almost deafening. I could only see about twenty men, but it sounded like hundreds.

"It's time for you and the girl to leave."

"Jack?" Alex sniffed and looked up at me. It was hard to see the hurt in her eyes. I had to think quick.

*   *   *

I paced outside by the SUV. Alex followed my movements every time I turned around. I didn't know what I was going to do. Could I have snuck in and somehow found the room Lisa and Rex were in and rescued them without anyone seeing? Doubtful.

Man that sentence had a lot of and's.

"I wonder how long Lisa can fend for herself."

"If Rex is involved...she'll handle it." Alex's response to my question meant for no one startle me.

I stopped for a moment to look at her. All the fear from before seemed to have drained from her face. she was even kicking her feet aimlessly.

"Could she... Could she, like...kill someone?"

"Aunt Lisa? I wouldn't be surprised."

I was impressed. "Damn. That's hot."

"You're weird." Alex's words were laced with humor. She didn't really mean it.

Hmm... I was getting off track. What could I do to save them?

Could I have just gone in straight massacre style with guns blazing? No, that wouldn't work because I only had...

"I only have one gun." I finished my thought out loud as I stopped pacing.

"What is it?" Alex's brow was furrowed. I shot her a grin and approached the passenger side of the vehicle.

"I've got a plan."

*   *   *

I watched Alex from a distance. She was a brave one. Willing to stand alone outside with those men all around. A trooper is what I would have called it. She wanted to help so badly that I had to give her the opportunity.

I snuck around to a window under the tower of the building. They were all boarded up, but I used it to my advantage. After taking a deep breath, I pounded my fist against the raw boards for three seconds. That was Alex's cue.

I rounded a pillar and pressed my back against it. When I heard the casino door open, I peeked out enough to be able to see their feet. There were four of them.

Alex began crying. It was a horrible sound. She wailed like a cat. In between the tears, she sputtered, "He left me! He just left me!"

She was a pro.

"It's just the little brown girl." One of the men shuffled his feet. "I'll get her. Tell the boss." The other three pairs of feet walked off. Perfect.

I followed the guy's movements as he stepped out into the open air. He was in my territory now. He wasn't wearing much, either. Just a cross belt of ammo and some ripped shorts.

I could see his ribs. His feet were bare. Each footstep kicked up a bit of dirt.

Alex was faced away from him, but she knew he was there. I told her how I predicted the plan would go. The man inched forward until his shadow fell over her.

"You're ours now, little brown girl." He snarled at her.

Alex immediately stopped crying and spun around. "I think not." I'd given her a rusty screwdriver that was in the glove box. She did exactly as I told her – blindly aimed it toward his face. She caught his cheek, ripping a nice sized hole and leaving some of the orange rust behind on his skin.

"You little brat!" The man held one hand to his cheek while drawing a pistol out of his cutoff jeans. But before he could even pull back the hammer, I slammed the butt of my shotgun into the side of his head. There was a massive crack and he fell over into the dirt. Blood began to pool, turning the sand orange.

"That's not... You just got... Damn it. I was hoping to say something really cool right now." I picked up his gun and checked the chamber as Alex giggled. I tucked the gun into the back of my jeans, then gave her a thumbs up. "You kick ass, Seabass."

She gave a little nod of her head with a knowing smile. "My gramma taught me good."

*   *   *

Alex told me she'd seen the location of Rupert's "throne room" when she was trapped inside. I thought I could use that

information to my advantage. I just had to find a way to be quiet about entering the building.

"How many of those guys are there?" I asked her. I'd put her into the SUV and told her to stay put with the doors locked.

"I don't know. I didn't see very many, but they were mostly in the front of the casino. They like the dark."

That was all I needed to know. As long as I stuck to the shadows, I could quickly eliminate anyone I came into contact with without alerting attention. Before shutting her in, I loaded up on supplies. I took a hunting knife and about two feet of nylon rope. I left the screwdriver with Alex.

"Okay." I turned to her. Her face held an expression of anxiety. "Your mom ever let you drive?"

She shook her head. "But my daddy did."

"So you know which pedal is gas and which is brake?"

She nodded. "And I know you have to put it in drive and take off the...emergency brake?"

"You got it. If I'm not back in thirty minutes, you take off. Drive as far as you can. Find someone or something that looks safe."

"Okay." She nodded.

I stood and shut the passenger door, leaving my hand pressed against the window for a second more than I should have. Seeing her watch me about to do something stupid was difficult. I had to choke back some emotion. There was a chance I wouldn't be back. Leaving her by herself was better than leaving her with those men.

As I walked backward, I made the motion to lock the door. She nodded. I gave her a thumbs up and she returned the gesture.

The metal door at the side of the casino was still open, so I slipped through without widening the opening and quietly shut the door. Surprisingly, the casino wasn't dead quiet as I thought it would be. There were sounds of shuffling, yelling and...chewing. I looked up to the second floor stairwell and saw Rupert pointing to something. He looked flustered. There was a moment's pause, then he threw up his hands and walked into a room in the middle of the hall. I counted. Third door on the right. That's the one.

She'd also given me the general direction of where she'd been held so I could check there for Rex and Lisa first. I pressed against the wall and began making my way to the staircase. The sounds seemed to become louder once Rupert was gone.

I was almost to the stairs when I noticed one of his men hunched over facing away from me. He was eating something – hoarding it like his life depended on it. I unsheathed my hunting knife and crept toward him. In a swift movement, I slid the blade across his throat while holding a hand over his mouth until he was limp. Killing someone so brutally on purpose was difficult, but I knew it was necessary. I glanced at the wad of meat the man was chewing on and hoped it wasn't Lisa.

The staircase was right in front of me. There was no movement the entire way up, but I could see two people in the

shadows at the top. They seemed to be arguing quietly over something. I turned and picked up the stringy pile of meat my late friend had been chewing and tossed it up where it landed between the feet of the two.

They immediately stopped arguing and stared at it. Then, they looked up at each other. That's when the fighting began. They clawed and screamed at each other, ripping off hair and chunks of flesh. One of them let out a low groan and fell to the floor while the other grabbed the meat and ran off.

I shook my head before ascending the stairs. The entire casino was covered in dust. It smelled like blood. There were brown stains all over the carpets. Chunks of meat hung from railings, slot machines and chandeliers. The hotel room doors were mostly broken off their hinges or completely gone.

At the top of the stairs, I came to the loser of the earlier argument. It was female. Her hair curled into greasy strings. Clothes hung from her bones. Her eyes were sunken. She was still breathing. Her gaze focused on me and her eyes widened. She lifted her hand, beginning to close her first to point at me. I showed her the knife, making sure it glinted off the dull light, and shook my head. Her hand fell back to her side as her head lolled the opposite way.

I stepped over her. The whole air of the place made me feel as though I had to wash my hands. Ugh.

I peeked into one of the hotel rooms without a door. The carpets and beds were completely splashed red with blood. Chains with shackles on the ends of them hung from the walls.

Lisa and Rex were in a room like this. If they were even still living.

"Go and don't come back until you've retrieved what I want!"

My head turned toward the sound of Rupert's voice. There was a frightened looking skinny man cowering at the open door to his chambers. The man nodded and shook, hobbling off toward the opposite end of the hotel.

Using the shadows to conceal myself, I crept toward his open door. There was a faint sound of classical music coming from inside. I positioned myself in a way where I could see how the room was setup. The bed was opulent to say the least. Gold sheets and a canopy. Everything looked like it was made of silk. A stereo was propped up on one night stand and what looked like an executive chair was facing the window – away from me.

As I silently approached the chair, I could see him waving his arms about, trying to conduct the music. I wanted to roll my eyes, but I had more important things to do.

The closer I got to the chair, the more I straightened myself until I was right on top of him. He looked up at me, but it was too late to scream. I threw the nylon rope around his throat and pulled as tightly as I could.

He struggled hard, clawing at the rope but only tearing skin from his neck. He tried to stand and nearly knocked over the chair. I caught it with my foot, letting it slip to the ground quietly. When I was focused again, I tightened the rope more and pressed my knee into his back for leverage.

Two Men and a Lift Auto Garage

"We Auto Know"

"This is for *her*."

After what felt like hours, he finally quieted down and stopped struggling. I slowly dropped him to the floor and, with one last tug to tighten the rope and make sure the deed was done, took a moment to make the sign of the cross over my chest.

"Now to find them."

"Shut the kid up!"

I glared up at the man who'd thrown us into the hotel room. Rex was screaming as I'd imagined, but they'd separated us so I couldn't soothe him.

"I can't! He won't!" The other man struggled to secure my son.

"Momma!"

"Just hit him!"

"Don't you dare touch him." While my blood was pumping and my heart thundering, I kept my voice low and still.

"We can't. Boss doesn't want them bruised, remember?"

The man on my side of the room looked down at me, hunger burning in his eyes. "How do you shut him up?"

I started at him for a second more. "I need to be with him."

He sneered. "Yeah, right, lady. I know this trick."

"It is not a trick."

He prodded me with the wooden stick he used for a crutch. "Give me a break."

"*Momma!*" Rex's scream was ear-shattering. Both men covered their ears.

"Just let her go! She can't get past us!"

The man on my side let out a guttural growl and bent down to unshackle me. I held my breath. I was going to do something risky, but necessary. As soon as both my hands were free, I clenched my right fist and aimed for the man's temple. I caught it at just the right angle and he went down. The other man didn't even have time to react. I grabbed the walking stick and jumped to the other side of the room. Without hesitation, I began beating the other man with the stick as hard as I could. Rex continued to cry but was no longer screaming; the other man was. I pummeled and pummeled until the screaming stopped. Then, I hunched over to catch my breath.

"Momma!"

And then I felt a sharp pain in my side. It was dull at first then white hot, spreading into my left arm and down my leg. My vision went a bit fuzzy. A loud shot resonated throughout the room. I slowly turned, clutching my side where the pain began throbbing.

The man was now on the ground, bleeding from his left shoulder. In his hand was a dagger with a red tip. No, the tip wasn't red. That was my blood. He'd stabbed me.

"Lisa!"

It was Jack. I turned my tunneled gaze to him, but could barely get a word out. All I could do was lift my hand to show him the wound. It needed to be treated right away; that much I was sure of.

Jack stared at it hard for a second or two, then turned to the man.

"What's on that knife?"

The man cackled. "Something wonderful."

Jack's jaw clenched as he stooped down. Placing the barrel of some pistol against the man's groin, he asked again. "What's on the knife?"

I could see a ribbon of fear travel through the man's body. "Okay, okay. It's LSD, man. Just chill. She'll be fine in an hour."

Just as I slumped to the floor, I heard the blast of a gun and the man's head exploded into a kaleidoscope of colors.

"Impressive." I felt as though I'd said the word, but didn't hear it.

Jack's face suddenly swam in front of mine. It literally swam. It seemed like he had no body. His eyes were too large. He held up a hand in front of me.

"How many fingers am I holding up?" His voice sounded distorted.

"Eighteen."

There was a pause. "Not only is that very, very wrong, but I think you may have a brain tumor."

"I'm serious. There are eighteen. You should see a doctor about that. You should only have ten. Twenty if we're counting toes."

He gasped comically. "You know the situation is bad when Lisa makes a joke."

"I'm actually not. You literally have eighteen fingers."

"No, I don't. I was holding up three."

"What on Earth are you talking about?"

He just wasn't making any sense. A garbled cry caught my attention. When Jack stood, a rainbow dripped from his knee.

"You might want to get that checked out as well. Rainbows can turn septic."

"I think the only person who's been higher than you are right now was Jack Kerouac." He held out his eighteen-fingered hand and helped me up.

"Solid reference." I used him to steady my feet. I couldn't understand why my left leg refused to move. "I didn't know you'd read any Kerouac."

"I haven't. But I've watched *Fear and Loathing in Las Vegas* about a thousand times."

"Good film."

"Momma!"

I looked toward my son and felt utter and complete horror grip my heart. "Oh, my God! There are snakes on him!" I lunged toward him and tried to fight off the rattlesnakes winding themselves around his wrists, pinning him in place. I didn't care about my safety.

"Lisa..." Jack's hand fell on my shoulder. "They aren't snakes."

In my panic, I stared up at him. How could he not see that my son was going to get bitten?

"Yes, there are. Please help me, Chase."

He slid me gently out of the way. "The name's Jack, but anyway..."

"No. You're Chase."

I watched as he removed the snakes from my son's wrists. They fell to the floor, hissing and spitting, but stayed away from him. It was as if he'd done it thousand times before.

"Chase is dead, baby." When he stood up with Rex in his arms, I tried to stand too. But a pull in my side stopped me. I looked down and noticed a rainbow leaking from my shirt.

Rex's eyes were also too large for his face. "Momma bleed."

I couldn't understand what he was saying. "Does he have any rainbows?"

There was a laugh under Chase's next words. "No. No rainbows on this buddy, huh?"

Rex chomped at the air.

"Come on, pal." He lifted my son onto his shoulders, but turned to look at me before he left. I didn't remember Chase having hazel eyes and light brown hair. I remembered him dead. "Need help?"

I shook my head. "Has anyone ever told you that you look like that actor?"

He tilted his head at me. "I could guess, but give me more?"

I searched my mind. "Van Wilder."

His mouth twisted into a smile. "Yeah, everybody says that to me. It's probably because we share a last name, though."

My footsteps fell into place with theirs. "No you don't. You're last name is Barclay."

"Bzzt! Wrong! Best two out of three?"

"What are you talking about?"

*   *   *

Birds. I heard birds chirping. I hadn't heard birds in months. The sound to sunk into my very core. My muscles loosened. I allowed my eyes to flutter open. I was on my back in the soft grass. I could smell it – sweet and earthy. The sky was visible through the tree above me. The clouds lazily moved in formation. Had I dreamt the entire apocalypse?

Then the pain awakened my senses. The smell of grass and sound of birds ended abruptly. My side was on fire. I gasped in a breath of stale air.

"Oh, hey..." Jack's face hovered over me.

"Where are we? What happened?" I tried to sit up, but the wave of pain radiated into the entire left side of my body. Jack placed a hand behind my head.

"It's ok. Lie back." His voice was soft and soothing. "Were in Las Vegas. At Paris Paris. You were stabbed."

"I distinctly heard birds and smelled grass."

Jack's features suddenly turned anxious. "Yeah...the blade was tipped in LSD. You might...hallucinate for a while."

I pushed myself up slowly onto my elbows. He watched me the whole time. "Did I call you Rex's father's name? Were there snakes?"

"You did and you thought there were. No snakes." His smile caught me a little inside.

As I moved, a new pain arose – a stinging burn. I winced.

"I also had to use super glue to stitch you up."

"Super glue?"

"Yeah. You're the doctor here. What was I supposed to do? I wasn't going to let you bleed out."

The concern in his face was warming. "That was incredibly idiotic to risk your life to save ours, you know."

"Glad I could be of service." He grinned at me and I felt something form in the pit of my stomach. I pushed it away immediately.

"Where's Rex?"

Jack held out a hand and helped me stand on both feet. It was a difficult process, but I could balance well enough. Rex was trotting along with Alex about three yards away. He seemed so randomly happy and at home in such a strange place.

"Wait..." I turned back to Jack. "What about all the men? Rupert?"

His face turned stony. "It's been taken care of. No need to worry."

"You killed him."

The surprise in his features was enough to tell me he had. "I had to."

I nodded. "I figured. Thank you for taking care of me."

He shrugged. "Hey, no sweat."

After feeling the wound under my shirt, I took a look around the casino. There were still a few men left wandering around cautiously – watching us.

"What about them?" I nodded toward one hiding behind a slot machine to Jack's left. He turned to look.

"They're not going to hurt us anymore. Or anyone else."

"But we'll starve!" A voice rang high above us on a stairwell. A few murmurs echoed afterward.

Jack rolled his eyes at me. "Then hunt shit."

A tickle of humor hit me.

"Hunt what?!"

Jack pinched the bridge of his nose. "Oh, my God..."

"Hunt the infected." I didn't think my words were offensive until everyone went quiet. Even Jack was eyeing me. "*What?*"

"Wouldn't they all get infected?"

I shook my head slowly. Did they really not know the basics? "Rabies can only spread through coming into contact with saliva or nervous tissues of someone who's been infected with the virus."

They all remained quiet and staring. Jack made a circular motion with one hand, urging me to continue.

"So, cook them well. Stay away from the brains, organs and bone marrow. And avoid the area where they were bit. Got it?"

There was some shuffling around the room. "We…we can eat them…"

"Yes."

An eruption of rejoice filled the casino. The man behind the slot machine jumped out and began to dance. Jack stifled an amused chuckle. The dancing man pushed past him and threw his skinny arms around me. My muscles tightened.

"Christ…"

He smelled like three-week old rotted food. He was sticky and half-naked. I shut my eyes tight.

"Thank you," he whispered in my ear.

I pushed my arms out to get him away from me. He was smiling while missing most of his teeth. "You're welcome."

An amused smile spread across Jack's face. "I think you have an admirer."

"Can we leave?" I tried to brush the dirt off my shirt, but all I managed to do was smudge the greasy human sweat into the cotton.

"Oh yes!" The man pointed to the locked entrance. "You leave through there."

"Thanks. Rex! Alex!"

The two children looked our way then came toward us. I grabbed Rex's hand and hurried toward the door without hesitation. The men unlocked the chains to open up our prison. The air smelled so sweet.

"Thanks, dudes!" Jack waved goodbye to them before the door closed behind us. Then, he caught up to us like a child running to their parents. "That was great. You're funny."

"Funny? How is narrowly escaping death funny? How is killing another human being with a walking stick funny?"

Jack screwed up his face. "I changed my mind. You're no fun at all."

Alex giggled.

"See? Even she thinks you're a stick in the fucking mud."

Even though I felt like laughing for the first time in months, I kept it to myself and shook my head instead.

"You said a bad word, Jack." Alex appeared at his side and gingerly took one of his hands. It was a sweet sight to see.

"Did I? I guess I did. Well, it's the end of the world, so not like it matters, right? Fuck it."

Alex giggled again. "Yeah. Fuck it."

"Hey! That wasn't an invitation to throw *your* manners out the window. Watch it, young lady."

Alex laughed, which made Rex laugh. Jack joined in, but all I mustered was a smile.

October 17

The school was huge. At least, I thought it was a school. It could have been anything. It was so overgrown with ivy and caked with dust that I couldn't decide on the spot. All I knew was that it was the only place we'd be safe. Okay, so maybe I wasn't one-hundred percent sure, but we were all dog tired and needed a shower. Plus, none of those...*things* were around.

I pulled the SUV to a stop on a gravel blacktop that looked like it used to be a basketball court. After switching off the ignition, I took a long look at Lisa. She was sound asleep against the glass window. It was enough to make my stomach hiccup. If stomachs can do that.

"Oscar, Uniform, Tango!" I used my "six-inch" voice so I didn't scare them or draw any attention to our position.

Lisa's eyes fluttered open. "What?"

"NATO alphabet."

She paused while brushing fingers through her tangled hair.

"Why?" Alex asked from behind me.

"Because it's cool. How's little Romeo doing back there?"

There was a hint of a smile behind Lisa's eyes, but it only lasted half a second before she tossed her gaze into the backseat. "How long has he been sleeping?"

"Pretty much since Vegas," Alex said. "Hey, Jack, what's my nickname?"

115

I peered at her using the rearview mirror. "Well, J is Juliet. So I guess you guys are Romeo and Juliet."

"Cool!"

Lisa's and my gazes met briefly and all sound stopped. I could feel the electricity between us, but I'd always been bad at that kind of stuff and figured it was probably just static from the floor mats.

Lisa shifted in her seat. "Oscar, Uniform, Tango?"

"Out!" Lexi squealed.

"That's right!" I reached back and we bumped fists.

For the first time since we'd stopped, Lisa looked around. She placed both hands on either side of her. I could tell she was nervous because her knuckles went white. That seemed to happen around me spontaneously.

"Why'd we stop?" There was mild panic in her voice.

"Stopping is a good thing as long as we didn't run out of gas."

"We ran out of gas?"

Oops. "No. Sorry, that was a joke."

She seemed to relax just a bit.

"See that school...or whatever?" I gestured out the front windshield. "We're staying the night."

"Is it safe?"

"I don't know what you mean. I can't tell you something's safe or not, unless I know what you're talking about."

116

She was silent for a long moment, just looking at me. "Movie quotes now. We're kind of in a dire situation here. I think we should check it out, yes?"

I smiled. "Yeah. I'll go check it out. You stay here with Romeo and Juliet and lock the doors. If you see one of those things, just duck down."

She nodded. The fear in her eyes had waned. She was almost used to this; I could tell. That revelation made me sad. No one should *ever* be used to something like what we were going through.

I took a second before popping open the driver side door. Throwing one last look at her, I stepped out into a dry heat.

"Don't take your time, Rain Man."

I raised an eyebrow. "Was that a *joke*?"

She shrugged. "I thought I'd try it out."

"How'd it feel?"

"Dry."

"Sounds about right. And it was *Marathon Man*."

"Rain Man sounds better." Her voice went back to serious.

"Definitely better."

We shared a brief moment of humor as I shut the door. But her tight smile quickly faded, replaced by anxiety. I knew she was anxious because she'd get these tiny wrinkles around the corners of her mouth. I think I may have spent too long

thinking about her without going anywhere, because I heard a knock behind me.

"Are you all right?" Her voice was muffled.

I nodded and turned toward the large building. Lisa had done a decent job at patching up my leg with what we had in the glove box, but it was still pretty sore. The dryness of the earth threw up dust with each step I took. I could taste the packed dirt as the last of the sun's rays heated the ground. A cough escaped me, but I kept going.

The door to the building was standing open.

"Shit."

"No kidding."

A felt a dull throb in the back of my head as my peripheral vision filled with my dead friend. "I can't talk to you right now." I spoke through gritted teeth even though I was yards away from the SUV where Lisa, Alex and Rex were waiting.

"Is that any way to treat an old friend?"

I stooped down to pick up a rock from the dry dirt. Throwing it into the open hallway would attract the attention of any Biters if they were right inside.

"And the wind up! And the pitch!" Silas narrated my every move with gusto.

The rock flew about three or four feet, then skittered to a stop, echoing across each wall. For that brief moment, Silas and I were both quiet, waiting for a sound. Any sound. When

nothing came after thirty seconds, I finally tossed a glance his way and swallowed hard.

"You're not looking so hot."

We wandered slowly into the dark hallway. The building was indeed a school; with lockers lining the halls and class doors off to each side.

"Who me?" Silas's voice sounded surprised. He glanced down at the deep, pulsing hole in his chest. I could see dark red lines spreading outward from the wound where his shirt had ripped away. His skin had also started turning gray. "I got blood poisoning because you murdered me."

I shut my eyes as the throbbing in my head continued. After meeting the dead end of the hallway, I decided to head back toward the stairs.

"What...ignoring me now? That's not very polite."

I rolled me eyes back in my head as I neared the stairs. Everything was dirty; the walls, the lockers, the railings. There was a thick layer of dust on the floor. I knelt down.

"No footprints...means no one's been here in a while."

"Man, that Lisa you found...she's one hot piece."

Even though Silas's words made my blood thicken, I ignored him still as I started down the dark stairwell.

"If no one's been up here in a while, there may be another way in down there."

"Let me tell you...if I could have an hour with Angel Lisa, I'd do things to her that'd make God blush."

I stopped mid-step. "You know, you're a pain in the ass for a figment of my imagination."

"Imagination?"

I started down the stairs again.

"I'm *not* a figment of your imagination, Jacky Boy. I'm for real. I'm *in* your head. You're going crazy, man. Face the facts. All work and no play makes Jack a dull boy."

"I do plenty of playing."

I stopped when I heard the faint noise of what sounded like a footstep. Both Silas and I stood still for a few seconds before hearing the sound again.

For a random moment, I became tired. I was tired of everything going on. I was tired of the monsters, of the lack of sleep, of being scared. Essentially, I was done.

So, I cocked the shotgun – the very same shotgun that I had used to kill my best friend – and began toward the sound.

All I could hear was the blood rushing in my ears and one set of footsteps – my own. All around me were classrooms with large glass windows. I could see discarded equipment like Bunsen burners and heating coils. Science classrooms.

I stopped when the scratching noise came once more. It was around the corner. I waited. And then after waiting for three seconds, I decided enough was enough. If I was going to face this shit, I was going to do it like a bastard.

"Hey!" I shouted. My own voice startled me as it bounced off the glass windows. "Come out!"

Two Men and a Lift Auto Garage

"We Auto Know"

What I heard next filled me with a sense of ridiculousness. A caw. It was a crow. It hopped out from behind the corner and pecked at the ground. It took a brief look my way, cawed again, then flew up to sit on an open door frame.

"A black crow. Bad omen."

I turned toward Silas. "Speaking of bad omens, get lost, Damien."

"Ooh. Someone's a grump."

It had been too long and I was starting to worry about Jack. He seemed to stop at the door of the building as though he'd heard something, then disappeared into the darkness. I looked back at my sleeping son and realized I was so not ready to face this world on my own.

It had been oddly quiet in the car and the surrounding area. I figured those things just hadn't made it this far. Or if they had, there was nothing to keep their interest and they left. Unless they were all huddled up in that school.

"Do you think Jack's okay?" Alex's scared little voice came from the backseat.

"I don't know."

"I hope he didn't get hurt."

I shook the thought out of my head. If there were infected in there, we'd all have known by then. Instead, I took a deep breath and held it until it hurt. Then I let it out slowly. A therapist had taught me how to deal with anxious feelings so far back that I'd almost forgotten. But I utilized them in that car.

I fell back into the leather seat and held my breath once more while rolling my shoulders to work out the kinks. I touched each ear to each shoulder while closing my eyes for five seconds. As I was rolling my head to the side, I saw Jack stepping out of the building.

My heart leapt, pumping blood into my face for some reason. I couldn't quite make out his facial expression, but his posture made him seem exhausted. Hell, we were all exhausted.

He tossed his shotgun in the dirt like it was a broken toy and whipped off his over shirt to reveal strong arms, beaded with sweat. I choked down the thoughts quickly as he approached the SUV, wiping dirt from his face.

"We're all clear, Foxtrot."

He'd given me a nickname, too. "Good."

"Just a pesky crow." He went silent a moment, his mind seemed as though it were elsewhere.

"Jack?"

He snapped out of it. "I might not be a gourmet chef, but I know there's some canned food and heating coils in there. What do you say we eat then get some rest?"

"Yeah!" Alex pushed open the back door and jumped out.

I couldn't get out of the car fast enough. Rex stirred as I took off my seatbelt. I thought I was in for some screaming when he noticed where we were, but Jack seemed to pick up on his distress right away.

"Hey!" He excitedly clapped his hands to get my son's attention. "What do you say to a...piggy-back ride?"

Rex's eyes didn't seem so sure, but he reached out his hands anyway. Jack scooped him up and put him on his well-toned shoulders. But I almost forgot about those when I saw how happy Rex was.

"Hold on, Romeo! We're goin' in! You ready?"

"Yeah!"

"You sure? It's dark. Aren't you afraid?"

"I'm no scare!"

"Me neither!" Alex bounded around them in a circle.

I watched them run about in the waning sun with an ache in my chest. I wanted so badly for Rex to have a father figure in his life, but I didn't want to be that mom who had a new boyfriend every week. And Alex...she was an orphan now. She was mine. I suddenly had a daughter.

I followed after them once they disappeared into the building. It was not a good idea to be alone outside.

I noticed the door to the school was completely missing and wondered how we were going to keep things out while we slept.

Jack, Alex and Rex's playful voices met me in the hallway. I could sense they were in the very last room at the end of the corridor. I picked up my pace.

It looked as though the room used to be a Teacher's Lounge. There were two sofas in the main area and a cot in a separate one. A fridge stood in one corner as well as a microwave and coffee machine. The clock on the wall was still ticking.

Rex had Jack by his index finger and pretended to know where and what everything was.

"And *this* is a purge." He pointed to the fridge.

Jack cocked a half smile. "Purge? Is that how you say it?"

"Yeah! Puuuurrggggeee."

Jack scratched the back of his head. "See...I always thought it was called a budge!"

"No, a budge is what cars cross over," Alex said as I walked into the room.

"Uh-huh." Jack raised both eyebrows. "I see."

I crouched down to my son. "Rex, are you hungry?"

Rex's eyes widened. "Yeah! Num num num!" He stretched out both arms and began zooming about the room. "Brrrmmm brrmmm! Vroooom! I'm a pain!"

Jack choked on a laugh. "A pain."

"Let's eat something."

*   *   *

Tucking my hands in the pockets of my filthy jeans, I took one last look at my peacefully sleeping son. Alex was reading some tattered old book next to him. I walked back out into the hallway to see Jack at the entrance moving lockers and tables to block the door.

"What if we need to make a quick getaway?"

Without looking at me, he said, "There's a door in the basement that has a padlock and chain on it. If we need to, we can go out that way."

We were quiet for a few moments. I watched him shuffle a few tables around and finally block out what was left of the light coming in from the door. We'd both gone around and wiped a few windows clean so we could get what daylight remained. While on that task, I'd found matches and a few candles, which I'd placed in the hallway and room we'd chosen.

"Jack, are you all right?"

He kept working. "Yeah, why?"

"You seem distracted and I want to make sure you're not ill."

Finally, he stopped and stood up straight. After rubbing some sweat from his eyes, he looked at me. "Do I seem distracted? I guess I am feelin' kinda...funky lately."

"Would you like to talk about anything?"

He hesitated as though he wanted to tell me something. Then, he just shook his head and turned to survey his work. He was evading me for some reason.

"So...he has a problem with words?" He asked suddenly. Whenever someone else would ask a question like that, it would be hinted with disgust or condescension. But his tone sounded genuinely curious.

I nodded. "Yes. And it has nothing to do with his autism, either."

Jack was silent, so I continued.

"He could never go to a 'real school' because the other parents were worried their kids would contract some autistic disease." I emphasized the words "real" and "school" with air quotes. "So I've had to teach him whenever I've had the time. It's certainly not ideal, but he seems content most of the time."

Jack sat down on a desk and ran a hand over his face. "So, how do you teach him the right words?"

I gave a half shrug. "Just by telling him the right way to say it over and over again until it sticks."

Without glancing at me, Jack widened his eyes. "Oh. Whoops."

"It's fine. Sometimes a bit of silliness is allowed."

An awkward moment passed. As Jack opened his mouth to say something, Rex began to scream for me. "Sierra, Hotel, India, Tango," he muttered.

I shot him a knowing look as I walked off. "You've got *that* right."

October 18

After about an hour of trying to calm Rex back into a state of sleepiness – which included two lullabies, Alex walking him around the hallway and three bedtime stories – he was finally quiet again. It had gotten dark and the flickering candles were creating odd shadows on the dingy walls.

I realized that Jack hadn't come in at all and wondered if he'd decided to sleep downstairs in the basement.

I walked out into the dark hall and looked to my left, where the glowing flame of a lighter shadowed his face. He was standing beside an open locker, studying something. I approached him.

"What are you doing?" I asked.

"Wondering why the hell this guy decided to join the cheerleading team as a *cheerleader*." He tapped a knuckle against a grainy photo inside the locker. A fuzzy-haired person was only slightly visible behind a couple kissing on some grass.

I squinted in the dim light. "That's a female."

Jack scrunched up his face. "What?" His voice started in a high-pitched joking tone. "How can you even tell that?"

"She has breasts?" I tapped on the chest of the girl in the photo.

"Oh…" He drew the word out. "Yikes."

"No, it's refreshing considering many men prefer staring at breasts in their free time."

He looked hard at me for the first time since we'd gotten inside the building. Sometimes it was difficult to tell if he was wearing a joking or serious expression.

"Nah. I'm more of an earlobe and left pinky finger kind of guy." He flipped the lighter closed. The humor of his statement caught me so I smiled.

"Are my earlobes passable?"

"I dunno. It's too dark to tell."

I nodded, my smile fading. "So, why are you rooting around in high school students' lockers?" I gestured toward the photo again.

Jack cleared his throat. "Finding this." He opened his hand, revealing a thin white object.

"I see. There's no way you plan on using that."

"Of course. God wanted us to find this joint. I'm telling you."

"You're actually going to smoke that?" My voice became near scolding.

Jack chuckled. "Yeah right. No, man. *We're* going to smoke it."

"You're kidding."

"Nope."

"You are. You have to be."

"I solemnly swear I am telling the complete and honest truth whether you can handle it or not, Foxtrot."

"No way."

"Yahweh."

"I don't think so."

Jack leaned back against the locker and sighed. "Okay, how long are we going to do this before you give in?"

I spread my arms out to the sides. "Jack, I'm a doctor. It would be against everything I know as a medical professional to even be near a lit joint."

"You *were* a doctor."

I shook my head. "How do you know it's not laced? Is it even safe?"

Even in the dim candlelight, I could see a twinkle in Jack's eye.

"It's so incredibly safe that you wouldn't even believe it."

I mulled it over in my head for a moment too long before I asked, "You're going to make me do this, aren't you?"

Jack smiled and stood up straight. "Hey, this is a high school. It's the land of peer pressure. You practically have to smoke ten of these before you're even *cool*." He grabbed my hand and we walked toward the stairway. "Besides...you need to relax a little."

The warmth of his touch traveled up my arm and into my spine. I felt it spread up to my heart, almost making it stop completely. It was as if we really had traveled back in time to high school and I was a girl with a crush.

Jack sat down on the top step and invited me to join him. Once I was firmly seated, he put the joint in his mouth and flicked the lighter on once again. But he paused first. "You want the first go?"

"No. You found it, so you take the first...toke." I scolded myself for using such a juvenile word.

He shrugged. "Suit yourself."

The lighter hit the white paper and began to glow in the darkness. When Jack inhaled, he clicked it closed once again and the tip grew bright for a moment. Then, it was my turn.

"This is such a terrible idea." After too long a hesitation, I put the thing in my mouth and inhaled a bit too hard. I came up coughing while Jack just laughed at me.

"It shows."

"Oh?" I coughed. "What..." cough, "have you been a..." cough, "smoker your whole life?"

"Smoker for six years." He took another drag.

"Smoker or stoner?"

He handed the joint off to me again. "What's the difference? Nicotine and marijuana are both drugs. Once is just more harmful than the other."

I studied him for a second. "I don't think I've ever heard someone say that before."

"People either go one way..."

"Or the other..." I finished the sentence for him.

The joint was winding down as he passed it to me again, so he handed me the lighter to spark it up. I did, and then noticed the engraving on its scratched surface.

"What is the S for?"

"It's my...friend's." Jack was suddenly somber.

"Oh." I knew he'd meant the friend who'd died during the rabies outbreak. I could sense he wasn't ready to divulge.

"So what kind of girl are you?"

"I'm sorry?"

"Well, I'm an earlobe and left pinky guy...what are you?"

I looked at him. "I'm nothing."

"Yeah you are." He playfully snatched the lighter from me. As he tried to light the joint again, the silver box refused to spark a flame. He sighed and tossed it on the floor beside him. "Fuckin' thing." Taking another long drag anyway, he looked my way and leaned toward me. "So?"

He was so close, I could smell the sweat and dirt. For some reason, my entire body flushed and I was filled with something I hadn't felt since before Rex had been born. I took a deep breath.

"Fine. I'll go with penis size." And then laughter burst from my chest before I could stop it. Jack didn't follow suit. Instead, he tossed the mostly spent joint on the stair.

"Well, fuck."

I stopped laughing and we looked at each other. But after a second or two of silence, a smile broke out across his face and the good humor flowed once more. We both let off quite a bit of stress on the stairs before the high came down and we realized it was getting late.

"I should have a shower." I stood up to stretch my arms above my head. Jack watched me with careful eyes.

"Yeah?"

"Yes. Then I'll go to bed. Are you coming?"

"Uh...no. I'd rather just sit here and stare at..." He gestured toward the open locker once again. I tossed him a confused glance. "On...second thought... That sounded really pedophilic, so, yeah, I'm coming."

October 18

The TV in the teacher's lounge was broadcasting nothing but static, but I didn't care. The uniformity of the sound relaxed my body somehow. I found myself laying my head back against the sofa and just reveling in the quiet.

"150 channels and there's *nothing* on!"

Damn it. I ran a hand over my face. I wasn't in the mood to deal with Silas's crap.

"Aren't you wondering where I've been?"

I rolled my head to the left and looked at him. "Nope. In fact...I was hoping you'd fucking stay there."

The dead man recoiled ever so slightly. "Ooh. Still grumpy, I see."

"Yeah..." I could hear the exhaustion in my own voice as I put my head back against the couch. "Very very grumpy."

"Dude...you have nothing to be grumpy about with that beauty back there," he said, referring to the running water just behind the closed door next to us.

I said nothing.

"You know...I'm a fucking ghost. I can just go in there and take a peak then come back out and tell you all the good bits."

"Do whatever you want. I don't care." I had to close my eyes; the dull throb in the back of my head was returning.

"Really? You really truly don't care?"

I drew in a deep sigh. "No. I really truly don't care."

"You don't care about what?"

My eyes snapped open. I had been so out of it that I hadn't heard the water shut off. I lifted my head off the couch and took in all that was Lisa. She was wearing a short white shirt with a heart on it. It showed a bit of her midriff. The sweatpants she'd found were a bit too big and sliding just off her hips. Her hair was wet and hanging down her shoulders in shiny waves.

"The uh...the news." I collected myself as quickly as possible. "I don't care about this crap. All reruns."

She glanced at the screen then back at me. "Are you going to rinse off?"

"Uh, no. I'm just too beat."

"Okay."

I put my head against the sofa again. If I looked at her any longer, I wouldn't have been able to hide that I liked the way she was looking. A second later, I felt the sofa cushion next to me depress. I didn't lift my head, but instead opened my eyes and looked her way.

She tucked her legs under her. Our bodies were too close to touching. "Jack."

"Yeah?"

She tucked her hair behind an ear, but didn't answer.

I took one hand off the back of the sofa and nudged her shoulder. "What...?" I egged her on like I was a baseball coach telling my star player not to choke.

But she didn't smile, just remained silent.

"Where'd you find those clothes?" I tugged at one of the sleeves on the white shirt.

She finally looked at me. "There's a lost and found in the other room. I needed to change."

"I see that."

"We should have sex."

That got my attention. "What?"

"Listen."

"I never stopped listening." I couldn't decide whether there was excitement in my voice or anxiety.

"Obviously there's something between us," she said. This time, her full attention was on me. I must have had a dumb look on my face, so I relaxed my features a bit.

"Well, yeah, but...I mean...we barely know each other."

"You've been amazing with Rex and Alex and you're extremely resourceful. You've saved our lives many times." She was as still and serious as she had ever been.

"It's only been three."

"I'm serious."

"Me too!"

"I had a lot of time to think about this while I was in the shower—"

"Oh, God, Lisa." I groaned out loud. "Don't make me start picturing you naked. That's all I need right now."

"Then don't just picture it." In one swift movement, she removed the white shirt she'd been wearing. I averted my eyes.

"Ooh-kay, those are yours."

She touched my hand and I felt a jolt of electricity so forceful that I almost tore it away.

"Nope. Nope." I shook my head while trying not to look at her. "You don't want to do this."

"That's not your decision to make."

"I mean it. I don't perform well under pressure."

"No one does."

Before I could issue one more protest, she climbed on my lap and pressed her lips against mine. Oh, God, the warmth of her skin and the soft touch of her fingertips just did me in. I was at full attention immediately. When she came up for a breath, I tried more reasoning.

"Seriously, Lisa...this isn't right. You...you won't like it."

She had started planting soft kisses on my neck as I spoke. "Why not?" She didn't stop.

"Because, I...I'm not good...I'm not a good person." I felt her breath against my skin and a shiver ribboned through me.

"Feelings of inadequacy stem from lots of logical places." She finally stopped and sat straight on my lap. "We can talk about it if you want."

I could feel my mouth hanging slightly open. "If you think I can even remember what I had for breakfast with those things in my face, then you've got another thing coming!"

"Then shut up."

When she shifted her hips, I felt the pressure of her pelvis on mine. I couldn't help it and let out a groan that sounded more like the growl of a hungover college student.

137

"You want this just as much as I do."

"Just because you want something doesn't mean it's right."

She looked at me for a solemn moment. I couldn't read her face at all. The candlelight danced around us and gave her skin a soft yellow glow.

"I'm not your type," she finally said.

"I didn't say that."

"You don't have to. I studied psychology for a semester in college."

"What *didn't* you study?"

She sighed heavily. For the first time, I could see sorrow and hurt in her features. My heart dropped to my stomach and the blood rushed in the same direction. She tried to get up.

"No." I held her down. "Don't leave."

I felt her fingers tap impatiently against my shoulder. I grit my teeth as she shifted her weight once again. He was not behaving.

"Okay, okay. Look...I'm not...that big..."

"What?" She tucked a strand of hair behind her ear as if she hadn't heard me.

I grabbed both of her hands and brought them to my chest. "Size matters to you. I'll disappoint."

She blinked out of turn. "You thought I was serious." It wasn't even a question.

"You're always serious."

Two Men and a Lift Auto Garage

"We Auto Know"

Lisa screwed up her face for some reason. I couldn't tell what was happening until she cleared her throat. She'd been stifling a laugh.

"Jack. I've been with one other man in my life and I haven't had sex in three years. I can tell it's been a while for you, too."

"Thanks..."

"I'm not in a position to be choosy."

"Double thanks."

"Besides..." She freed her hands from mine and ran them down my stomach to the zipper on my jeans. "What I'm feeling in here is far from average."

I'm pretty sure my brain just gave up when she said that. It just stopped thinking altogether. There was nothing. Nothing except pure passion.

"Oh motherfuck." I groaned and pulled her against me. I felt her shudder under my hands as they ran up her naked back. When she bit her bottom lip I nearly lost it. "Fine. Let's do this."

I barely got the words out before my pants were unzipped and hers were completely off. I mean, she wasn't wrong when she "guessed" that I'd been celibate for a while. But it'd been longer than three years. And it was obvious.

As soon as she straddled me there was no going back and I lasted about half a second. Although I cringed, I felt the faint hint of a shiver on her side.

"I'm sorry..." I sighed and let my head fall back against the sofa again.

139

"It's all right." Her tone was soft and I could tell she meant it. I felt her nails brush down my arms and wasn't sure if it was a caress or an accident. "You're thinking about it too much."

"Yeah!" I brought my head up to look at her. "I don't even think the clock on the wall had a chance to tick."

"No, really. It's completely fine."

I took a long look at her. She was everything I could never get. She was gorgeous. Her dark hair was growing past the bob stage and just brushing her shoulders. She was smart, too. I had zero education. The last serious relationship I had ended up with her stealing my car and my favorite t-shirt. Plus she sucked in bed.

No. I wasn't going to screw it up. If this was going to be the only night we had together, I was going to make it count. I wasn't just doing it for her; I was doing it for myself too.

"It's completely *not* fine." I grabbed a handful of her hair and brought her mouth to mine. She tensed at first, but relaxed when I touched her cheek. Her breathing quickened and she was making small hums of desire between kisses. I stopped.

"I wasn't ready last time. This time I'm ready and it's gonna get done right." I reached behind my head and tugged my shirt off. The entire time, Lisa watched me with one hand to her chest as though she were catching her breath.

As I tried to wiggle out of my jeans, they got stuck on my right foot. I tried to shake them off, but they stayed. "God...fuck!"

"Hey..." Lisa's voice was back to its soft tenor. It was the voice that made my thoughts melt. "It's okay."

I gave one last forceful kick and the jeans finally flew into the corner of the dusty room. Before they even landed, I had snaked my left arm around Lisa's waist and practically flipped her onto her back.

"Oh!" Her tone was one of surprise, but it quickly faded back to relaxed. "Oh."

"Know what I found out while you were in the shower?"

"What?" The question emerged breathy.

I grinned as I placed one hand on the top of the couch and the other on her left side. Then, I pushed down hard. The couch groaned loudly but eventually gave way and flattened out with a cloud of dust.

"Jesus!"

I grinned. "This is a futon."

"So it seems."

We stared at each other. "Fuck...you're beautiful."

Her face twisted into a slight grimace. "I've never heard anyone put it so forcefully before."

"I mean it." I allowed my hands to follow the curves of her waist and hips. Her breathing began to deepen again. "And I may not be an Adonis, but I can at least give you one night you deserve."

And it seemed that I did just that. I was positive it was going to be a one-time thing, so I made sure I touched every inch of her with the tips of my fingers. I was careful to whisper

141

to her exactly how she made me feel when she made me feel it. And in the final moments, she said my name. *My name.*

"This won't mean much, but you have nothing to feel inadequate about." Her voice was barely above a whisper as I caressed her bare arm.

"I appreciate that."

"Do you think we'll make it?"

Sadness welled up inside me. Lisa was vulnerable and she was showing it to me. She was unrated. I had to make her feel better. If I didn't, I'd fail miserably.

But my words were stuck in my throat. No matter how hard I tried, I couldn't speak. All I could do was put my forehead against hers.

"I know. We can't know for sure. We should get some sleep."

I fucked it up.

It wasn't the sun that woke me the next morning. When I was able to muster the strength to open my eyes, I noticed Jack had covered me with a blanket at some point during the night. He was lying next to me, on his back with one arm above his head. He was going to wake up to it numb.

The giggling caught my attention again. It was Rex. I sat up and tried to rub the sleep from my eyes. I was having an incredible nights' sleep so I was slightly upset that it had been interrupted.

"Peek-boo!"

Rex was ready to get out of bed. My hair had dried naturally overnight and was in messy waves. I tried to smooth it down before I reached for my clothes. Perpetual mornings without coffee weren't conducive to a productive day, but I fought through it, lazily slipping on my jeans and pulling my t-shirt over my head.

"Peek-boo!"

I sighed. "I'm coming, Rex." As I stood, I felt the overwhelming urge to just flop back onto the futon and sleep for twelve more hours. But that wasn't going to happen. I turned to see Rex standing on the arm of the other sofa, looking out the dingy window giggling.

"Oh, my God."

"Peek-boo!"

Rex was playing peek-a-boo with a rabies infected man clawing at the window outside. Bloody streaks followed his fingers. His moans were barely audible.

"Jack."

I inched toward my son while keeping one arm stretched toward my sleeping partner. Alex stirred in the next room.

"Jack."

Rex giggled louder as the diseased man outside seemed to be getting more desperate.

"*Jack.*" I raised my voice the slightest bit.

"Peek-boo!"

The man outside pounded hard against the window with a closed fist. The glass rattled in its frame, a crack stretching across the bottom pane.

"What the fuck?" Jack had heard the sound and bolted upright. Alex let out a tiny shriek.

"We have a problem."

He turned around and looked at Rex giggling happily and banging a tiny fist against the wall. Jack smiled. But that faded when he saw the bloody near-corpse clawing to get inside.

"Holy fuck!" He scrambled out of bed and began furiously gathering his clothes. In his haste, he banged his right arm against a door jamb. "Fuck!"

"It's numb."

"Yeah, what the fuck?" He wiggled it around after making a frustrated sound in his throat. Alex jumped out of the cot and ran to him.

"You slept with it above your head." I grabbed the numb arm and dragged him to the middle of the room with Alex still attached at his waist. "Hold still." I stood him up straight and paced two fingers on either side of his neck. While trying to coax Rex away from the window, I massaged Jack's neck lightly.

"Rex! Rex!"

My son finally looked at me. "Peek-boo, momma!"

"Yes, peek-a-boo, sweetie. But right now we have to go, okay?"

He shook his head. "No."

"Jesus Christ…"

Jack stomped a foot on the ground. His face was twisted into a grimace. I let him go and he hopped over to my son.

"Pins and needles…" he muttered. "Hey, buddy, wanna play an even better game?"

Rex hesitated, but eventually nodded. The man outside continued to claw and bang on the window. Jack instructed me to grab the shotgun he'd put in the cabinet the night before. While I did that, he explained the rules of his game with my son.

"Okay, so this game is called Burn or Bust."

"Yeah!" Rex jumped up and down.

"The rules are all three of us have to get out of here because the floor is turning into hot lava," Alex said.

"Oh no!" Rex stopped jumping and listened.

"Yeah. Also, that guy out there…" She pointed out the window. "If you touch him, you lose automatically!"

"Fun!" Rex clapped his little hands together.

I handed Jack his shotgun. He grabbed it and winced. "Pins and needles…"

Rex ran to me and I picked him up in my arms. For a moment, I envied him. Ignorance was bliss. He wasn't frightened at all.

"Do you think there are any of them in here?"

The four of us backed slowly out of the room.

"No way. I blocked us in tight."

"So where's this other way out?"

The man pounded against the window a final time and the glass gave way. Pieces hit the floor as his hand made its way through. The shattered edges of the broken window cut through his arm, but he didn't seem to mind.

"Ok. Time to go!" Jack grabbed me with his free hand and dragged us out of the room. We didn't have the luxury of taking our time, so we had to fumble down the stairs and through the dark hallway. A crow cawed and flew over our heads to the second floor.

"Fucker's gonna get eaten." Jack skidded to a stop just outside a metal door with a large padlock on it. "All right, guys...cover your ears!" He aimed and shot the padlock. The deafening sound rang through the hallways of the school. It was quickly followed by the howls of what sounded like hundreds of diseased people.

"Fantastic." Jack kicked at what was left of the padlock until the chain fell to the floor with a loud clatter. He looked at me briefly before pulling the door open a crack. "Fuck."

"That's not good. What?"

"They're all over the car."

"Jesus."

"Wait." He held a hand back and scooted forward, opening the door wider and letting the sunlight in. "Look at this."

I approached him with caution. Rex began to squirm. I held him tighter. When I stopped next to Jack, I followed the nose of the shotgun. My gaze landed on three vehicles sitting vacant in another part of the lot we didn't see the day prior.

"We'll take one of those."

"Who knows where they came from or if they even work. They may have been abandoned because they were out of gas."

He shook his head. "Cars can run on fumes, man… My bet is on the Toyota over there." He pointed to a blue sedan about a hundred yards ahead.

"How do we get to it?" Alex asked.

Jack was silent for a moment. I studied his features. He was thinking hard. "Ok. I'm gonna sneak around the side of the building this way toward our car. I'll get within range and set off the alarm. If there are any more of them around, they'll all swarm to it. When you hear the alarm go off, you high-tail it over to those vehicles and if the Toyota isn't unlocked, find one of them that is. I'll run over and hotwire it."

I didn't like the plan, but I logically knew it was the only way to get out. I nodded and set Rex down. "Okay, Rex. Ready to play for real?"

"Yeah!"

"Okay…when you hear the car alarm go off, we're going to run."

"Yay!"

I looked back at Jack. He was surveying the outside, trying to find an opening. When he'd found one, he looked back at me.

"Here I go." He grinned, but it was weak. He was scared.

I took a deep breath and grabbed the back of his head, pulling him into a kiss. "Be careful."

His eyes were wide with what looked like surprise, but he nodded before slipping outside into the bright sun. I watched him for as long as I could until he disappeared around a corner of the school.

"When we go, momma?" Rex was bouncing slightly on his feet.

"Soon, honey." I pulled Alex close to us. She was shivering.

We waited in the dark for what seemed like days. I was sure thirty minutes had passed when I heard the car alarm and the howls of those things. I grabbed my son and Alex and ran as fast as my legs could carry me over to the group of cars at the other end of the parking lot. I didn't dare looked behind me.

I was nearly out of breath when I reached the Toyota. With my free hand I pulled at the passenger side door. It was locked.

"Fuck!"

"Bad word..." Rex mumbled the sentence.

"I know." I swung around. The next closest car to us was a brown van with no windows in the back. I hesitated. There was no way that thing had gas. An ear-splitting howl startled me out of my thoughts.

When I turned my head, I saw the one that was banging against the window dragging itself toward us. I spun around as fast as I could and launched myself at the brown van. By the grace of whatever god I believed in that split second, the door was unlocked. I threw myself and Rex into the passenger seat. Alex scrambled in after us, shutting the door as hard as she could.

"Game over?" Rex asked.

"I don't know." I was busy looking out the window for the creature following us.

The driver side door flung open and a scream escaped me. Jack hopped in, locking the door behind him. Then he wiggled under the seat and tore off the panel beneath the steering wheel.

"Didn't think you'd be *that* excited to see me."

"I'm just glad you're in one piece."

A few sparks lit up his face before the engine roared to life. He jumped back into the driver's seat like it was nothing, put the van into gear, and floored it.

"Wee!"

Rex ran to the rear of the van where there were blankets and discarded clothes. He plopped himself in a pile of them and giggled.

Jack finally let out his breath and looked to me to grin. But the smile faded quickly. "What?"

"You just did that like you've done it thousands of times before."

"I have."

*   *   *

The sun was setting as we crossed the Utah border. Another night doing nothing but driving. I wasn't looking forward to it. Jack had been anxious all day about something. I had to figure it out because the incessant drumming of his fingers on the steering wheel was driving me crazy.

"You're anxious."

He glanced sideways at me as though I'd startled him. "No, I'm not."

"Yes, you are. What is it? Would you like to talk about it?" I tried to use my softest, most sincere tone.

"You getting all shrink on me? Because if you are..."

"I'm just concerned." The accusatory tone behind his voice had hit me hard. I didn't want him to be upset with me. Why was he upset with me?

After a few moments of excruciating silence, he said, "Okay, look... I know you've been waiting all day to break it to me and I've been waiting all day for it to come too, but I'll just put it out there to take the stress off of you." His sentence leaked out in one breath.

"I'm listening," I said after another pregnant pause.

"I know you're thinking last night was a mistake and that's totally okay. I've been through it before and it'll hurt my feelings, but I'm a big boy and I'll get over it."

I scrunched up my face for a moment, soaking in what he'd said. He may have said he'd get over it eventually, but there was already mild hurt in his voice.

"Last night wasn't a mistake."

"What?"

"Last night wasn't a mistake. I want to have sex with you again."

"Shh!" He straightened and looked in the rear view mirror.

"It's ok." I heard Alex's voice. "Momma used to talk about the men she'd bring home. I know what grown-ups do."

"She understands perfectly well. I'm confident there will be more."

Jack's brow furrowed. "What...are you talking about right now?" The question began with his voice at a high note, but made a decrescendo back to tenor at the tail end.

I took a deep breath to still my frustration. It felt almost as if he were playing a game of sympathy. Maybe he was. I didn't know much about him after all.

"I plan on having sex with you again."

"Why?"

"Are you serious?"

"As the holocaust."

"That's not very nice," Alex said.

"Well, the holocaust was *indeed* serious." I sucked in a breath and pursed my lips, trying to take the emotion out of my next statement. "Last night was amazing. You were amazing and I'd like to continue if that's all right with you."

He looked at me with one eye squinted. "You don't want to do that."

My frustration deepened. "I'd really appreciate it if you stopped making my decisions for me."

"Women of your caliber don't go for a guy like me." There was pain in his voice. He'd been hurt before.

"What do you mean?"

He sighed. "You're smart. Really smart. You finished college. You're gorgeous. I'm just a dumb mechanic."

I rested my elbow on the window frame of the van and placed my chin in my palm. My heart went out to him. This wasn't a game. He truly believed he wasn't good enough.

"The level of my intelligence didn't save us from those things. It didn't save us this morning. That was *you*. I didn't save us in Las Vegas. That was *you*. You have skills that are extremely important. If it weren't for you, we'd be dead." I gestured to the back where Rex had been playing pat a cake with Alex. "I don't know the first thing about hotwiring a car."

152

Even in the waning sun I could see the flicker of a smile. "Well, yeah, but..." He shrugged both shoulders. "You're just on a way higher level than me. I'm a 9mm bullet and you've got a first class ticket into a sniper rifle."

"While your analogy is definitely amusing, you have a very skewed definition of caliber."

"Well that was—"

"No, I know. Everyone's definition of 'better' is different. I'm not on a higher level. I'm on a different level. Everyone is." My explanation seemed to relax him just a bit.

"Yeah, but wouldn't you rather be around scholarly professors drinking brandy and talking about philosophy?"

I actually chuckled at that one. "Philosophy is a joke. It's just people asking ridiculous questions. You do know that all philosophers were inherently high on some kind of strong narcotic about half their lives."

Jack let out a belly laugh. It made me smile just the slightest bit.

"I'll tell you something that not even Sylvia knew about me."

"Oh, you have my attention now. Should I pull over for this?"

"No. Keep driving, please."

"You got it, Foxtrot."

I cleared my throat and took a deep breath. "Men don't typically entertain me."

"That... Did you just tell me you're gay?"

"I'm sorry? No. What I mean was that I've never met a man that could make me genuinely laugh."

"Pfft. I've heard you laugh once at my jokes and it was fake as hell."

"You amuse me on the inside."

"Oh-kay." He drew the word out with a grin.

"I enjoy your company. I enjoy you. I really, really like you."

Jack scratched at the stubble on one side of his face. "Oh, yeah?"

"Yes."

"Well…" He reached a hand over and touched my face gingerly. "I've really, really liked you since I saw you standing outside trying to start a car that wouldn't have started in a million years." His grin absolutely warmed my heart.

October 19

"I can't tell you how much I appreciate the fact that they at least left a Classical music station going."

I rolled my head to the side to get a good look at Lisa. Chopin's beautiful music floated lightly out of the car windows. The stars were bright and plentiful. The night was quiet. Out there, no one would have been able to tell the world had ended.

"Yeah." I took a deep breath, the hood of the van clunking incompatibly with my weight. There was no way I could've kept my mind off what she'd said on the drive. She liked me. She wanted me. That feeling was overwhelming. Oddly enough, for the first time in a long time I was happy. I felt normal.

"Staring up at the sky like this makes you really feel insignificant. The observable universe in itself is massive."

Every time she talked that way I felt a lump in my throat. "You know what else is massive?"

"I'm sorry?" She turned toward me. Apparently the hood of the car didn't appreciate her weight either.

I shifted myself slightly to face her more head on. "My..." I watched her for any signs that she'd gotten the joke. There were none. "My dick. Okay, let's move on. I like to cuddle. Do you?"

A quizzical eyebrow rose in response to my question. A smile even played on her lips. She was coming out of her shell because of me.

156

"I don't believe I've ever had the opportunity."

I sat up. "Say *what*?"

Lisa scooted closer and looked up at me. Finally seeing something akin to humor in her eyes was refreshing. I liked it.

"Do you know how easy it is for a woman to contract a UTI after sex?"

My thoughts ran away from me. I turned my head to the side and smiled. "Are you serious right now?"

"I'm alwa—"

"Always serious. I know." We looked at each other for a moment. "So you're one of those hit it, quit it and shower it off kind of girls?" I grinned at her.

"If you're inferring that I prefer to stay healthy with an active sex life, then yes."

Very softly, I brushed some hair out of her eyes. My fingertips lingered on her cheek for a second or two. She was so warm and inviting underneath that stony exterior.

"Jeez, Foxtrot, you are super hot when you talk all doctorey."

Her mouth dropped open slightly. Every fiber in my body pulled me toward kissing her. "Doctorey?"

I looked up, pretending to think. "Mm...on second thought..." I slipped a hand under her back and brought her as close to me as I could. Then I kissed her like I meant it — like my life depended on it. "You're just super hot."

Her right hand was holding onto my left arm. "No one has ever said something like that to me."

"Oh, yeah?" I took the hand from my arm and kissed her palm. "Why not?"

"I'm not entirely sure."

"Maybe they were afraid to."

She shrugged. "Maybe."

"Fireflies!"

The two of us sat up on the hood of the car to see Alex and Rex chasing after glowing pinpoints of light. They were both giggling happily.

"Do you think she misses her mother?"

"Half of her does."

I glanced at Lisa, but she was watching the children.

"Sylvia wasn't ready to be a mother twelve years ago. Of course, children are more intelligent than people give them credit for. Alex knew her mother didn't want her."

I turned my attention toward the little girl once more. The smile on her face did seem a bit pained, but she was a strong one.

"That sucks."

"Indeed. Alex spent a lot of time with me and her grandmother. That's why she knows how to take care of Rex. She's like a sister to him even though you can't tell on the outside."

"You caught one!" Alex jumped up and down while watching Rex marvel at the light in his hand.

He looked up at her. "Yay! I did it!" He began mirroring her movements. But in so doing, closed his palm and squashed

the bug. After contemplating his hand for a few seconds, his face began to twist into what I'd grown to know as the Tantrum Face.

"Hey! Rex! There's more, look!" Alex leapt in the air and snatched a bug. Closing her palms lightly, she brought it over to him and showed him the glow between her fingers. "I think there's a jar in the back of the van. Can we keep him?"

The two of them looked over at us. I felt some emotion rise from the pit of my stomach into my chest. "Yeah..."

"Yay! What should we name him?"

"Ba-ba-di!" Rex began to prance up and down while he followed Alex calling, "Ba-ba-di! Ba-ba-di!"

"Ba-ba-di?" I tossed a look at Lisa.

"You know the movie. Bibidi, babadi, boo."

*   *   *

I cut the engine outside a hotel at the end of a road. It looked pretty empty. I was surprised everything had been abandoned so quickly yet the infected were scarce in certain areas.

"Welcome to the Desert Rose Hotel in the middle of bumfuck, nowhere."

"Are we staying the night?" Alex asked from the back.

"Yep. It's better to be rested and alert than tired and driving."

"It's charming," Lisa said, unbuckling her seatbelt.

"Boo!" Rex crinkled his nose.

"What? You don't like it?" I turned in my seat. He shook his head. "Would you rather sleep in the van?"

Rex looked to his left, then his right, then up and down. When he looked back at me, his eyes were wide. "Nuh-uh."

"That's what I thought. Let's go, Romeo and Juliet!"

I hopped out and ran around to help Lisa out of her side. She was still a little weak from the wound in her side. At first, she swatted my hand away, but I forced myself in and grabbed her under the arms. She let out a little yelp as I gently threw her over my shoulder and began walking toward the hotel entrance.

"Okay, this has gone on long enough. Please put me down, Jack."

The kids were giggling behind us.

"No way, Foxtrot."

"Auntie Lisa, you look like a damsel in distress." Alex's smile was huge.

I pounded on my chest with a free fist. "Me Tarzan. You Jane."

I heard what I thought was a laugh from Lisa as we went through the double doors of the hotel. When I put her down, she swiped at me playfully even though her expression was serious.

"Wow...this place is huge!" Alex handed the firefly to Rex and ran to the center of the room. The lights were still on. I could hear the faint hum of a generator coming from somewhere.

"Whoever was here left in a hurry," I said. Lisa approached the front desk.

"Hello!" Alex shouted. "Can you hear me? Hello?"

"What are you doing?" I stood next to her, taking in the dirty furniture and stained carpets.

"I'm trying to hear my echo."

"I found room keys." Lisa straightened from behind the front desk and held out two key cards. I grabbed Alex in a pretend choke-hold.

"All right. Come on, knuckleheads, let's get some rest."

"But I'm not tired!"

*   *   *

"Not tired, my ass." I shut the adjoining door to our room and clicked the lock shut. "That girl went out with the lights. Asleep before her head even hit the pillow."

"What if they need help?" Lisa was perched on the fluffy king bed. She'd showered and changed into clothes that must have been left behind.

"I told them to pound if they needed anything. But their door is locked and chained. They know not to go outside."

She nodded. I could sense something was weighing on her.

"What's wrong, beautiful?" I pushed her back onto the bed and went down on top of her. She smiled – which made my heart beat faster – and I pushed the hair out of her face with both hands.

"Now that I have you I'm scared."

"Go ahead."

She grabbed the hem of my shirt and pulled it up. I slipped it off and kissed her everywhere skin was showing.

"I had a plan."

"What do you mean?"

"I was going to get Rex to safety then end my life."

I sat up quickly. "What?"

She closed her eyes while shaking her head. "Shh. No. Try not to take that tone. Relax."

"Uh, how can I relax when you just told me you're gonna kill yourself?"

"Please listen, Jack."

I studied her face but said nothing.

"I didn't know how things would eventually turn out, but the odds of me being alive at the end of this are slim."

"You don't—"

She put her index finger up. "Please. I need to finish. All I knew was that being a mother was all I had. I protect my son's life until I can't anymore."

I fell down next to her. She turned and faced me with that stony expression again.

"But when you walked into our lives that all changed."

I allowed my hand to glide down to her hip.

"You make me want to stay alive, Jack."

Scooting close to her, I said, "I feel the same."

Lisa's head inched back slightly. "Well, I know that. Otherwise we wouldn't be having this conversation."

I rolled over and groaned while covering my eyes. "We were doing so well!"

"I'm sorry. I ruined the mood."

I turned back to her. "Well, yeah, but you can make up for it." My hand slid down to her hips again and this time, I slipped it between her legs. She was so soft and warm.

"What can I do?" Her eyes were closed.

"Say something sexy to me."

"Something sexy."

I stopped what I was doing as a smile spread across her face. Just that tiny gesture of trust and humor made my pulse rush.

"I can't believe it."

"That's about the second joke I've ever told."

"*That* I can believe."

She smiled at me for another moment before pulling me down for a kiss. But before her lips touched mine, she whispered, "I want you."

"You have me."

Making love to Lisa felt like second nature. It felt like I'd done it a hundred times before yet it was still new to me. I could read her body as if it were my own. I knew when she wanted me to kiss her and where. I knew when to tease her and when not to.

She was beautiful and sexy no matter what angle I looked at her from. But when she was on top of me was my

favorite way to see her. Because I could see everything she had. Even beyond what was outside.

I took both her hands and laced my fingers with hers. Then I sat up so we were almost hugging while I was still inside her. When I let her hands go, she wrapped them around my shoulders. I kissed her below her ear.

"Why'd you stop?" Her question was short and breathy.

"Because I'm in love with you." My lips touched her skin as I whispered into her ear.

She made a funny noise in the back of her throat and squirmed a tiny bit. "Why...?"

I pulled her closer to me so we were still connected. The motion caused her to inhale sharply. "That's not exactly the response I was hoping for."

"I apologize." Her nails bit into the skin on my shoulders. She wanted to keep going and badly. "I don't know."

My fingertips caressed the back of her neck. Our bodies were so close that I swore our souls were touching.

"You don't know if you love me?"

"No, I...I don't know..."

I looked as deep into her as I could. "You haven't been unsure about anything so far. What's the matter?"

She bit her bottom lip. While it was the sexiest gesture I'd seen out of her, it meant something else at that moment. I could tell she was uncomfortable with not knowing.

"I don't know how much time we have."

I shrugged, pulling her closer and beginning to move again. "Who does?"

"Mmm...but what if I get bitten tomorrow?" Her questions became half questions as I laid back and let her do what she wanted.

"And what if I get eaten by a mountain lion tomorrow?"

"Cougar."

I would have rolled my eyes, but she was making me feel too good for that. "Well...then...what if I get...eaten by a cougar?" My grip on her hips tightened. We were both close. "So many things can...happen. Doesn't matter...if it's the end..."

"Oh...Jack..." She tossed her head back as pleasure rolled through our bodies.

"I don't think I'm ever gonna get used to that," I said as she flopped down next to me, her skin sparkling with sweat.

"What's that?"

"That you...*you* say my name during sex."

"I love you."

I rolled over and took her into my arms. "I know."

A sigh escaped her and she pushed me away with one hand. "Jack."

I laughed. "I'm sorry. I couldn't help it." I touched my lips to hers. "I love you."

She didn't smile on the outside, but it was there behind her eyes as she settled into me. Cuddling with her was odd at first because there was no discomfort. She always fit no matter

what position we were in. I felt as though that was the biggest sign of fate I'd ever experienced.

Other women I'd been with had either been too skinny or had so much hair that I'd end up eating it at night. I even recalled one former girlfriend who'd eat chips or crackers in bed. I'd wake up to crumbs. Sometimes I'd have to clean them out of my ass.

"What are you laughing at?" Lisa asked.

"Marry me."

"I'm sorry?" She sat up on her elbow and watched me.

"Let's get married."

"I think you and I both know that's not a good idea." She pulled the bedsheets up so they were covering her chest, but I pulled them down. She was too beautiful not to touch.

"Why not?"

The sarcastic laugh that escaped her stung. "It's the end of the world, Jack. I doubt anyone's going to be handing out marriage licenses. Besides, we hardly know each other. I don't even know how many girlfriends you had before me."

"Three."

She cleared her throat. "Okay."

"So, marry me."

After a long pause, a sigh and averted gaze, she said, "No."

The words stung. They felt like hot knives in my belly. I felt the burn of tears welling behind my eyes, but I wasn't going to cry. Not in front of her. Then again, she'd already told me she

Two Men and a Lift Auto Garage

"We Auto Know"

loved me. She'd shown me a vulnerable side of herself that I don't think anyone else had seen. But I wanted more than that. I wanted a life partner, no matter how short that life might have been.

"I'm sorry."

I shook off the sorrow my heart had pumped into me and shrugged. "It's ok. But I'm going to keep asking you."

October 19

    "Hey, Juliet. What are you doing up?" I didn't even need to stop what I was doing to see her out of the corner of my eye. Still clad in pajamas, she approached the car.

    "What are you doing?" Once she got to the passenger side, she stood on tip toes to look into the engine.

    "Well, there seems to be a hole in the brake line. Just can't tell which."

    She climbed onto the bumper and peered inside. "How do you know there's a hole?"

    I picked her up and moved her in front of me. While leaning against the hood, I pointed to the brake fluid reservoir.

    "See this?"

    "Yeah."

    "It should be full. The fluid should hit this line here. If we run out of fluid, we're Biter Meat."

    "So how do you find the hole?"

    "Here." I picked up the spray bottle full of water I'd been using and gave it to her. "Spray around the reservoir until it's soaked."

    She did as I told her.

    "Now, do you see any bubbles anywhere?"

    Alex leaned forward, searching all around for any sign of air. "No."

    "Okay, then that means there's no problem here. Want to take the wheel?" I grinned at her deer in headlights look.

    "You want me to drive?"

169

"I want you to get in and pump the brake while I'm under the car, ok?"

She nodded, hopping off the bumper and opening the driver's side door while I got down on the ground to look for signs of leakage.

"Ready?" I held my hand up for her to see.

"Ready."

"Go." I motioned with my hand for her to pump the brakes. Then I waited. After a few seconds, a drip began to form under the passenger side. I gave Alex the OK and she jumped out of the car. When she got down on the ground with me, I showed her the leak.

"Time to jack it up," I said.

"Jack it up?" Alex's face scrunched into a ball. "My mom used to say that when she would get in fights."

I couldn't help but chuckle. "This is different."

"Time to Uncle Jack it up!" She hopped to her feet. Together, we went to the back of the van to find the spare tire. The jack was the simple part. All we had to do was wind the crank. But when I went down on my back and wiggled underneath the vehicle, Alex hesitated.

"How safe is that?"

I looked out at her. "You jacked it up. What do you think?"

Her brows knit together. "I don't know."

"Hey, I'm under here. I've done this a thousand times, Juliet. Nothin' to it but to do it."

Two Men and a Lift Auto Garage

"We Auto Know"

Slowly, Alex got down on her knees and wiggled alongside me under the car.

"See? Told you there's nothing to worry about."

She smiled at me. "So what now?"

I handed her the spray bottle. "Same thing. See these two tubes here? Get them wet. No, get them wet, not me!"

Alex giggled while trying not to spray me in the face. We waited for air bubbles to form, but nothing came up.

"Okay, so it's not in the line itself."

"Is this one a head-scratcher?"

"Nope." I grumbled as I stood. My knee was giving off dull twinges of pain. "Let's remove the wheel." I grabbed the wrench to remove the lug nuts, then I removed the tire and hubcap. I showed Alex how to stand on the wrench to loosen the lug nuts.

"Why do we have to do it this way?"

"Because..." I stomped once more to get the last bolt out. "If they aren't on tight enough, the wheel goes flyin'."

"Oh."

"Oh-kay, let's see..." I checked around the inside of the wheel until I could see some fluid dripping down the side. "Got it. Have to fix the cylinder."

Alex and I worked on fixing the small crack. Since we didn't have any new parts around, we just had to make do with a Band-Aid. At one point, Alex nicked her finger. As it began to bleed, I put a clean rag over it. I admit I was a bit panicked — asking her if she was okay over and over.

171

She smiled up at me. "Don't worry. It doesn't hurt. And now my hands will look like yours!"

As much as her words warmed me to my core, I shot her a skeptical glance. "What's wrong with my hands?"

She dropped the rag and grabbed both my hands in hers. "They're all beat up."

I shrugged. I couldn't see anything wrong with them. Sure, there were a few scars here and there and they were dirty. But every mark told a story.

"They've been through a lot."

"I bet Aunt Lisa likes the way they feel." There was a devilish glint in Alex's eye.

"Whoa, now. Save that kind of talk for when you're twenty." We went back to work.

"I'm glad Aunt Lisa found you. She needs someone."

"Oh, yeah?" I pushed the sting of rejection away at the mention of her name. "Why do you say that?"

"She's lonely. She doesn't think I can tell, but I'm smarter than that."

"I see."

"I didn't like the way Rex's dad treated her."

We finished the repair and began to put the wheel back on. "Your mom liked to defend him. He sounded like a fine guy."

Alex scoffed. "She said that stuff because they were with each other behind Aunt Lisa's back."

Yikes. "No wonder she's afraid to commit."

172

"That's why I'm glad she found you." Alex smiled up at me. There was a spot of grease on her forehead. I grabbed the rag and rubbed it in.

"Go shower. Lisa will be up soon and you've got the mechanic look now."

October 19

  I awoke to an empty hotel room. Jack wasn't asleep next to me nor was he in the bathroom. The early morning sun was streaming in through the curtains. The night before played over and over in my head. I felt as if I hadn't done the right thing. But my head had never steered me wrong before.

  The realization that I was in love with Jack took a weight off my shoulders. It had made me realize I was lonely. I'd been lonely for a long time. My plan of suicide was no longer in the works. I had people that needed me. On one hand, that was a blessing. On the other – a curse.

  Every day I'd thought of suicide. What we were going through was not a life. That was my objective opinion. We were running. Constantly scared. Trying to stay alive. What kind of existence was that?

  But then there was Jack. And Alex. And Rex. They counted on me to an extent. I knew there wasn't much I could offer, but perhaps my presence was enough support.

  After putting on the clothes I'd found the night before, I stepped outside into the morning. There was a breeze, but the heat of the day could already be felt in the dry air. I was barefoot. The concrete was cool under me.

  Jack was fiddling around under the hood of the brown van. Sweat beaded on his arms as he worked. My stomach felt as though it were doing flips inside me. I'd never had butterflies before.

  "Hey." I leaned against one side of the car.

  "Morning." He didn't look at me. All he did was take the rag that was slung over his shoulder and wipe from sweat from his brow.

"Would you like some coffee? There's actually still some of the instant—"

"I'm okay, thanks."

For some reason, his short, curt answers began to hurt my feelings. "I apologize if I upset you last night, but I just don't think getting married is a good idea at the moment."

He stopped was he was doing and rested both hands on the front lip of the car, but he still wouldn't look at me. "I'd rather not talk about it."

"Keeping it inside really isn't healthy."

He went back to work. "Yeah, well that's how normal people do things."

That hurt. I wasn't expecting such a negative reaction from something that seemed so obvious to me. Neither of us said anything for some time. After a few long and intense moments, Jack stopped working abruptly after shooting me a glance out of the corner of his eye.

"Shit." He sighed. "Look, I'm sorry. I've gotten used to being rejected my entire fucking life, but for some reason it hurts more coming from you."

"I understand."

He looked at me hard. I couldn't tell what he was thinking, but his features were stressed. "I don't think you do, Lisa." He tossed the rag down onto the engine. "You have great control over your emotions and reactions. I don't. Tons of people don't. I love you...Christ...you're so...perfect, but..."

"You don't know how badly I wanted to say yes."

He shut his mouth. I waited for him to speak, but nothing came out. Even I didn't know what to say at that moment.

"Then...why didn't you?" His tone was soft.

"Because I can't be that person who gets married only to have their spouse die in days or weeks. And neither can you."

He seemed to mull it over. "Life is about taking risks."

"You really call this a life?" I stretched out my arms, indicating the world around us.

A half smile appeared on his face, but his eyes looked through me to something else. "Yeah...I do." He came back from wherever he'd been with a serious expression. "Rex and Alex are amazing. They're great kids and I like spending time with them. And I *love* you. This is absolutely my life and...I wouldn't have it any other way. Because if it happened differently, I might not have met you all."

I felt his words weigh on me. It was incredibly sweet of him to have those feelings, but I still had to stick to my decision. I went to him and put my arms around his middle.

"That makes me happy."

He hugged me back, then pulled away to look into my eyes. "I'm glad."

"Will you come inside and have coffee?"

"Will you marry me?"

"No."

He nodded, but smiled as he picked me up and pinned me against the van. "I bet you a thousand dollars I get you to say yes."

The way he was looking at me and the heat of his body caused mine to react. His arms were so strong yet gentle. Rex was happy when he was around. Our intimacy had a deep connection and he was extraordinary in bed.

"I knew it."

The words startled me out of my thought coma. "I'm sorry?"

"You're totally ready to go." He lowered his voice to a tone that vibrated through my entire body.

"No. I'm fine."

His hand moved from the side of the van to my arm. Fingertips brushed my skin until they reached the hem of my shirt. As he slid it underneath my clothes and over my bare skin, he learned forward.

"Then why are your nipples hard?"

The tone he used nearly caused me to lose control. But when he began touching me where I liked it most, the world dissolved away. When he kissed me it was pure passion – the kind of kiss you only experience once. It takes your breath away and spins your head like a top.

I wanted to touch him too, but before I could, he shifted so his leg was between my thighs. I knew he could tell how aroused he'd made me.

When we stopped kissing, I drew in a deep breath, unaware I'd been holding it so long. And I allowed a sigh of pleasure escape when he started using his mouth on me.

"You're enjoying this." His breath against my skin caused another shudder to wrack me.

"Yes."

He stopped and stood up. "Good. There will be more where that came from when we're married."

"Jack."

"Lisa."

"You can't just stop like that." I pleaded with him using my eyes.

"I just did. Now you can experience what blue balls are like." After a wince, he reached down and adjusted his jeans. Somehow, that gesture brought the flame back for a split second.

I set my jaw. "I don't think so. I'll just masturbate."

He leaned back, eyes wide. "What?"

I pushed past him and went for the hotel room. I wasn't about to let him control me or my feelings. I'd been pleasuring myself for three years and was perfectly fine. Sure, having a man do the work for me was a nice concept, but if he refused, then I'd do it myself.

After a moment of what I perceived as stunned silence, Jack ran to me. "Can I watch?"

Two Men and a Lift Auto Garage

"We Auto Know"

October 19

Lisa let me watch her masturbate. It was awesome.

I gave a short knock on the adjoining door between hotel rooms. There was no answer. I unbolted it and peeked inside. Rex was sleeping soundly with two fingers in his mouth. Alex's bed was empty, but the shower was running in the bathroom. I knocked, asking if everything was ok.

"Almost done!" Alex's voice sounded almost cheery.

I felt arms wrap around my waist and hot breath on my neck. "Where do you think you're going?"

I tossed Jack a backwards glance. "Not very far seeing as how your monstrous erection is pushing into my lower vertebra. That actually hurts."

"I know."

I turned around and allowed his hands to fall to my hips. "Men typically reach their sexual peak in their twenties."

He seemed confused for a moment — squinting his eyes at nothing in particular.

"Was...was that a question or...are you saying I'm an anomaly?"

"I'm just saying it's interesting that you can even have an erection that large at your age."

He let me go and stomped one foot on the carpeted floor. "*Man*, you're a boner killer."

I smiled. "I'm sorry. All I have is my medical knowledge, so sometimes it just spills out."

"You have medical jargon Tourette's."

I crossed my arms over my chest. "Tourette's isn't just yelling out random curses. It's—" Before I could finish my sentence, Jack pulled me into a passionate kiss. I fell into it and allowed my body to be overtaken by the butterflies in my stomach. He was such a gentle person. His hands were almost always touching my face gingerly or running through my hair. Anywhere else he touched me caused tiny exciting shocks of electricity. He finally stopped to give me air.

I took in a breath. "It also involves tics of the face or—"

"No," he said, kissing me again. "No. I did that to stop you from saying non-sexy things."

"But I—"

He shook his head. "Nuh-uh. Nope. It's just us. I have no idea what you're talking about. It sounds smart as hell, but you were going to go on for pages, weren't you?"

"Absolutely. I wrote a paper on Tourette's in college."

He nodded with a laugh. "Of course you did."

I tapped my foot. "So, may I continue?"

"Nope. Later. You can explain all about Tourette's Syndrome later. When I don't want to throw you down and have hot, sweaty sex."

"Which would be when?"

He shrugged. "I dunno. Maybe right after. When I'm coming down."

Tilting my head to one side, I found myself wondering if he were serious. "You're statistically less likely to be listening then."

His smile grew wider. "Exactly. You could go on for ages and I wouldn't care. Hell, you could read me the paper you wrote."

Surprise flooded me. "Really?"

He let out a belly laugh. "Whatever floats your Hindenburg."

Had I heard that correctly? "That's not very politically correct."

"Welcome to *Who's Jack Reynolds, Anyway?* Where everything is made up and being PC doesn't matter."

"Is that a reference to something I'm missing?"

"Yes."

"Aunt Lisa!" Alex's voice startled us out of our own world. The bathroom door opened and steam poured out. Alex was up on the seat of the toilet looking out the window.

"Shit. Are some of them out there?" Jack pushed into the bathroom while I picked up my sleepy son.

"No." Alex gestured to the window. "Someone's saying hello."

"What?" I slid past the door, but there wasn't much space left in the tiny bathroom. I could just barely see between their shoulders. A strange light was bouncing around the walls.

A few seconds passed before someone said anything. "It's morse code." Jack turned and searched for something.

"Yeah. I noticed the light and it was saying 'hello' in code." Alex handed Jack the beauty mirror lying next to the sink.

"You are amazing, Juliet. Very smart."

She giggled at his compliment.

"What are you doing?" I bounced Rex lightly in my arms so he'd sleep again.

"I'm gonna signal back." He positioned the mirror on the window sill and opened it. Cool air swept in, causing Rex to shiver. I held him closer to my chest. I watched Jack move the mirror back and forth for a few moments. Then we waited.

"What did you say?" Alex asked.

"I said 'hello' back and asked them if they needed help." They both turned back to the window to watch. I stood on my tip toes to see a bright point of light flash our direction. It clicked on and off at seemingly random intervals.

"No shit." Jack began creating a response.

"What is it?" I shifted Rex to my other hip. I didn't remember him being so heavy.

"Just a sec." He moved the mirror back and forth. When he was done, he tossed it back onto the bathroom sink. "There're people over there. They're alive. They're healthy. And they're offering us a place to stay."

"Really?" I watched as he and Alex pushed out of the bathroom. Alex began packing her and Rex's things while Jack went into our room. Rex began to fidget. He wanted down to help Alex. I put him on the floor and he wobbled off in her direction.

"Is it safe, Jack?" I leaned against the door frame as he checked his guns.

"I don't know." He stopped and approached me. Giving me a kiss, he said, "But we have to find out."

I nodded. "Just make sure you have plenty of bullets."

A coy smile appeared on his face.

"What is it?"

"Ammo. Pistols take bullets. Shotguns take shells. To cover it all, it's ammo."

I put out both my hands, palms up. "All right then."

He winked at me. "I'm the smart one this time."

Two Men and a Lift Auto Garage

"We Auto Know"

October 19

"So, how are we going to find these people?" Lisa was bouncing Rex up and down on her hip. It seemed so oddly instinctual that it took me a moment to digest it.

"They gave me coordinates." It was a good thing Alex and I had just finished fixing the hole in the break line of the van. I slammed the front hood shut, startling Rex.

"Jag! Jaggy bad sound."

"It's 'Jack', Rex." Lisa touched his nose with her forefinger.

"Could be worse." I began packing our things into the back of the van. "At least I'm a cool car, huh?"

"Jag!" He began to struggle with Lisa, so she put him down. He ran to me, throwing his arms around my leg. "Jaggy!"

Lisa shrugged. "It was a lot easier when he only knew 'mommy' and 'daddy'."

I was about to reply when Rex tightened his grip, laughed and said, "Daddy! Jaggy Daddy!"

For a second, I thought I hadn't heard him correctly. But when I looked at Lisa, I knew what I'd heard was true. And I knew because she had this look on her face. I couldn't describe it then, so I called it the 'I don't fucking know' look. One corner of her mouth stretched and downturned while looking at the ground with wide eyes. She raked a hand through her dark hair. It fell back into place in a feathery wave. Since I wasn't getting any input from her, I made a decision to bend down and pick him up.

188

Tossing him onto my shoulders, I said, "You can call me whatever you want, Romeo!"

Alex came out of the hotel room lugging two bags. She'd raided the mini fridges in both rooms and grabbed what she could.

"Not me." She lugged the cases into the van. "You're Uncle Jack to me. Because she's Aunt Lisa."

"I need more coffee. Is there more coffee inside?" Lisa was talking fast as she made a move toward the hotel room door. I caught her forearm.

"Ooh, look at you."

"What is it?" Her eyes were still wide.

"You're all flustered, Foxtrot. What's the problem?"

"My only problem is caffeine withdrawal."

"You had three cups of that nasty instant shit this morning." I couldn't keep my smile inside. Her eyes were pleading with me to stop teasing her, but I couldn't.

"Then I'm jittery because of it."

I nodded, letting my hand slide down to squeeze hers. I was only playing. "Yeah, probably."

I let her go when she breathed out a heavy sigh. But it wasn't a sigh of frustration. That was the sigh of someone getting off the hook for something. I knew that sigh very well. I couldn't tell if that fact was sad or not...

"All right, folks! Let's go!" We all piled into the car. Rex decided to set up camp in Lisa's lap while Lexi ripped open a king size pack of peanut M&M's. I gave a fake gasp and

watched her in the rear-view mirror. "Ooh, gurl. You gimme summa dem."

At first, she looked at me strangely — as if I'd reminded her of someone. But then she giggled loudly and poured a few in my open hand.

It had been months since I'd been able to taste chocolate. Who would've thought that to be the first thing to run out during the end of the world? Without taking my eyes off the road, I stretched my arm out to Lisa.

"Want?"

"No, thank you. But I'm sure Rex would like one, wouldn't you?"

Rex bobbed his head excitedly while she popped an M&M into his mouth. He squealed with delight as he chewed.

"So where exactly is this place?"

I kept my eyes on the empty road as I turned down a dirt path. "So damn close I want to cry."

The coordinates the beacon had given me were only a few miles away from the hotel. But the dirt road I'd pulled onto sent eerie shivers down my spine. Lisa must have noticed my sudden quietness.

"What's the matter?"

The woods seemed to be closing us in. It was getting dark. "I don't know. Something doesn't feel right."

Everyone had gone quiet except Rex who was mumbling happily in Lisa's lap. Just a few hundred yards ahead, it looked as though the forest opened up. Beyond the clearing, I could

see an enormous house at the bottom of a grassy hill that looked like something out of *Beverley Hillbillies*. No joke. The place was huge.

"Whoa..." Alex leaned forward until she was between the two front seats. "Someone's got some money."

"Not that it matters anymore..." I didn't realize that I'd slowed the car down until we were almost parked. As we inched forward, the sun began to creep its way up the hood of the van. The trees separated until the clearing came into full view. And that's when we knew we were in trouble.

Because there were Biters everywhere.

"Shit." I slammed my foot onto the brake in an attempt to stall for some thinking time, but nothing happened. And as the van reached the edge of tree line, it also reached the edge of the hill.

"What's going on?" Lisa sounded as though she were trying to keep her voice calm.

"Remember that hole in the brake line?"

"Yes. Didn't you fix that?"

I cleared my throat as the van picked up more speed. "Ah-yup. And now it's back."

"You've got to be kidding me." Alex gripped the sides of each seat.

"Well...I guess it's time to brace for impact. Everyone got their seatbelts on?" I glanced at them.

"I don't have one!" Alex squealed as Lisa buckled herself and Rex in tighter.

"All right." I kept my eyes ahead. "Just get down and cover your head. Behind my seat. There you go. You'll be okay."

One by one, the Biters were realizing something was coming their way. They began to turn and, upon seeing us picking up speed, started to growl and spit. There were more of them than I'd initially thought, too. I'd say hundreds. They littered the grass outside the mansion. Most of them were just shuffling along, but when they saw the van, they began to run.

"What the fuck? They can *run* now?" I put the van in neutral.

"Let's just get the hell out of here, please." Lisa was gripping her armrest.

The vehicle continued to speed up as we neared the front gates of the house. I could see the beacon blinking on and off in a side window. At least I knew it was the right place. I tried to steer the wheel so we wouldn't hit the wrought iron fence. There was a giant tangle of barbed wire surrounding the perimeter.

The Biters were closing in. While still yards away, I knew we'd have to make a break for it. About a hundred feet in front of the wall of barbed wire, the van hit a pot hole. The entire thing bounced. I couldn't control the wheel. It jerked to the left and sent us off toward the side of the house.

Before I could even get a curse word out, we slammed through the wire and into the brick wall. Luckily, the van's engine cushioned most of the blow and we were all okay.

However, I had no time to check for scrapes and bruises because I could hear the Biters closing in.

"All right, everybody! Out the back!" I scrambled toward the double doors with Alex in tow. But Lisa called out to us before we could touch the handles.

"My seatbelt is stuck!"

I turned back around to find her fumbling with what looked like a broken belt buckle. Rex seemed to think she was playing and bounced in her lap. I finally let out the curse and stumbled back to the front while Alex opened the back doors.

"Hold still." I grabbed a pocket knife I'd been carrying since we'd left Las Vegas and began to saw through the tough belt. Lisa kept amazingly calm while I cut with fumbling hands.

"Guys! They're getting closer!"

I glanced back to see a wave of Biters running toward us. We had probably thirty seconds to get through the front gate. Going back to my task, I sawed faster than I thought possible. I swore I saw smoke coming from the belt.

Finally the last scrap separated and Lisa was free. I grabbed her and Rex and ran to the back of the vehicle. We all jumped out and headed straight for the front gate. But those damn Biters were fast. They closed in on us from all sides, ready for a snack.

I didn't think twice. My gun was out in half a second and I was shooting any of them within range. One by one they went down, but there were just too many to count. By sheer luck, we reached the gate with seconds to spare. But it was locked.

Someone must have heard our crash and was running down the stone steps to open up for us.

"Hurry!" I yelled as I turned to shoot more Biters.

The man reached the gate with hundreds of those things surrounding us. He unlocked it quickly and began helping me shoot the ones directly in front. We scrambled through the gate.

"Jack!"

I turned back in time to see Alex get pulled back by a particularly large Biter. "Shit!" I leapt forward, instructing Lisa to get Rex to step back. I have no idea if she actually listened to me because I was busy slamming the big guy with the butt of my gun then shooting him square in the face. I'm pretty sure he lost half his jaw.

I grabbed a crying Alex and we rushed inside the compound. The man who'd unlocked the gate for us slammed it closed just as the Biters reached it, pushing their bloated hands through to grab what they could. The five of us raced up the path and into the house.

As soon as we poured inside, we all but fell to the floor in exhaustion. The man who'd saved us said something about finding the owner and left. Alex was still inconsolable.

"You okay, honey?" I put my arms around her. She nodded, but said nothing.

When I stood again, Lisa grabbed me and kissed me like she'd never see me again. It was filled with so much emotion that it startled me.

"When are you going to get bored of saving my life?" she asked when we came up for air.

"Never, Foxtrot. Never."

October 20

The owner of the house was an older, portly woman in her fifties named Gwen Huntington. She'd apparently lost her husband years before the outbreak. They'd had no children, so she devoted her time to filling their house with people. Anyone who came by was welcome. That was why they'd set up the light.

She was generous. She fed us immediately and made sure Rex was occupied. I don't know how she did it, but it seemed like she knew my son's mannerisms in the first few seconds of meeting him. She'd given him chicken tenders and followed that up with ice cream. Then she'd showed him a thousand piece puzzle the house guests had been working on. Even when he took it apart, she kept her smile.

When it came time to assign rooms, she gave Jack and me our own with an adjoining room for the children. It was strange, but after she left and we were alone, I felt at home – at peace. It was nice.

It was late by the time we'd settled in. Alex had finished Rex's bedtime story and was drifting off to sleep herself when I shut the door to their room. Jack was getting ready to sleep and his shirt was off. I felt pure need flood through each and every one of my veins like the virus that had started the outbreak.

"Jack."

He turned to face me. "What is it?"

I took a second or two to formulate my words. "Why do you keep saving us?"

He tilted his head to the side and came toward me. "Why wouldn't I?" His arms slipped around my waist. He was warm and inviting. I felt my blood run hot.

"You've put yourself in mortal danger every time I get stuck. And I've gotten stuck quite a bit."

His brow furrowed. "Okay..."

My gaze dropped to his chest. "I'm the epitome of natural selection. I should have died a thousand times already."

"Have I rescued you that many times?" He was joking. There was a smile on his face. "What are you getting at?"

"You should be looking out for yourself."

He scrunched up his face. "What...are you talking about right now?" It was the same voice he'd used in the car ride to Utah. I found my stomach in knots when he spoke that way.

Before I could say anything else, he picked me up and set me on the dresser. And that was when I felt his warm touch under my shirt. He placed a soft kiss on my forehead.

"Natural Selection has nothing on you." His words were mumbled as he continued to plant kisses on my mouth, cheeks and neck. "You kick Natural Selection's ass."

A soft moan escaped me when he pressed his hips into mine. I allowed my hands to wander down to his waist, barely believing I had that much of a craving for him.

"You beat a guy to death with a stick because he was threatening to hurt your son. You underestimate your own worth."

"Let's not talk about that right now."

"Mm-hm. And what should we talk about?"

I undid the button of his jeans. "Let's talk about how much I want you."

He snatched my wrists with one hand then used the other to wiggle an index finger at me. "Nuh-uh. Remember what we talked about?"

Frustration burned through my veins. That was odd. I'd never been frustrated that someone wouldn't allow me to have sex with them. He must have sensed this as his grip on me eased.

"But…" He pulled me off the dresser and toward the bed. "There are *other things we can do.*"

That night, we helped each other ease our sexual tensions. It wasn't what I'd wanted nor what I'd expected, but in my tired state of mind, I was confident his teasing wouldn't last. When we'd satiated each other enough, we went to bed together.

"Where have you been all my life?" My whisper cut through the silent darkness of the bedroom.

He chuckled. "Apparently across the street from your best friend."

November 10

Days melted into one another at the Huntington Mansion. People came and went surprisingly often. Lisa and I met folks from all over the United States. From them, we'd learned the outbreak had completely devoured our country. There were no businesses left. No homes. Entire families had been lost. Lisa took these conversations harder than I imagined she would've. She'd pretend like nothing was wrong, but I knew her being stuck in that house and not helping people was wearing her down.

One day about three weeks after we'd arrived, a mob of people came tearing in. A group of six popped up one day. They all looked tired, dirty and hungry. Ms. Huntington decided to throw a party in their honor and we were all to dress up in our best clothes for dinner.

A couple who had come in with the group became quick friends with us. They travelled all the way from British Columbia in search of a place to stay. Brian and Cheree. Even their names were cute.

"Almost ready?" I knocked on the door to Rex and Alex's room. From behind the wood frame, I could hear Rex in a fit. His screams almost drown out my voice. The door popped open with a very well-dressed Alex behind it. The screaming intensified.

"Is 'no' a good answer?"

"Bad?" I stepped in to see Lisa struggling to put her son into his dress pants. In the time since we'd met, I noticed he was getting bigger. With that, came strength.

"Rex, please. Just let me—"

"No!" He kicked his feet, allowing one leg to escape. He flipped over onto his stomach, squirming to get away. But Lisa grabbed his shoulders and pulled him back. Frustration was beginning to show in her face.

"Rex, *please.*"

"No!" His next kick landed square on her jaw. She let go completely and he scrambled back toward the bed, his face red and pinched.

"Are you all right?" I started to approach her, but she held out her hand. After clearing her throat, I could see the glisten in her eyes. She was holding back tears.

"I used to have such a good handle of him." She put her hands to her face and took a deep breath. Alex and I watched quietly while she composed herself. After a few moments, she scooted closer to her son. "Rex." Her voice was soft as she reached out to him.

But he swatted at her hand and screamed. "No!"

Lisa went stiff. I'd never seen her stand so quickly. "Then you won't go! You'll be alone all night!" With that, she stormed off into the other room and slammed the door.

"Sheesh. Is that normal?" I asked Alex as she went over to a sniffling Rex.

"Not for Aunt Lisa, no." Alex tried to get Rex's attention, but he was busy staring at the door his mother had slammed. "I've never even seen her yell."

Alex was about to help Rex to his feet when the boy jumped up and ran toward the door. With small clenched fists he began pounding on it. But instead of the screaming I'd expected, he was calling out for Lisa.

Alex and I exchanged glances, wherein she gave a shrug, so I opened the door. Rex ran to the bed, but she wasn't there. I could see the tears start to gather in his eyes until the bathroom door opened and Lisa came out. There were stress lines creased into her face, but I could tell she hadn't been crying.

"Momma! Momma!" Rex ran to her with his arms outstretched. She knelt down and her brow furrowed when he jumped into her arms. "I wear pants, momma."

Lisa pulled back and looked at her son. It seemed as though she wanted to say something, but only nodded.

"I love you, momma. No mad." Rex gave her one last hug and ran back into the adjoining room. Lisa just knelt there. Then, she looked up at Alex.

"Did you tell him to do that?"

Alex shook her head. Lisa looked to me, but I also affirmed a 'no.' Once again, she put her face in her hands. Neither Alex nor I were sure what to do, so we just watched her. And when she looked up again, she was smiling. A genuine smile. It was beautiful.

"He's never said that before. He's never hugged me like that before." She shook her head as if she thought she was dreaming. She bounced to her feet and ran to the door. Touching my shoulder, she said, "I'll meet you downstairs."

*   *   *

She was the last one to come down. And she looked off the charts gorgeous. She'd straightened her normally wavy hair and put on a sparkling white dress that hugged her frame. But the most beautiful thing she was wearing that night was her smile. Everyone seemed to notice when she entered the parlor. She literally brightened the room.

She spoke to Cheree for a brief moment until Rex found me. "Hey, kid. You learn all of Shakespeare, yet?"

Lisa moved toward me, a smile still on her lips. "I bet he could, because he's smart. Aren't you?"

"Yes!" Rex bobbed his head and ran off to find Alex.

"Can I speak to you for a moment?"

"Uh oh." I grimaced. "Did I do something wrong?"

She pulled me around a corner to an isolated spot under the staircase next to the broken restroom no one ever used. And then she kissed me. It was a hungry kiss; I could feel it. And she tasted like cherries.

"No," she said when she stopped. "You didn't do anything wrong."

"Good." I pulled her close to me. "Because you look so fucking hot right now."

She giggled for once and we continued to fool around like teenagers until she pulled me into the bathroom and locked the door. Then, she pushed me down onto the closed toilet seat and straddled me. If I hadn't been aroused before, I sure as hell was then.

"What has gotten into you?" I was barely able to get the sentence out between her kissing me. "I mean...not that I don't like it... I *really* like it." I caught her hands before they reached for my zipper. I almost didn't make it. She was driving me crazy. But I was going to get her to say yes to my proposal.

"I'm excited."

"Yeah...I can tell."

"Rex is starting to notice patterns in social behaviors. That's a huge step." For some reason, she pushed her chest into my face, then reached for my zipper again.

"You know the rules."

My statement was meant to be teasing, but it must have come out a bit ruder than I'd intended, because her smile just melted away.

She stood up after making a frustrated noise. "You're making decisions for me again, and frankly, I'm quite annoyed by it."

I gave a shrug. "Hey, I stick to my guns." After pausing, I added, "Sometimes literally."

"Jack, I'm not in the mood for jokes."

I stood up. "Point taken. But rules are rules."

"These are not rules I agreed to."

Another shrug seemed to come automatically. "I know what I want, and I'm pretty sure I know I can get it."

"By playing games with me." Her voice dropped low.

In defense, I put up my hands. "No games, Foxtrot. I'm serious."

"You can't be."

"I'm dead serious."

She let out a sigh that reminded me of the ones my mother used to give me whenever I ate a cookie before dinner. "A relationship cannot survive without sexual intercourse."

"Tell that to high school Jack Reynolds."

"Please stop joking."

"That wasn't a joke."

"Jack." Ugh. She even *said* my name like I'd spoiled my dinner.

"All right, if we're putting all joking aside, can we stop treating me like a kid, too?"

"I'm treating you exactly how you're treating me."

Jesus Christ, her monotony was driving me up the wall. My muscles were starting to tense and the blood began rushing in my ears.

"I'm just trying to get you to see my point. That's all."

"You're not doing it like an adult would."

That was it. I had to shut my eyes and bite my tongue to keep the anger in place. I didn't want to say something I'd regret.

"Look... I stepped toward her. She didn't move. "I love you, okay? Like...a lot. I think it's fair to have a discussion about getting married."

"And you believe frustrating me to the point of becoming angry is the way to do it."

My fists clenched. "You just know everything, don't you?"

"Well, I know quite a lot, yes. That's not a fair statement."

"Fair? Nothing about our relationship is fair."

She crossed her arms. "I see we're on the same page now."

I counted to ten in my head. Some of the numbers were replaced with derogatory rhyming words, sure, but it helped.

"What...do I have to do to get you to marry me?"

"You can't do anything. I won't do something I don't want to do."

I let her words sink in. "So, you've changed your mind?"

"I'm getting quite close to it, yes."

Raw anger settled into the pit of my stomach. I was tired of being rejected and unwanted. "So what you're saying is that my feelings don't matter to you?"

"Jack, please."

"I'm never going to be good enough for you to marry, am I?" I could feel my fists clenching into tighter balls.

Lisa sighed. "Jack."

"I need to know if our relationship is going anywhere."

She tilted her head to the side. "I don't understand why we have to get married for you to see that."

"Then you don't understand me." It was a harsh statement, and I could see it in her eyes, but I didn't care. I was tired of taking a backseat. "If this isn't going anywhere, then it's over."

I didn't even pause to give her time to react. My whole body was heated from the exchange. She'd humiliated me. Rather than respect me, she chose to break my heart. I was done. There was nothing more I could do to save our relationship. And Lisa only had herself to blame.

From the Desk of Dr. Lisa James

November 20

  He looked so distraught. Every time we bumped into each other at breakfast or lunch. Every time we'd run into each other around a corner. And every time we saw each other in the closed garden, it was torture. The kids loved spending time with him and it was already starting to feel more like shared custody than anything else. My mother would have called me stubborn. I called it resourceful. When I made decisions, I stuck with them. It was the easiest way to keep things in a rhythmic order.

  "Where's Uncle Jack going?" Alex stood up from playing in the pond with Rex. I followed her gaze through the window to the image of Jack with a backpack over his shoulder, saying goodbye to some of the house guests.

  "I don't know."

  "Uncle Jack!"

  Before I could catch her, Alex fled into the house closely followed by Rex. A dull ache pulsed at my side as I stood. It was almost as if I were getting older by the day. I followed them in slowly, carrying my empty tea cup with me. Tea was the only caffeine I could get.

  When I entered the parlor, our gazes met. His instantly petered out into a dark sadness. I felt it in my heart, but I would not acknowledge it. No matter how much it hurt, I wasn't going to back down.

  "Uncle Jack! Where are you going?" Alex looked up at him as the remaining house guests filtered back to their tasks.

  "Where go?" My son repeated her question.

  Jack knelt down and put a hand on each of their heads. "I'm headed out to explore the world, kiddos."

I leaned against the wall and gripped my cup tighter. He was leaving us.

"When will you be back?" Alex already knew what was happening, but the hope in her voice nearly broke me.

Jack paused as if he were trying to construct a proper sentence. "Well, Juliet...I won't be."

"Huh?" Rex's face suddenly turned downward. He knew what going away meant. His own father had done it and now his best friend was doing it too. Everyone was leaving.

"I want to go with you." Alex's little voice – filled with sorrow – felt like a knife in my side. But I was tired of being made to feel guilty for a rational decision. I approached them and took hold of Lexi's hand.

"You can't go, honey. You have to stay with me." I met Jack's gaze however difficult it was. There was enough pain behind it to render anyone speechless.

"But I don't wanna! I want to go with Jack!" Tears began to form in Alex's eyes. Rex had no idea what was happening, but he began to react as well. And I was too tired to deal with it.

"Kids. Enough. Let's go and let Jack on his way."

He stood up. "Guys, go play in the other room for a second, okay?"

Why was he undermining my authority? He was being ridiculous and the kids were actually listening to him. They skittered off to the parlor.

"You have absolutely no right to do this." I lowered my voice to a harsh whisper.

"Do what, Lisa?" His voice was as tired as his face looked.

"Just pick up and leave them like this. They love you. They love spending time with you. You can't just roll into their lives and then back out again like it means nothing to you."

Jack closed his eyes and breathed a heavy sigh. "I'm not obligated to do anything for them, Lisa. They're not *my* kids."

His words stung. But he was correct. "You can't just leave because I won't agree to marry you."

"Is that why you think I'm leaving?"

"Well, it is."

"No, it isn't."

"It absolutely is."

Without warning, Jack grabbed my upper arm and pushed me into the wall. It was a gentle push, but there was force behind it. He closed in on me until I could smell him.

"Would you *stop* acting like you know everything? It drives me crazy."

I looked into his eyes. "But that's what this is about."

Defeat flooded him. "Even if it was, would it matter?"

I stayed silent.

"If I said I'd leave unless you agreed to marry me, would you say yes?" He was searching my face hard for answers.

"No."

November 22

Empty boxes of soda crackers. Unopened cans of fruit cocktail. A very old, very moldy potato. A packet of instant coffee. I pocketed that one. Just in case. On my left there was nothing but a dusty old bar. On my right were empty shelves with clean circles every few inches.

"There used to be booze here."

My own voice surprised me. I hadn't heard it since I'd sat in the car, hitting the steering wheel and yelling every obscenity I could. That was twenty hours ago. Twenty hours. It'd felt like a lifetime without her. In that time, I couldn't even go a mile past the hotel we'd stayed in before finding the house. I just couldn't fathom being too far.

"Ah-ha!" I noticed the glint of some glass between the open door of a cabinet below me. Fishing inside, I knew I'd found something good. And what I brought out didn't disappoint.

"Holy shit. Red Label." My teeth tore into the cork someone had stopped it with. There was about three-quarters left. Enough to do the trick.

"Bottoms up." I spat the cork onto the dirty counter and downed a quarter of the liquor. A cough and a hiccup later, my stomach was on fire. But at least I was warm.

"Man, that is sad."

I jumped onto the counter for a comfortable seat. "Who the fuck invited you?"

Silas stared right through me. There was not a quip or a joke. "Your stupid ass."

"Oh, so now I'm stupid?" I took another swig of whiskey. "You're the one who's got half his face falling off."

My dead friend touched the skin around his jaw that had begun to tear. He was even paler than before. "I'm worried about you, bud."

I laughed, nearly spitting liquor on him. "You? Why?"

"I don't scare you anymore."

"So?"

"I don't give you headaches anymore."

"And?"

"You've gone full circle."

"Meaning...?"

"You're fucking insane." He stared me down for a few silent seconds. "Look at you... You should change your last name to Torrance."

"Oh, ha ha." My reply was sarcastic. I hopped of the counter and turned in a circle with my arms spread. "Here's Johnny!" My shout was muted by the heavy carpets in the bar.

"Drinking won't solve your problems."

I stopped and put my hands on the edge of the counter. "What, you're playing conscience now?"

"I've always been your conscience, you moron. You killed me and that's why I'm here."

I could feel my face twist into a sneer. "Enough with the killing business!"

"You're a murderer, man. What else can I say?"

"Nothing! You can shut your fucking mouth!" I was beginning to feel a slight buzz.

"Murderer."

"Stop it!"

"Murderer."

"Shut up!"

Silas leaned forward until he was as close to me as possible. I could smell the decay on him. *"Murderer."*

"Fuck you!" Without thinking, I closed my eyes and hurled the bottle of Red Label at him. When I heard the smash of glass, I looked up to find him gone and expensive whiskey dripping off the mirror across from me.

"Great...now how am I gonna get drunk?"

When no one answered me, I decided to head to the separate cabins in the back of the hotel to hunt around for whatever might have been left. Darkness had already settled on the world when I stepped outside. Even soft snowflakes began to fall from the clouds. The first snow of the season.

The familiar glint of Huntington's beacon broke my heart just a little more. But I had to keep going. And as soon as I consumed every single drop of alcohol left in that hotel, I'd move on. Where? I had no idea.

I was yards away from the cabins when I heard the breaking of glass to my left. Stopping in my tracks, I pulled the pistol from my belt. Instinctively, I put an arm out to stop

216

whoever was behind me from moving forward. But then I realized there was no one left to protect.

Something metallic scraped against the ground. I looked toward a dark corner of the building. A garbage can fell over and rolled half a foot away. I drew my weapon and pulled back on the hammer.

"Who's there?" The calm of my voice surprised me. Whiskey really was liquid courage.

I took a step closer to the garbage as the rummaging continued. The fallen can rolled a bit more, then settled. After a few seconds, a very thin malnourished-looking raccoon poked his head out.

"Oh…" Holstering my gun, I crept closer while kneeling down. "Hey, there, little fella."

The raccoon looked up at me, chewing a bit of something he'd found in the garbage. Snowflakes collected on the end of his fur. He didn't seem frightened, so I kept approaching him.

"How'd you get all the way out here?"

He continued to chew as I got closer.

"I don't suppose you found any liquor out here?"

The raccoon stopped what he was doing and scurried away. So much for that. I took a deep breath and sat in the dirt. With my back to the outside wall of the hotel I began thinking about next steps. Where was I going to go? I supposed Braycart. But what if Lisa went there too? I guess it didn't really matter.

Or maybe I could go find Raychel…

Something nudged the side of my leg. I looked down to find a furry animal looking up at me. It was the raccoon. We stared silently at each other for a second or two before he stood on his hind legs and offered me something. It was a can of beer.

"You understood me, bud?"

I took the beer from him and reached out my hand. At first, he flinched back, but once he smelled me, he allowed me to pet him.

"You sure are lucky to be alive." I popped the top on the beer and began to chug. It was warm and flat, but it didn't matter, because my buzz was deepening.

"Jack."

"Fuck you, Silas." I let out a sigh of relief as I emptied the can.

"No, seriously. Look. The beacon is saying your name."

I looked up at him. The blinking light illuminated his face in a familiar pattern. I counted them. I don't know why. Short blink, three long blinks. Pause. Short blink, long blink. Pause. Long blink, short blink, long blink, short blink. Pause. Long blink, short blink, long blink.

"Holy shit." I scrambled to my feet and looked toward the direction of the beacon. It was dark for about three seconds before it started to repeat my name. "Lisa?"

"You'd better answer," Silas said.

Without a second thought, I started to run toward the cabins. The first two doors were locked, so I threw myself in reverse, stepping on the raccoon's tail.

"Sorry, bud!" I ran past him. "Didn't know you were following me!"

The third cabin was unlocked. I kicked the door open with my foot and ran inside. Once there, I frantically searched through each drawer, hoping and praying to find something to signal back with. Somehow, there was a large flood flashlight in the cabinet near an old dresser. I flicked it on. Still worked.

Running back over to the window, I cleared a small wooden desk of clutter, then found a paper and pencil to write with. Then, I got to work. The raccoon watched me curiously.

.-.. .. ... .- ..--..

Lisa?

There was a pause. Whoever had been signaling must have been translating a response. Did Lisa even know Morse code?

.--- . ... -.-. .-

Alex.

Of course.

--- -.- ..--..

Ok?

I hadn't taught her much, but at least there was someone real to talk to.

Yeah. What are you doing up, Juliet?

Wanted to sure you were ok.

I'm fine. How's Rex?

Ok. Aunt Lisa sad.

Me too.

Come back?

Can't.

Why?

I just can't, Juliet. I want to, but I can't. You'll understand when you're older.

There was a long silence. Just darkness. I supposed she was done. I turned to the raccoon with too much feeling in my chest.

"At least I'm lucky to have you."

The animal regarded me silently. I wished for a moment it could speak, then allowed the silly thought to vanish. Then I wished there was more beer.

..- -. -.. . .-. ... - .- -. -.. / -. --- .--

I turned my attention back toward the window. *Understand now*, she'd said.

I'm sorry, kiddo. I can't explain it.

There was one last message before the end of the conversation. .. / .-.. --- ...- . / -.-- --- ..-

I love you.

I felt tears well into my eyes. What was I doing? I'd allowed a little girl to look up to me so much that she loved me and I left her. But if I couldn't have been her father, then it wasn't worth watching her grow up. It would have been too painful. I signaled back that I loved her too and that we'd meet

again someday. Even if it was a lie, I had to tell her something. After a deep sigh, I set everything down and got ready for bed.

December 15

Time seemed to pass quickly, but not quickly enough. Two weeks after Jack left, the kids seemed to be doing all right. Alex had sulked for days, but seemed to have the spring back in her step again. And Rex drowned himself in sleep, ice cream and butterflies. The interesting part of the whole thing was that he'd never been happier. There were times when he'd dream of Jack. And the only reason I knew that was because he'd talk in his sleep. I'd hear him mumbling through the wall at night or Alex would tell me the next day. If he could have understood, I knew he would have been hurting.

But I had to keep going strong. So I did. The plan to end my life kept creeping ever forward in my head, however. Day by day it became a louder voice inside me. And day after day I choked it back down. It wasn't healthy, no, but I'd find a way to deal with it when I had the time.

One night – about two and a half weeks after Jack had left – I was tucking the children into bed. Rex had had his bedtime story and was fast asleep. When Alex's turn came, she quickly hid a book she'd been writing in under her mattress and straightened up.

"What's that, sweetheart?" I knelt beside the bed.

"Nothing."

"A diary?"

She paused. "Yes."

I nodded. "Just know I'm here to talk if you need it, okay?"

"Oh, I'm fine." She smiled wide and puffed out her chest. "I talk to Jack all the time."

The poignancy of her statement weighed heavily on me. "Alex. It's not healthy for a girl your age to talk to herself."

"But—!"

"I understand you miss him, honey. So do I. but we have to keep going."

Alex was silent for a moment. "It sounds like you're trying to make yourself believe that more than me."

I smiled on the inside. She was a smart cookie. "It's bedtime."

"I know."

Even though I'd grown accustomed to sleeping in a bed by myself after Rex was born, it was difficult again. I felt the need for warmth and companionship. All because of Jack. He'd simply asked far too much of me. If I were to give in, who knows what would have happened. Having no plan is not a healthy way to live.

Writing has become very difficult. I find I may not continue with journal entries unless I deem it necessary.

December 17

Okay...what the ever-loving fuck just happened?

I was asleep. The bed was fluffy and soft. It'd been about two and half weeks since I'd left the house. I just couldn't allow myself to move on. I knew I would, but there was still food and water at the hotel. I couldn't let it go to waste.

My little buddy Lucky woke me. He was scratching at his thin fur. I assumed he had fleas. There was nothing I could do about it.

"Why don't you go find us some grub, buddy?" I rolled away from the harsh white of daylight through the curtains. The raccoon had somehow clicked with me right away. He'd brought me a beer the first night we'd met. And since, he'd been fetching things for me all over the place. He could get into places I couldn't, so he'd find random stuff to snack on.

The curtains parted and Lucky exited through the broken window. I sat up slowly, rubbing my temples. While I hadn't had a drink in three days, my body was still experiencing a hangover. I thought a shower may have helped, so I stood and stumbled my way to the bathroom.

The water was cold, but at least it woke me up. And at least it was still running. There were some clothes left behind, so I gathered those and dressed myself. It seemed like hours – me standing in front of the mirror, staring at my scruff.

"Maybe I should grow a goatee." I made a few poses in the mirror to cheer myself up. Then I remembered my cell phone. While I'd thought it was a useless brick since it couldn't

make or receive calls, it could still take pictures. I reached for it in my back pocket.

"Maybe I should take a selfie!"

"Or maybe you should do what's right for once." Silas was looking worse every day. His skin had turned a very sickly gray. Veins were noticeable just under his skin and I could even see shiny bone poking through his jawline. The hole in his chest had ceased pulsating but was exchanged by a thick, black drippy substance that smelled like sewage.

"What do you know about what's right?" I rolled my eyes while facing him.

"I know more than your dumb fucking ass."

I leaned against the sink. "Whoa...what's with the hostility?"

Silas took a step toward me. Something inside him made an awful gurgling noise. "You'd better do what's right, Jack. Otherwise it's gonna come and bite you in the arm."

That was an odd choice of words. "I think you mean ass."

A smirk slid across my friend's face, ripping some necrotic flesh from the corner of his mouth. "Nope. I definitely meant arm."

Without warning, the long glass window of the bathroom shattered into a thousand tiny pieces. On instinct, I shielded myself from it while cursing.

"The fuck? Did a bomb just go off or some—" I stopped dead when I saw what was once a woman clawing through the

new opening. Thick rivulets of foam dripped from her mouth. She was covered in blood, but I wondered how much of it was her own. And where was my gun?

I spun around, trying to remember where I'd put it when I went to sleep. Why the hell had I taken it out of my belt? I made a move to get it, but the bathroom door slammed shut in my face.

"What the fuck?" I grabbed the knob and pushed, but the thing wouldn't budge. "No!" I slammed my fist against the wood. Then I kicked it. I could hear the diseased thing behind me creeping closer. Throwing my entire shoulder into the door didn't even move it.

"I told you. Do what's right, Jack." Silas's voice mocked me from beyond the door.

"Silas! Silas, let me the fuck out! This isn't funny anymore!"

My friend laughed. The woman behind me grabbed my ankle. I kicked her in the face, but she didn't let go. A yank later, I was on my ass on the bathroom floor, struggling hard to get her away. But her bony grip held fast.

"Get. The. Fuck. Off!" With each word I spoke, I gave her a swift kick. I swore her growls sounded like laughter.

"Do what's right, Jacky-boy."

In a split second, the diseased was on top of me. She was strong as hell. Too strong. She hissed and spit at me as I held her at arm's distance.

"Silas! Help!"

A sudden hot, raw pain tore through my bicep. She'd bitten me. Her rotting teeth had torn right through my skin and into my muscle. I cried out, but no one answered me. Tears stung my cheeks.

A good chunk of my arm ripped off in her mouth. And the look in her eye as she happily chewed my flesh and the pain of the virus flooding my veins just pushed me over the edge.

With all the strength I had left, I shoved my knee into her stomach. She growled and fell to the floor. As I tried to use the toilet to lift myself up, more burning pain clawed at my shoulder.

The bitch had jumped on my back and sunk her nasty teeth into my neck. And that was all it took. My rage turned violent. I screamed and grabbed the lid to the toilet tank. Then I spun around and smashed her head with it. She went down, but I didn't stop. I didn't stop hitting her with the lid until her swollen brains splashed over the tile floor.

I threw the lid behind me where it landed on the floor with a loud clunk. The sound hurt. I was breathing hard. The ringing in my head grew to a deafening level until I had to hold my hands over my ears.

"Make it stop!"

I fell to my knees and began to cough. My body hurt all over. My stomach was in knots and I couldn't focus. A splash of blood came out of me. Then another. Suddenly I was vomiting a waterfall of red. Dizziness overtook me and everything began to

go dark. And then I fell to floor in a pool of my own blood. I was dead.

*   *   *

A faint tinkling melody roused me. My brain was a fog; my vision dark. When I opened my eyes, the room was a blur. I could only see a few tiles clearly. My phone vibrated three inches away, singing a tune.

I tried to move, but could only get one arm to cooperate. The tips of my fingers came into view. The phone stopped vibrating and the screen went dark. I made an attempt to pull myself up, anticipating the white hot burn of the bite on my arm.

But there was nothing. No pain at all.

I sat up in one quick motion and pressed a palm to my neck. There was no bite. The floor wasn't covered in blood and there wasn't the body of a diseased woman lying dead next to me. The bathroom door stood wide open and Lucky was munching on something happily. What the hell had happened?

The tinkling melody filled my ears again. My phone was vibrating. The screen was bright. The name "Raychel" was clear.

"Holy shit!" I lunged for the phone and pressed the answer key. "Hello?"

"Oh, my God, Jack! Thank you, Lord Almighty! The phones weren't working! I finally found a signal!" Her voice sounded like it hadn't changed at all.

"Raychel...where are you?" I stood slowly to steady myself. The back of my head ached.

"We're at your house! We didn't know where else to go..." Static crippled the line for a moment.

"Raychel?!"

"Jac...I...here...you...there?"

"Raychel, do you have a car?"

Static. "Yes."

"Okay, drive straight to Las Vegas and stay there! I'll meet you there. Don't get out of the car and don't talk to anyone, okay?" I began to search frantically for my gun and a jacket.

"Okay. See you."

I paused. The air hung empty with the words I knew we both wanted to say. "See you."

"I—"

The phone beeped loudly in my ear. I looked at the screen. No service. I didn't have time to dwell on what had just happened in the bathroom. I had to light a fire under my own ass.

I found both my guns, shrugged into a beat up coat, and threw open the hotel door. "You coming?" I turned back toward Lucky. He regarded me for a moment, then jumped up to follow me out the door.

December 18

Ten hours. Seven hours of driving. Two hours of stopping to piss and one hour spent syphoning diesel fuel with a hose. Man that shit tasted terrible.

It took me ten hours to get to Vegas. In that ten hours, I had way too much time to think about what happened between me and Raychel. So many hurtful words were exchanged and so much time had passed without a phone call that I wasn't sure how it was going to go.

"Now we're talkin'!"

I jumped halfway out of my seat, causing the van to swerve into the shoulder. Dirt and snow plunged into the air. The sound of skidding tires met me. I calmly took my foot off the gas pedal and turned the wheel back toward the road.

"You're lucky I know shit about cars." I rolled my eyes skyward, avoiding the disgusting corpse rotting in the passenger seat.

"Wait...how am I lucky? I'm already dead."

I opened my mouth to say something, but he was right. My jaw hung open for a few seconds more before I closed it again.

"Why the hell did you pull that stunt back at the hotel?" I kept my eyes on the road ahead. Only ten miles to go.

"Me? Man, that was all *your* imagination. You have a damn powerful one."

"Not the hallucination. You telling me I need to do what's right. What *is* right?"

"This. What you're doing right now is what you should have done ages ago."

I took one hand off the wheel to scratch the back of my head. "No shit."

Five miles.

"You know...I never met Raychel. Is she as hot as *Lisa*?"

My blood pressure spiked. "Why'd you say her name like that?"

There was no response from Silas. I'd almost forgotten what I'd said because a small Fiat car was coming into view on the side of the road.

"Must be them."

Slowing to a crawl, I could feel my stomach rising into my throat. Would it really take an apocalypse to bring me and Raychel together again? Would she even forgive me? There was no time to worry about that. She must have seen my car slowing down, because the driver side door opened and out she jumped in all her blonde glory.

"Jack!"

I parked the van. Raychel ran to me before I was even out and threw her arms around my middle. For a moment I was dumbstruck. It was if nothing had gone bad between us. It felt right to hug her — as if we were meeting for a movie or dinner or something.

I held her back at arm's length. She was obviously older than the last time I'd seen her, but her eyes were still that

vibrant blue. A few more wrinkles creased her face. It was as if life were showing how harsh it had been to her.

The large smile on her face suddenly faded. She pulled away before slapping me on the arm. "Why didn't you ever call?!" Crossing her arms over her chest, she turned away in a pretend huff.

"Did you have any trouble getting here? I hope you weren't waiting too long."

She turned back toward me with her eyes a bit wider. It was as if my voice or words had come as a surprise to her.

"Uh, no. The drive was boring. We've only been here for about an hour or so."

"Yeah, okay. Who's 'we' again?"

"Are you seeing anyone?"

"What?"

Her face went into blank mode. Her head tilted to one side. "Are. You. Seeing. Anyone?"

I leaned forward slightly. "What. Does that. Have to do. With anything?"

"Then that's a no."

I said nothing.

"No one since Claire?"

That caught my attention. "You never met Claire."

A coy smile appeared on her face. "I stalked your Facebook page. She was cute. Why'd you break up?"

After a deep sigh, I pinched the bridge of my nose. "What are you talking about?"

235

Raychel grabbed my hand and pulled me toward the small car. Through the window I could see a man and a woman in the back seat. I didn't recognize him, but I recognized her.

"Jack!" She began getting out of the car.

I swung back around to Raychel. "What the hell?"

Raychel shrugged. "She and I got to talking after you two broke up. She's sweet. We became friends."

Claire rounded the back of the vehicle with her arms outstretched for a hug. But I wasn't feeling it. "Sorry. I'm seeing someone."

Both Raychel and Claire's faces drooped. It was quiet for a moment until Raychel introduced the man as he got out.

"This is Gregg."

I studied the side of her face as she watched him. There was a soft fondness in her eyes. It reminded me of the way she used to look at me.

"So, what..."

She finally tore her gaze away from him. "Yeah?"

"What do you...what are we gonna do?"

"Well," Claire said, "we were kind of hoping you'd gotten somewhere safe and could show us where."

That was typical. Only calling when she needed something. I cleared my throat. "I was staying in a hotel in Utah. Seemed okay."

"Well, let's go!"

We debated for a few moments whether or not the two of them should follow me or if we should go in one car. In the

end, we decided to siphon the gas out of the van and take the Fiat. While it was a smaller, we could most likely save time by driving quicker, and if anything were to happen, I'd be there.

"So, Jack...where is your girlfriend?"

I turned my attention to the rear view mirror so I could see Claire. "What?"

She shrugged one shoulder. "You said you had a girlfriend, but she wasn't with you. Where is she?" That single question was loaded with a multitude of others. There was so much hesitation in in the air that it was impossible to sort everything out right then and there.

Closing my eyes for a second, I turned my head back toward the passenger side window. "She's in Utah."

"At the hotel we're going to?"

"No."

Out of the corner of my eye, I saw Raychel nod. "So, you lied."

"Can we talk about something else?"

She paused. I'd almost thought I'd hurt her feelings until she let out an exhausted sounding chuckle. "You are still the Dancing King. Dancing around the issues."

"Is my dating life really an issue?"

She smiled, reached over and flicked my ear. "Stop it!"

I flinched, waving her hand away. "I was seeing her, okay? But it didn't work out."

"Maybe she was turned off by your scruffy beard." Claire let out a snort of amusement.

I shook my head. "This is a new development."

"Yeah, well it should probably go. You look homeless."

I raised an eyebrow. "Aren't I?"

Her face went blank. "I think we all kind of are."

*   *   *

"So what is the four-one-one?" Raychel sat in the swivel chair at the bar and turned to face me. She still had that mischievous look in her eyes.

I grabbed the counter behind the bar and leaned forward. "About what?"

She shrugged. "Life, the universe and everything."

"Forty-two."

"I'm serious!"

"Me too."

After a sigh, she rolled her eyes. "All jokes aside—"

"Wait... When did we agree to that?"

She eyed me. "Just tell me how your life has been."

I took a deep breath. "Nothing out of the ordinary. Aside from these Biters on my heels ready to tear me a new asshole. What about you?"

"Same shit, different day."

I could have sympathized with that. "How's Ray doing?"

Raychel scoffed. It was a sound I knew all too well. "You are the only person I know that refers to his father by his first name." She paused. "He's dead."

"Good. When did that happen?"

"Two years ago. And you were right, so...no gloating."

Two Men and a Lift Auto Garage

"We Auto Know"

I put my hands up in a defensive pose. "I wasn't going to."

She gave me a half-cocked smile. It was the same one I remembered from years ago. A familiar ache inched its way into my chest.

"So...this girl you were seeing... Care to offer up a serving of what she was like?"

Leaning forward, I rested my elbows on the bar while crossing my arms. "Perfect."

Raychel slapped the bar with an open palm, alerting Claire and Gregg who'd been off exploring the lobby. "Wow! She musta sucked the soul outta you to get you to say that!" A laugh accompanied the sentiment.

"Dude. Gross. What the fuck?" I narrowed my eyes at her while she continued to laugh like nothing had happened between us or in the world.

"That must have been some blow job!"

I could feel a grimace cross my expression. "All right, all right. Are we done?"

"Aww!" Raychel stood to reach across the bar. Then she pinched one of my cheeks before I could swat her away. "Cheer up, Jackie. Give me a smile!"

"What's so funny over here?" Gregg took the seat next to Raychel who still thought she was the funniest thing since David Brent.

"Ray Ray got into the laughing gas again," I said. Claire giggled, so I nodded toward her. "C'mon, Charlie. Let's get out of here before Raychel's head explodes."

*   *   *

"You used my nickname."

I was in my own world when Claire spoke. The stars were so bright because lack of light pollution, I could see the Milky Way. Yum. Milky Way.

"Jack?"

"What?" I turned to look at my ex-girlfriend. She hadn't changed at all — still had that short brown hair and shy look to her.

"You used my nickname back there."

I blinked a few times. "Oh, yeah. I got used to giving people nicknames when I was with Lisa."

Claire was quiet for a moment. I knew that quiet. That quiet was the jealous quiet. There was no energy to handle that shit. So, I decided it was time to try and head to bed. But she followed me. Could not take a hint, that one.

"It's um...it's nice to see you again. How have you been?"

I sighed while opening the door to my cabin. "Just peachy. You?"

"I've seen better days."

I glanced at her. "You look fine. Haven't changed much."

A tinge of red filled her cheeks. "Thanks."

A long silence fell over us. I felt bad for being angry with her. Despite what she'd done to me in the past, she was a sweet woman and always kind. Just not that bright.

"I didn't mean for things to end the way they did."

I expected to feel upset at her statement, but I felt nothing. It was kind of refreshing. I sat on the bed and she followed again. "Well, cheating is a conscious decision."

She turned to me, her eyes wet. "And I feel terrible for that."

I shrugged. "The past is the past."

"I tried to get a hold of you a lot after that."

"I know."

"I wanted things to work." There was a slight waver in her voice. All I needed then was for a woman to cry at me. "Raychel told me why your last relationship didn't work out."

"Oh boy..." I knew she'd be looking to get back together, but I had no idea she wanted to take it so fast.

"You know I always wanted to marry you."

"Yeah, I knew that. But it wasn't right."

A tear fell down her cheek. "The only reason I cheated was because you wouldn't commit!"

I could feel my brow furrow. "As backwards as that sounds, I was twenty-seven, Claire. I wasn't ready to get married."

"Raychel says you were always ready."

I let out a low groan. "Jesus. Yes, I was always ready, but I didn't feel like you were the one. I was trying to spare your feelings."

Claire shut her mouth and fell back against the headboard. "Ouch."

"Sorry."

"Well now what?"

I turned to look at her. "Now what *what*?"

She met my gaze. "What about now? How do you feel about me now?"

Was that a trick question? "The same..."

Hope bubbled into her eyes. "You still love me?"

"Now, wait." I sat up and put out both hands as if to ward her off. "I didn't say that. Claire, you're an ex. We broke up for a reason."

"But I haven't ever cheated again and, even if I could, who the hell would I get? It's the end of the world and I don't feel like befriending a zombie."

I leaned back, oddly impressed by her choice of words. "That's...there is so much wrong with that sentence."

"Give me another chance. You won't regret it."

"This is weird. It feels like a movie. I feel like you're the expendable character only being introduced to throw a wrench between me and Lisa."

At the mention of Lisa's name, Claire went quiet. I could tell from the gleam in her eye that she was jealous again.

Jealous of what, I had no idea. The whole reason she'd come with me was pure weirdness.

"What if I could make you forget about her?"

I stopped for a moment. While forgetting about the heartache Lisa had caused me sounded amazing, completely forgetting about her and what we had was a scary thought. I wanted to answer, but I was frozen. My brain had crashed. Claire must have known it, too, because she took that opportunity to kiss me.

And it wasn't that bad. She'd always been very soft and gentle. Her warmth seeped into my already exhausted body. Our kiss deepened. It felt never-ending at that point. And when she pulled away and began kissing me elsewhere, she said my name softly. And in return, I said hers.

But she sat up and looked into my eyes with anger for some reason. Then she got up and stormed toward the door.

"I guess you really can't forget about her, can you? You're obsessed, Jack Reynolds!" With that, she slammed the door.

"Whatever." I sighed and went back to lying on the bed.

"Good job, bro."

"I didn't do anything. She's just upset."

Silas laughed from the chair next to me. It was a relatively good chuckle at that.

"Don't laugh too hard or your jaw will fall off."

"This?" He touched the shiny white bone peeking through his grey skin. "This is a fashion statement, dude. And

243

you did do something stupid just now. You called Claire by Lisa's name."

I squinted one eye at him. "I did *not*."

"Did too."

I thought for a moment. "Whatever. Doesn't matter. I'm used to not getting laid at this point."

*   *   *

A bright light woke me a few hours later. My first thought was a helicopter, so I jumped up, getting tangled in the sheets on the way to window. Stubbed my toe on the desk. Ouch. Across the way from me, I could see the lobby of the hotel. And the light was on.

"Shit!" I untangled myself as best I could and stumbled for the door. After throwing it open, I listened to the night. Then I heard it. The howl of a Biter. And it was close. So I kept to the shadows and ran straight for the lobby, Lucky on my heels.

When I slammed through the door with gun drawn, Claire, Gregg and Raychel stared up at me like deer in headlights. I ran straight for the opposite wall where the electrical panel was hidden.

"What are you doing?" Claire stood from her seat at the front desk.

In one swift movement, I switched every breaker to off until the lobby went dark. Then I turned to my companions.

"What the hell were you thinking?" I kept my voice at just above a whisper.

244

Two Men and a Lift Auto Garage

"We Auto Know"

No one said anything, because they were stunned into silence. The howls of the diseased were closing in. Shuffling footsteps rounded a corner.

Frantic, I looked around for something – anything – to wedge against the door so they couldn't make it in. all I found was a broomstick, but I figured it was enough if we were quiet.

Once the door was secure, I turned back to them and motioned them to lie low and be quiet. Raychel clung to Gregg while Claire hid behind the front desk. A few tense moments passed as the shuffling of near-dead feet crept closer.

A hand pressed against the glass doors. It gave a slight push, but the broom held. Another hand appeared and pushed harder, but the door remained shut.

That must have been enough to satisfy the Biter's curiosity because it shuffled away from the door. I stood from my crouching position and listened. I couldn't hear the howling anymore, but I knew they were still around.

"We have to get out of here. Where are the flashlights I gave you?" I reached into my back pocket for mine and clicked it on. The others followed suit. "Keep one hand over the light so they won't—"

I was interrupted by a crash from behind the front desk. Somehow, a Biter had entered the hotel and was stumbling toward Claire.

"Let's go!" I ran over and grabbed her just as the Biter reached out. Then, we all ran toward the entrance of the indoor pool.

245

Two Men and a Lift Auto Garage

"We Auto Know"

Halfway there, another Biter came from the shadows, lunging for Raychel and Gregg. They stupidly took off down the hallway instead of sticking with us.

"What the...? Fuck! Raychel, lock the door and hide!"

"I'm not stupid!" She yelled back at me before her and Gregg disappeared around a corner, the Biter still at their ankles.

"Come on!" I pulled Claire into the swimming area just as more howls echoed down the dark hallways.

I shoved her inside, then bolted the double metal doors shut. Then, using the Allen wrench hanging from a string off the handle, locked them tight, taking the "key" with me. An eruption of pounding caused Claire to yelp, but the doors didn't budge. It was only a matter of time before they got bored. We just had to wait it out. But Claire was having none of that. Before I could even react, she'd grabbed the Allen wrench from me.

"What are you doing?"

"Let me keep it safe. You always misplaced stuff."

Was she trying to start a fight? "I do *not*." I tried to grab the wrench from her, but she backed away.

"Yes, you do. You were always putting things down and forgetting where they were." She inched backward toward the pool. I stopped myself, watching the dark water lap at the sides.

Swallowing hard, I kept my voice calm. "Claire, please give me the wrench back."

246

Just like a bad dream, she tripped. Damn clumsy woman. Trying to control the damage before it was done, I leapt toward her, trying to get the wrench from her hand. And my fingers just grazed it before it went flying into the water.

"Fuck!" I backed away from the dark sea of water. I could already feel my head getting fuzzy and my breath short.

"I'm sorry!"

I put my hands out, backing away from the pool. "Okay... Okay... It's...it's not that big of a deal. All you have to do is go in there and get the wrench back."

"Who, me?"

I spun around to face Claire. She was making my blood boil. The sheer stupidity that followed her around was insane!

"Yes, you!"

"Um... I don't think so."

"You *know* I can't go in there."

She was silent, her eyes wide like a doe in the forest. I wanted to shake her. I wanted to grab her and shake the stupid out. But I couldn't. Instead, I sighed and looked around for another way out.

Lucky tugged at my jeans. I looked down to find him staring up at me. I wish I could say that we had this mental connection where we could understand each other's thoughts, but I didn't speak Raccoon.

"Not now, buddy. We have to get out of here."

I swear he made a frustrated little grunt before running off toward the opposite side of the pool. I watched him scurry out of sight. Welp, so much for that.

I turned back to Claire. "All right, then. I guess we wait for Raychel and Gregg to come rescue us."

"I'm sorry, Jack." Claire's words were quiet. I tried to feel sympathy for the situation, but she was so freaking dumb.

I forced a smile. "Still a chance to redeem yourself."

She stared at me like she had no idea what I was talking about. So I just offered her a shrug and a sigh before heading over to sit next to the door.

The Biters had gone quiet. There was no noise outside the double doors. I wasn't even sure how long we'd been sitting before someone spoke.

"Remember our first date?"

I looked up at the pools of light swimming on the ceiling, reflecting the water. "Oh, you mean the date where you broke my toilet?"

To my surprise, Claire began to laugh. Her laugh had always been infectious, so I soon found myself chuckling as well.

"I hadn't meant to! I was nervous!"

"Nervous about going on a date with a mechanic?" I nudged her with my elbow.

"You're always underestimating yourself." Her tone turned serious. "You've never learned to appreciate yourself like everyone else does."

I was quiet for a moment. Deep words like those were rare coming from her. "Nah." I decided to joke instead.

"My mom adored you."

"Allegra liked everyone."

"Well, you especially." She tucked her knees under her while turning toward me. "First thing she said to me when the outbreak happened was to go find you, because you were probably my last hope at getting married."

"Snap."

"And then she got attacked." Claire went silent again, staring at a wet patch of concrete.

"Bummer." It was all I could offer as far as sentiment went.

"As usual, mother was wrong." We looked at each other. "A guy like you doesn't stay single forever."

Told you she was nice.

For some reason, no words came to me. Probably because Lisa wasn't one for doling out compliments like they were candy. One here and one there was how she did business. Being flattered was, well...flattering.

A bang on the door interrupted our moment. Claire jumped while I scrambled to my feet.

"Jack!" The whisper was harsh, but I recognized the voice. Raychel and Gregg were waiting for us outside the doors.

"Raychel?" I kept my voice low. "Are the Biters gone?"

"For the most part."

"We're kinda stuck in here right now. Can you maybe—" I stopped when I felt a tug on my jeans. It was Lucky. And in his tiny little hand was another Allen wrench. I knelt down. "Oh you beautiful little creature. I could kiss you." I stood with the wrench in hand. "But I won't."

When we were finally outside, the non-chlorinated air smelled sweet. Raychel and Gregg were right outside in the dark, waiting for us. I look at Raychel's flashlight. There was blood all over it, casting an eerie red glow on the walls.

"That's not yours, is it?" I asked, keeping my voice low.

She shook her head. "I got one of those things."

I nodded. "Good. Let's get the hell out of dodge."

The lobby was clear as well. While the lights were still off and it was dark, we could see a little with flashlights. We were almost to the door when Claire screamed.

We all swung around to see a Biter reaching out to her. I tried to grab her, but couldn't get there fast enough. The thing grabbed her by the shoulders and sunk its teeth into her throat.

I cocked my shotgun just as it was tearing a chunk of her flesh out and shot it square in the chest. It fell to the floor as I rushed over to Claire.

She'd fallen against the front desk and sunk down. A streak of red painted the wood behind her, reminding me of Silas – alone and rotting in his own home. Claire gasped for breath and clung to me. Blood gushed with every beat of her heart. That thing had bitten right through her artery.

I pressed my hands against the wound. "Just hold on. Hold on, Claire. You'll be okay."

She kept gasping. Blood poured through my fingers. I wasn't putting enough pressure on the wound. Claire's grip loosened. Her head fell to one side and life faded from her eyes. Her last breath escaped her in a long whisper.

I sat there and stared at her for a few seconds, blood still pooling beneath my hands. I felt as though my own heart had stopped.

"Fuck!" I moved back and slammed a fist into the ground. "Fuck! Shit! Fuck!" I felt no tears but a raw emptiness built inside my chest. I wasn't able to dwell on it much longer, because Raychel screamed behind me. I spun around just in time to see the diseased monster taking a big bite out of Gregg's ankle.

"Fuck you!" I pointed the gun at it, making its head explode in a cloud of blood. Red splashed on the both of them. Raychel was sobbing while Gregg writhed in pain.

I stepped over the thing's body to get a closer look at his bite. "Jesus Christ. It bit right through your Achilles tendon."

"Oh shit. Oh Jesus. What's that mean? I'm I gonna die?"

"Will he be okay, Jack?" Raychel's tears were coming in torrents.

I looked up at them. "I know a doctor."

December 19

The days were beginning to shorten. Darkness fell upon the Huntington house around five every evening and the children were asleep by seven. Ms. Huntington always invited me down for tea afterward and we'd talk about anything and everything. Besides Jack. Whenever his name was brought up, I'd change the subject. I didn't need to be made to feel guilty for him anymore. He wasn't my responsibility.

Snow had started to sneak into our lives. During the day it was a refreshing sight. While it didn't match my moods most the time, I grew accustomed to the transition. Inside was very warm and inviting. People would come in and out of the house. For some, it was just another pit stop on their way somewhere else. For others, it was a permanent residence. I'd met many new faces.

The nights we're only getting more and more difficult. I never did have a chance to figure out why. I suppose deep down I knew. But I hadn't made a mistake. My head had never steered me wrong. The heart was weak. There was no way I could follow it to a correct decision ever again after what had happened with Chase.

And because of that, I had a decision to make.

It was a Tuesday. There had been a snowstorm sometime during the night. The driveway was muddy and puddles had built up. Rex and Alex were out jumping from one dirty gray patch of snow to another. I watched them from the window. Clouds still hung low in the sky, but it seemed the snow had stopped for the most part.

I can't recall how long I stood in the kitchen, but it felt as though hours had passed while I steeped the green tea in my cup. The kitchen was bustling as it was right after breakfast, so I waited until everyone had filtered out to go to the far cabinets.

Inside, I found a large box of rat poison. Taking another quick look around, I dumped several spoonfuls into my tea and stirred it up.

"I'm telling you, Scotty, you have no idea what it's like."

I looked over my shoulder to see the chef and his friend waltz into the room. Scotty, the chef, was the taller of the two. He was a young redhead full of ambition and hope.

His friend, Tango, was short and scruffy. He seemed to like arguing and making up stories. The two of them stopped at the kitchen sink.

"Dude, I know." Scotty's voice sounded exasperated.

"No, man, seriously. I was on the SWAT team that raided that guy's house, man. You have no idea what weed does to you."

Scotty picked up a rag and slung it over his shoulder, then he turned to face me.

"Oh, hi Lisa. How are you?"

"Hey, Lisa." Tango glanced at me briefly, seeming eager to continue the conversation.

"Hello. I'm fine. Just going to have some tea."

Scotty's eyes glazed over with something that looked like concern. His features went from excited at my presence to wonder.

"Ooh, make sure you don't get any of that in there." He came over to grab the box of poison. After placing it back in the cabinet, he tossed me a flashy smile. "Can't be good for you."

I nodded my agreement.

"Oh, yeah, yeah. I know what you mean." Tango began to rant once again while Scotty rolled his eyes. "I swallowed rat poison once in the army and was sick as a dog for days, man."

I excused myself while the two continued to argue about arbitrary things. Eagerness flooded into every fiber of my being. I just wanted to end it.

Alex and Rex had moved to the sun room to play, so I sat in the loveseat across from the window, watching them teach each other about life.

I stared down at my reflection on the surface of the tea. Deductive reasoning told me I looked tired and haggard. But I felt oddly at peace. The children were taken care of. My presence was no longer a requirement of their wellbeing.

I took the first sip of tea. It was bitter. Not awful, but enough to cause my cheeks to pucker on the inside. I'd had a good run.

Somewhere upstairs, a door slammed. Running footsteps echoed around the hall. Scott and Tango emerged from the large kitchen.

"What's all the noise?" He wiped both hands on his apron.

"I'm not sure." I looked toward the stairs as Ms. Huntington stumbled down. I stood as she passed the sitting room.

"Oh, Lisa! Dear, I need your assistance!" She seemed frantic. Ribbons of her hair had come loose and were falling around her face.

"What's going on?"

"Someone's been bitten. They're bringing them in."

"Oh, shit! I'll help! I have training." Tango ran toward the front door.

"I see. Scott, please boil some water and fetch me as many towels as you can find. I'll need antibacterial soap, something to make a tourniquet with and we'll need to tie the patient down in case they turn." I handed him the cup. "And please pour this out. Make sure all of it goes down the drain."

Scott nodded, confusion knitting his brows together. Then, he disappeared into the kitchen. Ms. Huntington showed me to a room adjacent to the kitchen where they would keep individuals who were ill. We cleared a bed for the newcomer. Scott came back with a large bowl of steaming water and towels.

"I couldn't find anything like a tourniquet," he said.

"It's fine." I turned and snatched a sheet from the neighboring bed and began tearing it into pieces. Ms. Huntington paused for a moment while watching me. "I'll gladly replace these."

She nodded just as the front door smashed open. There were voices and cries of pain. Scott and Ms. Huntington rushed toward the parlor while I continued ripping the sheets into pieces. A few moments later, the shouts continued, but Tango and Scott were carrying someone I'd never seen before. They brought him into the room and laid him carefully on the bed.

"The bite is on his right ankle." I said the words more to myself than anyone else. The man squirmed. "Can you both please restrain him?"

Scott and Tango nodded and they each held down his legs and wrists. Luckily, the man did not fight.

"I'm sorry, sir. This is for everyone's safety. When were you bitten?"

"Uh...um...about an hour ago?"

"What's your name?"

"Gregg."

"Okay, Gregg, I'm going to wash the wound. It's going to hurt very very much. The water is quite hot, but this could potentially stop the spread of the virus through your bloodstream."

"Whatever you say, doc."

I instructed Scott to find some kind of liquor for Gregg to dull the pain. He didn't seem to be struggling, so I made the decision to not restrain him as harshly.

"Mmm." Tango came around to see the wound. He then put one hand to his chin as if he were thinking. "That's a nasty bite, son. A dog bit me there once. Not fun. Needed stitches."

Scott came back with the whiskey and shoved the bottle at Gregg. He happily began chugging it down.

I grabbed a towel, dunked it in the hot, soapy water and pressed it against the bite wound. Gregg immediately tensed and shouted a curse. But he kept as still as he could. I occasionally squeezed the towel to allow more hot water into the wound.

"Who found him like this?"

"A guy named Jack Reynolds brought him here," Tango said.

I tried to still the jump of my pulse.

"Jack said you were the best doctor he knew. He said you could help me." Gregg's voice was hoarse with pain.

"I'm the only doctor he knows." I turned for more hot water.

"Should I tell them anything, Lisa?" Scott took a step toward the door.

"Them?" I didn't look up from my task.

"Jack and Raychel. I'd assume they'd want to know your, uh...."

"Prognosis." Tango finished the sentence for him.

The thought of Jack with some new woman was not one I had time to dwell on as much as I wanted to.

"Tell them I'd like to speak to them. I won't know anything until I clean the wound. Have them come see me when they're ready."

Scott left. Tango stayed and helped me work. It took about fifteen minutes to properly clean the bite. I tied the tourniquet just below the knee and placed fresh towels under Gregg's leg as he drifted in and out of consciousness.

When I was done and Tango had gathered the supplies to bring back to the kitchen for a thorough cleaning, I went to the window. It overlooked the garden and outside I could see Jack speaking with a lovely young blonde woman. They smiled at each other while they spoke. She touched his face.

He'd grown a goatee, but it was neatly trimmed around the sides. The two of them talked for a few more moments before turning to go inside. I fell back from the window.

"Jack was right."

I looked toward Gregg.

"You are the hottest doctor I've ever seen."

"Thank you. Try and rest, Gregg. Your body requires some hibernation after such a trauma."

"You got it, doc."

Jack's voice came to me from the hallway. Ms. Huntington was asking him about his female companion. He introduced her as Raychel. He hadn't mentioned anyone by that name to me. For some reason, the realization I'd made caused my heart to sink a few metaphorical inches into my stomach.

I stepped out into the parlor and shut the door to the room myself. A twinge of dull pain spiked in my insides. I'd have to remember to induce vomiting at some point.

The three of them stopped talking and turned toward me. Jack seemed to visibly deflate when he saw me. The woman's expression registered some recognition, but I was sure I'd never met her before.

Ms. Huntington turned back toward them. "Raychel, dear, I'll show you to your room—"

"I've got it." Jack interrupted the woman and grabbed Raychel's hand. "She'll stay with me."

With that, he whisked her up the staircase and out of sight. Her gaze seemed to linger on me, but I didn't even get a chance to gather my thoughts at seeing Jack again.

"A snack, dear?" Ms. Huntington's voice interjected into my thoughts.

"Tea would be fine, thank you. I'll take it in the sunroom. Where are the children?"

"Ah. Mr. Davis took them into the backroom to put that thousand piece puzzle together while they brought the poor man in. Is he going to be all right?"

"Only time will tell."

*　　　*　　　*

I had nearly finished off my ginger tea when the French doors opened and closed. Out of the corner of my eye, I noticed two people. When I turned my head, I saw Jack and his female friend approaching me. Neither of their expressions told me what they could have possibly been thinking, so I gave them a polite yet guarded smile then went back to watching the snails crawl on the concrete.

The two of them sat down and for a few excruciating moments, none of us spoke. Finally, the blonde woman made a funny noise in the back of her throat before standing up.

"If you're not gonna do it, I will."

Jack said nothing, so she approached me.

"I'm Raychel." She held out her hand, so I shook it. Her voice was raspy but quite full of happy energy.

"Lisa James. Nice to meet you."

We were quiet again. She sat back down next to Jack.

"I brought him here because I knew you could help him." It was Jack who'd spoken. I studied his face, but he kept his expression stonily blank.

"I appreciate it."

"Ugh. Would you look at that?" Raychel gestured toward the French doors. I turned and saw a mangy-looking raccoon rummaging around in the flowers.

"Did he come with you?" I was curious.

"He came with Jack. That's his baggage, not mine." Her voice was drenched in humor, but Jack didn't seem to find it amusing.

"His name's Lucky."

"I kept telling him it's super gross. I mean, Raccoons are the number one carriers of rabies. How can you be so silly?" Raychel nudged him.

"Actually the number one carrier of rabies is dogs. But raccoons are on the list." I watched Lucky try to munch on a flower then spit it out, using his paws to rub the end of his nose.

"Oh."

"How long have you had him?" I turned back to Jack.

"About a month." He didn't look at me.

"Then you're fine. He would have shown signs by now. Unless he gets bitten, we have nothing to worry about." I watched the animal scratch at his patchy fur. "He has fleas."

"Yeah, I know. But there's not much I can do about it, is there?" Jack's question was flat.

"Ms. Huntington keeps boxes of Dawn dish soap in the shed on the other side of the house. If you stop up a tub and put him in the water with some of it, it'll kill the fleas."

He finally looked at me. I thought I saw a sparkle of humor in his eye, but it vanished as quickly as it had come. "Let me guess... You studied veterinary science in college?"

I took a deep breath. "Yes. For a semester." If I wanted answers as to who this mystery woman was, I'd have to ask difficult questions. "So how long have you two been seeing each other?"

Both of them snapped their gazes to me at the same time. They were silent for a second or two before Raychel burst into almost hysterical laughter. Jack rolled his eyes.

"You can stop now."

Raychel put her hands to her mouth and tried to control it. "I'm sorry. I'm just...I'm not done laughing yet." She wiped a tear form her eye while quelling one last chuckle. "Jack is my brother."

I felt instantly stupid. "Oh."

"I'm involved with Gregg in there, actually."

"Oh! I apologize. I don't have a fountain of information for you yet. The next twelve hours is very critical. I've cleaned the bite as best I can. The good news is it's as far away from the brain as it can possibly be, so it could take quite a few days to spread. I should know more by tomorrow morning, and hopefully we won't need to amputate."

"Thank you." The words emerged quietly from her mouth.

"Of course."

"So, does he have a leg to stand on?" Jack asked.

Raychel groaned. "Grow up."

Jack lifted his shoulders in response. "It's a legitimate question! Gregg might have to learn partial arts."

"Are you serious right now?" Raychel stared at him, but he just kept a straight face.

"Completely. He'll at least get half off on pedicures."

"Oh, my God!" Raychel sounded exasperated, but the two of them had small smiles on their faces.

"Once he can walk again, he'll be having problems with stares."

She was silent for a moment. "Oh...that one took me a minute."

Jack ran a hand through his hair. "I'm trying to think of another amputee joke, but I'm stumped."

"That's it!" Raychel stood up with her hands in front of her. "I can't take any more of this. How do you put up with it?" She was speaking to me.

"He has good timing."

"Someone thinks I'm funny." He smiled at his sister.

"Oh, you're funny, all right. So funny that I can't take it anymore. I'm going to check on Gregg. You two have a nice chat!"

Jack watched her walk back into the house. When she was gone, he made a move to stand.

"Wait! Gregg will make a fortune as a Bell Hop!" He waited for a moment. "Damn. She didn't hear me." He sat and watched the raccoon hunt around in the garden.

Once the humor inside me died to a tolerable level, I spoke. "So, how have you been doing?"

He still didn't look at me, but shrugged one shoulder. "As good as can be expected."

I nodded. "You never mentioned Raychel by name before."

"I never even knew if she was still alive. We were both pretty stubborn about contact."

The French door slammed open, startling the raccoon and causing it to squeak then run to hide behind a bush.

"Uncle Jack!" Alex ran to him.

"Juliet!" He smiled for the first time since he'd gotten in. It was warming to see. He picked up Alex and spun her in a circle. "How you been?"

She giggled. "You know how."

His expression seemed impressed. "This is true."

Rex had also come out when Alex had, but he instinctively hid behind my legs. He didn't remember Jack right away. I patted his head, but he whimpered.

Jack set Alex down. "Hey, Romeo. How about you? How you doing?"

Rex cowered away, but I caught him, pulling him in front of me. "You remember, Jack, honey. Don't you?" Our gazes met and a wave of heat washed over me. One corner of Jack's mouth twitched upward.

I cleared my throat and turned back to Rex. "Jaggy?"

That resonated with my son. "Jaggy!" He cried as Jack lifted him up.

"I knew you just needed a reminder. Way to go, mom," Jack said. His smile seemed genuine.

"Way go, momma!" Rex imitated him.

"What do we do next, Aunt Lisa?" Alex sat down in the chair Raychel had previously occupied.

"Yeah." Jack turned back to me with my son still in his arms. "What do we do now, Aunt Lisa?"

I sucked in a breath. "Well, dinner is being put out soon. Would you like to join everyone? How long are you staying?"

Jack looked at Rex and bounced him once. "Dunno. That's up to Raychel."

"I see."

"But I see no reason why we can have dinner together. Do you?"

Rex shook his head. "Dinner."

"Do you, Juliet?"

"Nope!"

He turned back to me. "Then it's a yes."

*   *   *

"It certainly has been some time since you left, Jack." Ms. Huntington smiled proudly at her guests. We'd gained some new faces and lost a few, but the house still felt like a family. Jack had already begun eating – it seemed he was famished – so he abruptly put his fork down and gestured a 'thank you' with his mouth full.

"And it's lovely to have you here, Raychel, dear."

"Thanks!"

I found Raychel's zeal incredibly sweet. She was bubbly and happy. She made jokes all the time. She was the female version of Jack. I felt like nothing could bring her down.

"All right, everyone. Let's eat!"

The table erupted in a cacophony of conversation and clinking silverware. There were smiles and laughs. People were happy.

"When is the last time you had a decently cooked meal?" I watched Jack hungrily devour his food.

He paused to swallow. "When I was here."

"Oh."

"Who are they?" He nodded toward a couple who were cuddling together.

"They're Sam and Jennifer. They came here shortly after you left."

"What happened to Cheree and Ben?"

I glanced down at my plate. "They aren't together anymore."

"What?" Jack gave me a skeptical glare while he chewed.

"Ben left about a week ago and Cheree went shortly after."

Jack swallowed. "What happened?"

"I don't know."

Scott swung over and asked me if I'd like more bread. I tossed him a polite smile and accepted. Then he bent down.

"Can I talk to you for a sec?"

"A more appropriate time would be tomorrow morning. Would that be all right?"

He nodded and whisked away to offer others more bread.

"And who's *that*?" There was a tiny hint of malice in Jack's voice. I turned to him in surprise.

"That's Scott. He's the new chef."

"What happened to Jeffrey?"

"He left."

"Hmm."

"What is it?" I managed to maintain a patient tone.

"Does he talk to everyone the way he talks to you?"

"I'm not sure what you mean."

"He's like a lost puppy. I notice him following you around and taking every opportunity to speak to you."

I blinked a few times. "He's nineteen-years-old, Jack."

He squared his shoulders. "So?"

"He just lost his parents." I lowered my voice even more. "I talked him through it when he first got here. He was suicidal. It wasn't healthy."

Jack seemed to want to say something, but he kept silent. I couldn't tell what was going on inside his head.

"He's jealous."

We both looked up to see Raychel smiling at us.

"I am not."

She laughed. "Yep, you are. It's super obvious, bro. When are you going to stop being mad?"

"I am *not* mad."

"Yes you are." I chimed in, keeping as calm as I could. The truth of the matter was that heat I'd felt hadn't stopped coursing through my veins. Every time he looked at me my entire body craved him.

"See?" Raychel stuck her tongue out at him. "Even she knows you're mad."

"That's because she studied psychology for a semester in college." He glanced at me, making my heart hammer in my chest.

"So you admit you're mad!" Raychel continued to egg him on.

"Okay, how long is this going to go on? Is this like an initiation thing or are you two girls going to say things about me to each other until I crack and put you in the brig?"

"Oh, God. The brig." Raychel put a hand to her head and leaned back.

"The brig?" I was curious.

"We used to have this stupid tee-pee thing when we were kids." She smiled at the memory.

"It was a wigwam." Jack cut in. "It was made out of sticks and some ripped up jeans or something. Whenever one of us would get in trouble, we'd get sent to it. We called it the brig."

"Eventually we started stapling things to the inside so we wouldn't get bored."

"Remember the posters?"

Raychel laughed again. "Oh, God. I'd put up posters of James Bond and then he'd tear them down and replace them with Raquel Welch. It was like a cold war."

They continued discussing their childhood while I listened. It was a very sweet conversation. I knew they'd had some issues between one another and it was comforting to see them remembering good times and not bad.

The dinner lasted quite some time as the guests were enjoying the conversations. I'd taken a break to put the children to bed, but they wouldn't sleep without a Goodnight from Jack. When I came back down, we enjoyed a round of desserts before everyone decided to turn in.

December 20

It was 1:30 in the morning when I ventured downstairs for the final time. The house was eerily quiet. But the silence was thick. It was as if all ears were trained; waiting for something to happen.

"How's it going?" I checked the straps on each of Gregg's arms. They were still secure.

"So far, so good. It's throbbing, but I don't feel sick or anything."

"Did Scott give you some water an hour ago like I asked?"

"Yes."

"Did you drink it?"

"Yes."

"Without issue?"

"Yeah. It was a Godsend."

I nodded. He was safe for now. But the timing was critical. I needed to know how the wound was progressing and if it seemed to be healing or spreading. I rounded the table, ready for the worst but hoping for the best.

I'd kept the lights off in case the virus took him during the night. But I made sure to carry a Maglite with me. I clicked it on to study the wound.

Each tooth mark was individually apparent. They were swollen and puffy. That was normal. What wasn't normal were deep purple veins visibly sprouting from all sides. I moved the restraint away from his foot to see they had reached the heel already.

"Shit."

"You're going to have to take my leg."

I looked at him and he gave me a weak smile. He smelled a bit like liquor, but I couldn't have blamed him at that point.

"Yes. The virus is poisoning your blood. It's reached your foot already, but not your knee. If we can change that, we can save the rest of you."

"All right, so...what do we gotta do?"

I inhaled and held it for a moment. "I need medical supplies."

Gregg sighed as his head fell back onto the pillow I'd given him.

"For now I'll move the tourniquet up to your knee. That should keep it from spreading any more the rest of the night." I put the restraint back in place and moved the towel to tie around his knee. "Now, since we're going to anesthetize you in the morning, you shouldn't eat anything else. Water is fine, but try to limit your intake. The last thing you want after major surgery is to be nauseous."

"Okay."

I placed a hand on his shoulder. "This is a lot better than losing your life."

"I know... I just hope Raychel still wants to marry me when I only have one leg."

Two Men and a Lift Auto Garage

"We Auto Know"

December 20

Lisa was super impressive the next day. She scrambled around giving orders to everyone who offered to help. For most of it, I held onto Rex while Alex followed on our heels. From what I could gather, Lisa had told two people to clean out one of the industrial size freezers and sterilize it from top to bottom. Scott was instructed to turn it off and wheel a steel table inside. People were running everywhere gathering towels and boiling water on the stove.

Ms. Huntington had told us there was a Dr. Brown who lived in the house. Neither of us had ever seen him because he apparently kept to himself. His room was at the end of the hall of the East Wing, so that was our first stop.

"I have a question."

Lisa was in the process of knocking on the door, but her closed fist stopped an inch away when I spoke. "Yes?"

"Why didn't this doctor guy come out and help you with Gregg?"

She narrowed her eyes. "I'm not sure. But my impression is that he prefers solitude." She knocked three times.

"A doctor who prefers not to treat patients. Interesting."

The door opened a crack. "What is it?" A raspy voice met us.

"Dr. Brown?"

"Yes."

Two Men and a Lift Auto Garage

"We Auto Know"

"My name is Dr. James. We have a patient downstairs in need of an amputation and—"

The door opened all the way to reveal a short old man in a brown tweed jacket. His spectacles were slipping halfway down his nose. "Yes. I heard last night. You need supplies, I assume."

"Yes, sir."

"Then come in." He waved Lisa inside. She disappeared and I started to go after her, but Dr. Brown held his hand out. "Only one guest in my room at a time." Then he shut the door in my face.

"Old Man River."

Waiting outside was no easy ordeal. At first, I watched the door for about five minutes, hoping it wouldn't take much longer than that. Then I began humming to myself. I had no idea what song I had in my head, but it was catchy.

When that still proved fruitless, I began to run *Die Hard* in my head. Man, that was a good movie. I found myself wondering if Bruce Willis was still alive. About fifteen minutes after that, I checked my watch. Then I realized I didn't have a watch.

"Huh..." I tapped my wrist. "I should draw a new battery for this thing..."

The door swung open. To my surprise, Lisa stormed out in a huff. Well, to Lisa, a huff is slightly lowered eyebrows and a deep frown.

"No, thank you, Dr. Brown. We're fine." When she shut the door, I noticed a few tools in her hand. But they didn't look right. And when she turned to face me, I could tell she was upset.

"What happened?"

"Dr. Brown's name ends in DDS."

"Oh, shit."

"Exactly. All he had was lidocaine. We need to knock Gregg out not numb his tongue!" She inhaled and shut her eyes. She was calming herself.

"But you got something from him?"

"Yes. Suction, latex gloves and a syringe." She opened her eyes. "What are we going to do?"

The entire way back to the kitchen Lisa was silent. I could tell she was working things out in her head. She'd told me that if we couldn't knock Gregg out for the procedure it was likely he'd go into shock.

No one could give her any advice as to where to find medical supplies. She handed over the tools she'd received from Dr. Brown and instructed someone to sterilize them in boiling water. Then she sat heavily into a kitchen chair and sighed. Raychel came out of Gregg's room and immediately knew something was not right.

"What's going on?"

"We don't have drugs to put Gregg to sleep," I said.

My sister looked from Lisa, to me, to the ground and back at Lisa. "What does that mean?"

"I'm not sure yet." Lisa looked up, putting her chin in her hands.

"Hey, you should probably eat. Want me to get you something?"

She nodded. "Sure."

I looked for Scott to find him in the kitchen slicing what looked like fish. I had no idea where he'd gotten any from, but I figured I was better not asking.

"Hey, Scott. Lisa needs some brain food. Whatcha got?"

At the mention of her name, Scott stopped what he was doing and turned to face me. "She's hungry?" There was a hint of urgency in his voice. It caught me off guard.

"Yeah... But don't have a heart attack, man."

Scott's eyes darted around, searching the countertops. He spotted something behind me and lunged to get it. I almost didn't move in time. He pulled out a platter of bagels and rushed out of the kitchen.

"All right." I followed him back to the dining room.

Lisa was still sitting at the table staring into space. Raychel gave me a weak smile. She was scared. She'd always hug herself when she got scared. That hadn't changed a bit.

"Lisa..." Scott was too close to her in my opinion, but I didn't say a word. "I brought you something to eat." He placed the platter on the table next to her and handed her a bagel.

She took it with a tight, polite smile. She was totally in another world when she bit into the bagel. "I just don't know where we're going to find any medical supplies."

"Medical supplies?" Scott asked.

She looked up at him.

"I passed a hospital five miles east on my way here."

Lisa paused, her eyes lighting up as much as they could. "What are we waiting for?"

December 20

"This is an incredibly terrible idea." I looked up at the hospital through the rain-soaked windshield. The wipers flicked back and forth with an audible tick. Lisa unbuckled her seatbelt.

"We have no others."

"I'm sorry, what?" I tore my eyes away from a shadow passing in front of a second story window.

"We have no other ideas." Lisa stated her sentence slower than the first time.

"No, I know." I gave my tone a higher pitch. "I'm just sayin' this place is probably haunted by ghosts and demons and Willem Dafoe, so it's up to you whether or not you actually need medicine."

"You are a strange man," Scott said from the backseat.

"Baby Face is right." I let out an exaggerated sigh. "We need a plan."

"I never said—"

"Medical supplies have specific closets, don't theu?" Another kid who'd come with us piped up next to Scott.

"Normally." Lisa nodded.

"This place has three floors, Doc Hotness. Where do we start?"

"Hey, don't talk to—"

"Not now, Sierra." I put my hand up, not taking my eyes off Lisa.

"We start on the first floor."

Two Men and a Lift Auto Garage

"We Auto Know"

A sort of frustrated anger bubbled up inside of me. She was treating me like a kid again. And I was pretty sure I wasn't born the day before, so I broke my gaze with her and looked back at the wheel.

"Junkies have probably already cleaned this place out. We probably won't even find anything."

"Well, we have to try."

"Took the words right outta my ass. Sierra! Protein bar me." I put my hand back, palm up and wiggled my fingers at Scott.

"What?"

Turning slowly, I tried to keep my voice at an animated control. "You wanna give me a protein bar from the bag or you wanna keep making lovey eyes at my doctor friend, here?"

Scott sighed and began to dig through my backpack.

"I doubt anything is really on the first floor. That's probably the lobby and maybe a lab or two. So we can probably just poke around the back a bit and head upstairs," Lisa explained.

"Okay, sounds like a plan."

"There are no protein bars in here." Scott interrupted us from the backseat.

"What is in there?" I faked a roll of my eyes at Lisa.

"Fun Dips."

"And...?"

"That's all, man. You have like eighteen packets of fun dip in here. What the fuck?" Scott's voice began to rise into

280

what sounded like a panic. Oh, now he didn't trust me. Just because I liked sour candy.

"Listen to me, Sierra!" I turned around to face him. He was hilariously pale. "What flavors are in there?"

He seemed confused by my sudden curt tone, so he took a moment to answer. "Uh...cherry and blue."

I sighed. "Blue's not a color, Sierra."

"Blue Raspberry, Jesus!"

"Gimme a cherry."

*   *   *

I'd forgotten how good Fun Dips were. Especially the cherry ones. I was really enjoying my packet while Lisa searched a back office and we stood watch. Lucky clawed at my leg. He wanted some too.

"Do you mind?" Scott glanced at me from his side of the door.

"Nah. Want?" I held out my backpack.

"No." Scott shoved it away. "I mean do you mind finishing that thing up. You're really annoying me."

"You kidding? These things are rare today. And these are the ones that change color, see?" I showed him the blue stick.

"Do you ever get tired of being fucking weird?"

"You know...." I tilted the packet back until most of the sour powder fell into my mouth. "The statistical probability of you surviving this mission is slim to none. Given how you were just introduced."

"What the fuck are you talking about? Slim to none isn't even a probability measure."

I tossed the candy stick into my mouth. "You just upgraded to 'divided by zero'."

Our other companion snickered.

"See, Chuckles over there thinks I'm funny. What's your name anyway?"

He flashed an unhealthily toothy grin. "Everybody just calls me by my last name. It's Tango."

I felt my brows shoot up. "Well, hell. Now I can't give you a nickname."

Tango laughed again. "If you really want to be different, you could use my first name. Tinder."

I dropped the spent packet to my feet and kicked it away. Lucky ran after it, sticking his nose inside. "Like...building a fire Tinder or finding romance the not-so-old-fashioned way Tinder?"

"My parents were survivalists, so the first." His tone suggested mild smugness at his own short comings.

"Well, Tinder Tango, it's nice to meet you. You want a Fun Dip?"

Lisa stepped out of the office, holding a bottle of some liquid. "Well, I found insulin. It may come in handy, but it's not what Gregg needs. We need to keep looking." She tossed a glance at all of us. "What's going on?"

"What do you mean?" I played ignorant.

Two Men and a Lift Auto Garage

"We Auto Know"

"I mean Scott looks like he's ready to commit a felony." She pointed to him while looking at me.

"I don't like his mouth, Lisa. He's gonna get us in trouble."

Lisa put her arms out before the kid could take a shot at me. "Jack has saved my life many times, Scott. He's very handy with his weapon."

"Shh... Not in front of the children, honey." I winked at Scott, but he rolled his eyes.

"So what do we do now?" Tinder Tango looked at each one of us. "Upstairs?"

"Yeah...about that." I put a hand on my trusty shotgun. "I saw someone or something up there while we were outside. Tinder Tango, you and me should head upstairs to check it out. Sierra, you stay here."

"Now, hold on a second! I'm just as capable as you are!" Scott was whining. Whining made me want to vomit up all my Fun Dip.

"Well, there can't be that many. I mean, the door was closed and there's none of them down here. Maybe Scotty and Lisa should just come with us." Tinder Tango had a point. There weren't any Biters on the first floor. And I'd only seen one shadow. If there were living junkies up in the place, they probably would have ambushes us when the Scott kid started whining.

283

Lisa pushed past us and started up the stairs. I bounded over to her, grabbing her upper arm in a gentle hold. "Whoa, there, Foxtrot."

For some reason, saying her nickname to her made my heart do a somersault. She looked into my eyes as if the feeling was mutual.

"We need the medicine, Jack."

I stared at her a moment longer, trying to search for an answer to all our problems in her face. When I couldn't find it, I looked back to Scott and Tinder Tango who were whispering together.

"Let's do this, kids."

They stopped whispering long enough for Scott to toss me a grin. "Anything you say, Juliet."

I allowed my mouth to fall open comically accompanied by an exaggerated gasp. "Oh my shit! You're learning, Sierra!"

As everyone began ascending the staircase, I stopped the little shit in his tracks and lowered my voice enough so the others couldn't hear.

"Listen to me, Scott. This isn't some fucking Yoga class you can just squirrel your way through. We're talking about face-biting monsters. They don't care who you are, what your fucking name is or how old you are. They will kill you without so much as an angry grunt."

Scott looked me up and down with a sneer, then backed an inch away. "Whatever, man. You act like I'm doing this for you. I'm doing this for Lisa."

284

"Yeah? Aren't we all?"

"Difference between me and you is that I'm still fucking her."

It took me a moment to understand just what he'd said to me. How could that have been right? Wouldn't Lisa have told me? This kid? Really?! He was such a punk.

"I'm gonna shoot you in the ass."

"That's cute." Scott turned and started up the stairs after the other two.

"God, I wish you wore a red shirt today."

"Whatever."

With each step, the air became hotter and more putrid. The smell of rotting paper and mildew was enough to choke a small child. That was morbid.

About halfway up, I heard the distinct shuffle of booted feet. I stopped everyone and got in front, pushing my back against the wall. It seemed as if the world was holding its breath.

The sound came again. It sounded metallic – like someone hitting a tuning fork against a railing. Then the howl met us. It was pitiful, just like every other time I'd heard it.

"I got a plan." Tinder Tango moved past Lisa and Scott to me. "Scotty and I can go this way and you and Lisa go that way." He jerked his thumb toward the sound of the Biter first, then pointed down the safe-looking part of the hallway.

"Are you serious? Have you ever shot a gun, Tinder Tango?"

"Tango's got a good idea. Let's just do it." Scott was beginning to get on my last nerves.

"Listen, guys, I realize I'm not Chuck Norris here, but—"

I was cut off by another loud howl of the Biter. And in the midst of that ear-piercing music, Scott and Tinder Tango got it into their heads that it was the perfect time to defect. Scott yelled, "Go!" and the two of them rushed past Lisa and me toward the sound.

"Jesus Balls. Come on, Lisa."

"Right behind you."

With shotgun in hand, I began down the hallway toward where Scott and Tinder Tango had run. Babysitting made my head ache, but they were the only volunteers willing to go. But what good were volunteers when they didn't even listen?

"Hey, Lisa, I know there's been a lot of tension between us." We were finally alone, so I took that as an opportunity to ask her about what the kid had said. I peered into an empty room, then moved on.

"What happened to you and me sucks ass, I'll say that, but it wasn't just my decision." I passed another empty room. The Biter was now quiet. "But that kid said something to me that I don't like." I was almost to the end of the hallway. "If I ask you a question will you be one-hundred percent honest with me?" Another empty room on my left. And silence behind me.

"Lisa?" I turned to find empty space where she should have been on my heels. "Mother fu—"

"Help!"

286

The cry came from my right. I spun back around and ran toward the end of the hallway, Lucky on my heels. At the very back was a circular room full of cages. Some of them were empty, but others had Biters locked up in them. Scott and Tinder Tango were in the middle of it all. An enormous Biter with pounds upon pounds of flab was standing over Scott, ready for a meal. Tinder Tango was backed against and open cage, white as a sheet.

"Hey, Bitch Tits!" I cocked my shotgun as the heavy Biter turned toward me. "Come get some."

The thing roared something fierce and began lumbering toward me. The footsteps boomed on the concrete floor, almost shaking the entire hospital building. And I took my time. I savored the moment when the big nasty thing would hit the ground dead because of my awesomeness. So I waited until he was about two feet away before I pulled the trigger. Buckshot sprayed in an arch, hitting him in the chest.

He stumbled backward for a moment, but then regained his composure and started for me again. Before I could aim, Lucky leapt on the Biter, sinking his little teeth into the thing's neck.

But he was so small. All the Biter had to do was shrug him off. With a whip of a hand the size of a baseball mitt, he flung my companion across the room where he hit the wall with a thud, then slid to the floor.

"Lucky!" I turned back toward the overly stuffed rabid man and aimed again. I fired, splitting open his fat head and

lodging metal pellets in his jaw. Indeed it was pretty satisfying when he hit the floor.

I ran over to Lucky, but it was too late. The little guy was breathing his last breaths in my arms. He looked up at me with a sadness that struck me right in the heart.

"It's okay, buddy." I stroked the fur on his face. "It's ok."

With one last longing look, my pet raccoon died. I sighed, wanting to cry, but not in front of two stupid kids. I gently placed Lucky's body in my backpack and stood to face them.

"Okay, what the actual fuck, you guys?!" I dropped my gun to my side and approached Scott to help him up. He seemed weak. I looked him over, but couldn't see any blood or bite marks. Something didn't seem right, though. I ignored it for a moment to grab Tinder Tango.

"Come on, guys."

The two of them were still white. Tinder Tango was shaking so bad the cage he was against rattled. I took another look around the room. The Biters were gnashing their teeth. One of them banged on his door, startling the poor kids.

"There are people here," I hadn't even realized I'd spoken.

"What do you mean?" Tinder Tango breathed a sigh of half-relief.

"These things didn't put themselves in cages. There are people here. And they have Lisa. Let's go."

December 20

I'd realized not following Jack was probably a bad idea, but I figured they could handle those diseased things on their own. In addition, I'd seen a nurse's station on the opposite side of the hallway. There'd most likely be a map of the hospital there.

So, I told Jack I'd be behind him and went the other way. There were papers scattered all over the nurse's desk. Charts were left open on the counter. Many of them stated the patients all caught the virus. The victims we'd heard were probably all that was left.

Another howl emanated down the hallway. It startled me into faster action. I rounded the station to see a directory taped to the desk. Looking it over carefully, I found the Chief of Medicine's office was down and to the right. The medical supplies would be around there, so I abandoned the station.

Suddenly, it felt like an earthquake rattled the building. A roar followed by shuddering walls made my footsteps quicken. I could see the office. I was inches away when I felt strong arms wrap around my waist and pull me into an empty room.

The door slammed shut as I tried to kick my way out of the stranger's grasp. But he held tight. He was very strong.

"Been waitin' for ya." A gravelly voice whispered in my ear. Chills shot down my spine.

"Let me go." The firmness of my voice surprised me.

"If you insist."

I heard what sounded like a zipper, then a click, then the man stepped away from me. He was indeed very large with a scruffy thick beard and a very dirty bandana wrapped around his head.

"You're cuter than I thought." He smiled as if showing off how many teeth he was missing.

"I'm not the only one here." I remained standing with two feet planted. I gentle tug of my arm made me realized I was handcuffed to a bed. The man appeared to live in the hospital. There were food wrappers and broken beer bottles everywhere.

"Oh, I know that, sweet pea." The words stung. My father used to call me that. "But my pets will keep your friends busy for quite some time."

"Pets?" I tried to stall him.

"Shush, now, sweet pea. Papa's gotta present for ya." The man closed in on me. My mind raced with a thousand thoughts. All of them culminated in a fight or flight response, but I was cuffed to the bed. I backed away as far as I could, but I could smell his putrid body odor from feet ahead of me.

Twisting my body slightly, I felt around with my free hand for something to attack him with. My palm closed around the sharp edge of a broken bottle. Pain stung up into my arm, but I managed not to wince. I didn't want to tip him off.

He was closer. About six inches away. His smell clouded my brain. I heard shouting. The man hesitated, but didn't stop coming for me. His fingertips grazed my cheek just as Jack, Scott and Tango busted into the room.

The man spun around to face them. That's when I jumped onto his back and jammed the bottle shard straight into his eye. Blood began to gush from the wound, spraying partially onto the warped ceiling tiles. He screamed, clawing at the glass sticking out of his head. My three companions stood in the doorway dumbstruck as the large biker doubled over. The blood began to blind him. He stood and aimed for the open door, but instead rammed into the wall with all his weight. When he fell over, I could see the glass shard had embedded itself deep into his gray matter. He was dead.

"Will someone please search him for a handcuff key?"

Scott got to work before the words had even left my mouth completely. Jack stepped around the big man and approached me, his eyes sparkling with what looked like surprise.

"You go girl."

"He threatened my life. It was survival instincts."

Jack put both hands up as Scott came toward me with the key. "Hey, I'm impressed, not judgmental."

"Thank you." I used the sentence to appreciate them both at once while I unlocked the handcuffs. I explained to them where the medicinal supplies were kept and they followed me to the closet while regaling me with what they'd done while we'd been separated.

The man had apparently been keeping diseased victims hostage and making them attack anyone who entered the hospital. It also seemed as though he'd been waiting for a woman stubborn enough to enter by herself.

The medical cabinet's lock had been broken – no doubt by the biker man. I expected the worst when I opened it, but was pleasantly surprised to find a few drams of morphine inside. Enough to put Gregg to sleep.

"Lisa." Tango startled me. He was close. "We have a problem. Jack's trying to kill Scotty."

I couldn't believe my ears. I rushed out to the lobby of the second floor to see Scott sitting against the reception desk with Jack's gun pointed straight at his head.

"What's going on?" I gave the drams to Tango. He put them in his pack.

"Scott, tell her what's going on." Jack never looked at me.

"I swear I have no idea what he's talking about! He's crazy, Lisa! Help me!" The boy's eyes pleaded with me.

"He got bit." Jack finally tossed me a glance.

"Is that true?" I studied Scott's face.

"No! I swear! Help!"

Jack sighed, dropped his gun to the floor and knelt next to the boy. Then, he pulled out a pocket knife, clicked it open, and went for Scott.

"Jack!"

The knife cut through the soft fabric of Scott's shirt, sawing a large chunk out of the sleeve. Jack pulled down, revealing a fresh bite mark in Scott's bicep.

"Jesus Christ…" Tango whispered the words behind me.

Tears coursed down Scott's cheeks. "I don't wanna die, Lisa. Help me."

"I'm sorry." There was nothing more I could say. He cried harder.

"You have a choice." Jack stood, picking up his shot gun. "You can either stay here and turn or I can end it for you right now."

Scott sniffled, wiping dirt and tears from his face. "I…I don't want to die."

Jack looked to me for guidance.

"Stay here, Scott." With one last glance at the floor, I started toward the stairs. Tango followed. I could hear Jack giving Scott a bit of a pep talk.

"You did good, Scott. Your parents would have been really proud. You can pray or cry or sit here and jack it, but you probably don't have a lot of time left to..."

His voice trailed away as Tango and I exited the building.

*   *   *

We pulled up outside Huntington House with only hours of daylight left to spare. Many of the diseased had wandered off of the property, making it easier to get in. Tango immediately jumped out and ran to the front, eager to give the morphine to Ms. Huntington.

I started to exit the vehicle, but Jack said my name to keep me back. I owed him quite a bit of my time, so I obliged.

"If I ask you something, will you give me a one-hundred percent honest answer?" he asked.

"Of course."

He took a deep breath. "Look, I know things have been tough. There was no easy way to... Well, I guess I'm just trying to say I understand if you moved on."

"That's not a question."

He seemed surprised when he looked at me. "Oh, shit, you're right."

"So what was the question?"

He screwed up his face for a moment, then looked back at the house. "Scott told me something at the hospital."

"Go on."

"He said you two slept together."

Had I heard correctly? "I'm sorry?"

Jack took his hands off the wheel and turned to face me again. "He said you two slept together. You had sex. You did the deed. You vulcanized the whoopee stick in the ham wallet. You retrofitted the pudding hatch with the boink swatter. You cannonballed the fiddle cove with the pork steeple. Foxtrot Uniform Charlie Kilo. Aren't you going to stop me?"

I raised an eyebrow. "I didn't want to interrupt. Continue."

He opened his mouth, but nothing came out for a few seconds. "People usually stop me way before that. So, I guess I'm done."

"Well, the answer is no."

"Oh."

We were silent for a few moments.

"Why do you think he told me that?"

I shrugged one shoulder. "Perhaps to make you jealous. He saw me as a mother figure and he was probably just being a territorial nineteen-year-old."

Jack made a face. "Kid had a real Oedipus complex."

I commended his usage of literary history. "Indeed."

*   *   *

My hands were shaking as I pulled a syringe full of the anesthetic. I'd tried to make enough in relation to Gregg's weight, but I wasn't even positive of that.

"Shouldn't we test it first?" Gregg seemed agitated.

"There's no time. The virus is spreading almost up into your knee now."

He nodded. I took a brief look around the sterilized freezer. Tango was there to help hold the leg in traction. He'd given me a razor sharp paring knife as a scalpel. Jack had found fishing wire in the cellar and had given me a flame torch used for welding to act as a cauterizer. He would be performing that action while I cut. Sam had volunteered to suction and Jennifer was going to keep track of Gregg's pulse. Everyone's hands were gloved.

"All right, doc. Give it to me."

In order to make sure the syringe was free of bubbles, I tapped it twice to release the air. I'd found some rubber tubing in the cabinets and tied it around his upper arm. Finding a vein, I took a deep breath and slid the needle in. He made no sound. None of us did. We watched him for a few moments.

"I think it's kicking in..." Gregg's eyelids seemed to be a burden on him and his speech slowed. When he finally closed his eyes, I checked his pulse and we were ready to go. I looked out the tiny freezer window to give Raychel a nod.

"Okay, everyone, cutting is going to be the hard part, so let's get it over with." I moved next to Tango. Jack came to my right while Sam was across from me. I instructed Sam to begin suction as I began cutting into Gregg's skin.

I started by creating a long incision around the circumference of his upper leg. I left the bottom untouched for the moment. After the cut was made and the blood siphoned off, I pulled the skin away from the connective tissue and slid it as far down his leg as I could, exposing the muscles beneath. Jennifer looked away.

"I'm going to cut away the lateral muscle, here. That will expose the bone." I went to work, trying to be precise and quick. When the muscle had been cut away, the artery became visible.

"We need to clamp the artery shut." I held out my hand. Tango put something in my palm. It was a binder clip. "Seriously?"

He shrugged, so I made it work. I then had Jack cauterize around the clip then separated the two ends. An electric carver was the only option I had when it came to cutting through the bone. That took the longest.

I moved to the other side to repeat the process for the fibular bone. I cut away the muscle then the bone. Once everything was separated and sealed off, I cut a flap of skin on the underside of the leg, then instructed Tango to take it.

"Put that on ice, please. I'd like to look at it later."

Tango hesitated, but eventually removed the leg from the table with caution. I checked with Jennifer on Gregg's pulse and she tossed me a thumbs up.

"I need the sewing needle and fishing wire, please."

Jack handed it to me. I folded the flap of skin over the front of his leg, sewed it up and was done.

"Now we wait for him to wake up."

Two Men and a Lift Auto Garage

"We Auto Know"

December 21

It was late. Around midnight when we started up the stairs. Lisa was guarded about giving any more information on whether or not Gregg would wake up without gangrene. But the three of us spoke in length about it before turning in.

"I'm looking for signs the body has rejected the surgery. That includes darkening of the skin farther up from the wound or visibility of the veins. Any dark red streaks are a bad sign as well, but not as bad as the virus spreading."

"What do the streaks mean?" Raychel asked. We were already at the top of the stairs.

"Blood poisoning." I answered with my voice low. I knew what it meant because Silas had showed me on his visit in the school. It seemed like years ago.

"Right." Lisa nodded. "But at least I can treat that."

The three of us stopped outside Lisa's room.

"This is me." She seemed to be stalling.

"I'm off to bed! See you tomorrow." Raychel pranced away. I knew what she was thinking, but it wasn't going to happen. Two grown adults can be alone together without anything intimate happening. People did it all the time.

"Goodnight."

I turned back to Lisa as she was saying the words to Raychel. When she looked at me, I felt an odd flutter in my chest. It was as if my heart were trying to escape.

"I suppose."

To Lisa, that simple phrase was an entire sentence.

"Thank you for doing this for us. For Gregg."

299

Two Men and a Lift Auto Garage

"We Auto Know"

She nodded, and I leaned in to give her what I thought would just be a goodnight peck on the cheek. But as soon as I felt how warm she was and how good she smelled I knew I'd made a mistake.

When I pulled away, we looked into each other's eyes. And that was when I threw away everything I'd promised myself I'd stand up for. Without a second's more hesitation, I kissed her. I kissed her like I'd never see her again. And she kissed me back. It was like no time had passed.

I felt the flood of emotion wash over me. I wanted to hold her forever; I wanted to kiss her forever. I wanted to be her lover and husband. I wanted to be the one to make her smile and laugh every day. Why had I been so stupid?

With one hand, I reached behind her and turned the doorknob. Then I pushed her through, shutting it behind me. And yet we hadn't stopped kissing. I could think about nothing except taking all her clothes off with my teeth and tossing her on the bed.

She threw her arms around my neck, so I slipped my hands under her skirt. But I only got as far as hooking my thumbs into her panties to pull them off, because she stopped and pushed away.

"What's wrong?"

For a second, she said nothing. The room was only half lit by a smoldering candle, but I could see stress lines crease into her forehead.

"Why did you have...to leave, Jack?" As soon as she said my name, tears began pouring down her cheeks. I was so

surprised, I froze right where I stood. "Why did you leave us?" She slid down onto floor, covering her face.

"Hey, hey, no..." I knelt down and took her into my arms. "Don't cry, baby, don't cry."

She sobbed harder into my chest. I shushed her, smoothing her hair and planting light kisses on her head. My heart ached. I'd had no idea how much she'd been hurting. It wasn't obvious on the outside. While we were sitting there, a few tears escaped me as well.

"I'm not going anywhere, Foxtrot. Never again. I promise, okay?" I held her at arm's length. I'd never seen her as upset before and it felt like my heart suddenly weighed a hundred pounds. Her eyes had become red and swollen. The wrinkles between her eyebrows were deep and long.

"I've lost everyone else." She sniffed, trying to fight off more tears.

"You've got Rex and Lexi." I brushed some hair out of her eyes.

She shook her head. "That's not what I mean."

"Okay." I nodded. "I understand. I just...I didn't know me leaving affected you this much." I stood and extended a hand to her. She took it. I pulled her to the bed. As we lay down, she finally seemed to calm a bit.

"I want to marry you."

I thought I hadn't heard her right. "What...you...you do?"

"Yes. But not now. I don't know when."

Adrenaline pumped through my entire body. My brain stopped working. I couldn't believe what she had said.

"Oh, honey...that's...that's all I wanted." I kissed her. "You've made me so happy."

She smiled at me through her emotion and it melted my heart. I squeezed her as close to me as physically possible. In that moment, life could have only gotten better if there weren't any Biters around. My life would have ended happily.

"I love you, Jack."

The pressure inside my chest increased. "I love you too, Lisa."

"I have to check on Gregg."

I sucked in a breath with a groan. "I knew it wouldn't last." Even though I was slightly frustrated, I gave her a smile.

"I apologize." She sat up and I joined her.

"It's ok. I admire it. You're dedicated to your work."

"Yes."

"Well, get down there. Because the sooner you finish checking him out, the sooner you can come back up here and we can take a shower."

Her eyebrows rose. "Oh. I see."

"I'd fucking rip you to pieces right now. So you'd better go." I grabbed her hand and pretended to bite her fingers. My action was met with a sincere smile. "Go."

She nodded, standing from the bed. At the door, she turned. "You'll know when I'm ready."

"Got it."

December 21

When I got back upstairs, Jack was asleep on the bed sitting up. The dark circles under his eyes told a story of their own. He'd been through a lot while he was gone. And seeing him comfortable enough to fall asleep caused adoration to wash over me.

I crept up to the bed and tried not to wake him as I crawled over to the other side. But when I laid down, he stirred.

"Hey." He stretched his arms above his head. "How long was I out?"

"I was only gone for about twenty minutes."

He nodded and pretended to fall back asleep in my lap. I ran my fingers through his hair.

"How's Gregg?"

"His pulse is strong, but he's not awake yet."

He rolled over to look at me. "Where's the shower you promised me?"

"I thought *you* promised *me*."

He sat up. "Nope. When you were leaving you said you'd come back to shower."

I felt an amused smile spread across my face. "Okay."

Before I could add anything else to the conversation, Jack kissed me while softly running his hands up my outer thighs. We fell into a rhythm in an instant. He knew how and where I liked to be touched without me saying a word. He followed my noises of pleasure. Even the simple act of removing my dress was enough to send tingles through my entire body.

We found that I was much too ready for him as soon as we began. The sweet words he whispered to me were enough to send me even farther over the edge.

He kissed me. "I know this should be a really soft intimate moment, but...you feel really good."

I allowed a sigh of ecstasy to escape me. No man had ever made me crave intimacy the way Jack had. He was everything I never understood about couples who enjoyed sexual relationships. I wasn't even able to give myself the kind of pleasure he did.

I adored the way he moved when we were together. The sounds he made in the heat of the moment made me never want to get out of bed. I was with my first lover when I was twenty. And it had taken me eleven years to find someone who I enjoyed seeing naked.

Jack grabbed my waist, turning so I was straddling him. I liked that position. I was able to reach my peak in less time. I felt my entire body shudder.

"You okay?"

When the moan escaped me, I didn't even realize it. All I knew was he'd given me the best orgasm I'd ever had.

"I'll take that as a yes." He flipped me back over and continued. When he was close, he let me know. I didn't even think I'd appreciate that kind of thing until he said it. Because it made the blood in my veins thicken. I made sure to kiss him as he climaxed. I could tell he enjoyed it.

When it was over, we allowed ourselves to soak in the moments until morning. For a few hours, we pretended like nothing was wrong in the world and we were the only two left. With that thought in our minds, we fell asleep together again.

*   *   *

I'd been buried in the oldest anatomy book I could find with the amputated leg next to me. I had cut away some of the tissue around the bite so I could see the bigger picture. But my eyes were starting to lose focus.

I moved from the anatomy book to the bite wound on the leg. The veins within an inch radius had turned black. And when pressed upon, they spewed a thick, opaque substance. I just couldn't understand how it worked. I'd never seen a virus that did that in all my medical practice years.

"Hey there."

Feeling almost blessed by the distraction, I looked up from my book to see Jack standing in the doorway of the cleaned out freezer.

"Hi." I blinked a few times to clear the fuzziness from my vision.

"How's it going?" He approached me and began to lightly massage my shoulders.

"I can't really do much without a microscope." I sighed. "But I can tell you that I've never seen a virus show these kinds of pathways. It's very obvious where it was going and how fast it was travelling. That could help with studying it."

"Didn't you say there was a doctor trying to find a cure in Colorado?"

I took a deep breath. "Yes. There supposedly is." I spun around in my chair to look at him. "We need to go there, Jack."

He gave me a slow nod. "I know. But can it wait until next week?"

"Why?"

"Because apparently Raychel and Gregg are getting married Saturday by Pastor Samuels."

I stood. "So he's awake? How is he doing?"

Jack ushered me out of the freezer. "He's in pain, but we're feeding him ibuprofen."

"Good. That will reduce the swelling."

We stopped in the kitchen. No one was around and the house seemed silent. "So, what do you say? We leave Monday?"

After a moment of thinking, I knew what we had to do. "Yes."

December 24

In just a few short days, Gregg had learned to walk again with our help. Lisa checked him daily for any signs of infection, but she always gave him a clean bill of health. His color was even coming back.

The weekend was drawing near and I could tell my sister was nervous. She had an anxious glow around her. It was as if someone had given her a halo. And when I told her that, she joked that it was supposed to be devil horns, but they'd gotten it wrong.

Lisa spent most of the days in solitude studying book after book. Getting her to eat her meals was difficult, but getting her to come to – or should I say *in* – bed was pretty simple. While diligent in her studies, she was hellfire at night. It was like all the stress that had built up was released when she was with me.

And it was incredibly difficult to pull her away on the day of the wedding.

"Lisa..." I followed her pacing with my gaze. "Come on. Raychel needs you right now."

"I just don't understand how this virus works." She turned around again to pace to the other side of the room.

"But...we're going to Braycart. The doctor there is going to help."

"But what if I find something out between now and then? What if it's big?"

"That's what she said." My words were met with silence. "What can I do to take your mind off this thing so we can go help Raychel set up her wedding?"

Lisa stopped mid-pace and looked at me. "Do we have time for sex?"

I leaned forward. "What?"

"Do we..." She came toward me. "Have time for sex?"

"Hmm..." I tapped a finger on my chin. "Let me think about that. Yes."

"Okay."

Before I had a chance to react, she was removing her clothes.

"Holy shit, wait!" I turned around, feeling laughter bubble into my chest. "We should probably close the doors to the parlor first."

As soon as I turned back around, she was already on me, kissing me hard. We didn't even get my jeans completely off before I was inside her.

"Rabies normally travels through nerves." As she spoke, her sentences were staggered and harsh from our actions. "But this time it's in the veins."

"This is so not what I had in mind for sexy talk."

"Shh." She pushed me down onto a desk in the center of the room. It was the strangest act of intimacy I'd ever experienced. She was very much into what was going on, but managed to think at the same time. Her enthusiasm was pretty damn exciting too.

"There's no way it can mutate inside an animal... It had to have mutated before or after a bite from an infected animal."

My grip on her hips tightened. She began to respond as well. Her sentences became even more disjointed and breathy.

"It's coming to me... It's coming to... I'm coming! I've got it!"

In that moment, she leapt off me and ran over to the bay window where her books were stacked.

"What just happened?" I sat up in bewilderment.

"It's prions!"

"Prions made you come?"

She tossed me a cynical look. "No."

"What's a prion?"

She picked up a book and walked over to me while reading. "Prions are neurodegenerative disorders. Very very rare. It's pathogenic and sporadic, but sometimes genetic. That's why the incubation period is so much longer." She was getting excited. The pitch of her voice had increased.

"Okay."

"And *that's* why this particular strain of rabies lasts so long once symptoms start to show."

"What's why?"

"What?" She looked up from the book with that crease between her eyebrows.

"What's why rabies lasts so long?"

Her face scrunched up. "Oh, apologies. Prions are transmissible spongiform encephalopathies – TSE's. Once it gets to the host's brain, it acts almost like Alzheimer's. It causes brain damage, forgetfulness, etc. But it also fails to induce the inflammatory response."

I kept quiet. I had no idea what the hell she was talking about, but she was looking at me like I should have.

"It means infected tissue doesn't swell!"

This time, I pretended to understand by widening my eyes and nodding. She seemed satisfied, so she turned to grab another book.

"Rabies causes swelling of the brain. So when these two diseases are introduced, rabid victims will stay rabid for a far longer time since the swelling response isn't immediately targeted."

"Oh. I get it now. So...what does that mean? In the long run?"

"Well... It simply means that someone with either Creutzfeldt-Jakob disease or fatal familial syndrome contracted rabies. Then the prion-manipulating TSE piggybacked on the virus somehow." She looked back at me, her eyes serious. "I'm not even sure if this is curable."

"But we have to try, right?"

The seriousness was replaced by a glimmer of what looked like hope. "Exactly."

December 24

I wasn't even sure how I'd act when my little sister finally got hitched. The family had always agreed I'd go first and she'd be divorced a few times over. Weren't we a lovely group? I was just happy I got to be a best man for once. Everybody knew Silas was going to be a bachelor forever. And now he was dead forever.

"Are you all right?"

Lisa's question startled me. I looked at her in her beautiful blue maid of honor dress. That color looked amazing on her.

"Yep. Just in my own world for a sec."

She nodded as Gregg came down the aisle with the help of Ms. Huntington. He was walking so well that I had to smile. When he made it to the altar, he leaned against his crutch for stability.

I leaned forward. "Hurt her and it won't just be your leg that's gone."

He tossed me a look. "What? What does that even mean?"

After a roll of my eyes, I said, "Your life will be gone, man."

"Oh, 'cause you'll kill me..."

I gave him a thumb's up and straightened. Lisa had one eyebrow raised, but all I could do was shrug as music began to play.

I had no clue what song Raychel had picked to walk down the aisle, but it was fitting. Very elegant yet playful. But when she stepped out all I could focus on was this...thing she had on her head. It was like...some sort of crown of beads or jewels or...

"Jack."

I must have been making a face because Lisa grabbed my attention and gestured to me to smile. So I put on a big one that was only one-quarter goofy. But I couldn't keep it to myself when she was finally standing next to Gregg.

"What are you wearing?"

She batted her lashes. "It's a Norwegian headdress."

I squinted hard at her. "We're not Norwegian."

"Reynolds is a Norwegian name."

"Yeah, but—"

"Dearly Beloved!"

I shut up when the pastor started to speak. But Raychel was able to get in a quick raspberry in my direction.

"All of us have come to this place as a result of recent unfortunate events. Those of you who've stayed have done Ms. Huntington a great service by keeping her company. And to those of you new faces, we hope you stay just a little longer as well.

"While the events of late are certainly frightening and difficult to become accustomed to, somehow these two people have found each other. And in each other, they have found protection, peace, safety and love."

315

I tossed Lisa a wink, but she was busy watching Raychel glow like a lamp. Her smile was just infectious.

"Gregg, please look at your lovely bride to be."

"Okay."

Some of the folks in the audience laughed.

"Do you, Gregg, take Raychel to be your loyal bride, to have and to hold, in sickness and in health until death may take you?"

"I do."

"And Raychel, do you take Gregg to be your loyal husband, to have and to hold, in sickness and health until death may take you?"

"Any beyond." Raychel giggled.

"Well, by God's great will, I now pronounce you man and wife. You may kiss your bride."

I looked away while my sister kissed her new husband. And with what I'd call a rebel yell, she and Gregg held onto each other as they walked back toward the house.

"Well, if anyone else would like to get married, now's the chance! All the flowers are set and there's a nice photographer who won't charge you a dime for prints."

I began to step down onto the runway.

"Wait."

I looked back at Lisa. Everything I felt for her bubbled into my chest in that moment; with one glance. I knew I wanted to marry her. I wasn't sure if I'd make a good husband, but I wanted it.

Two Men and a Lift Auto Garage

"We Auto Know"

"Jack."

She told me I'd know when she was ready. And I knew.

"Do we have takers?" The priest's eyes sparkled.

"We're more doers than takers, but yeah, I get what you mean." I tossed a smile at Lisa. She bit her lip but quickly stowed away any anxiety and gave me a smile. Her eyes shimmered. "Oh, Foxtrot, now don't cry. You're going to make me lose it."

She let out a half laugh half sob. I grabbed both her hands and faced her in front of the priest. In front of a hundred people. Strangers. But I didn't care.

"Today is a beautiful day for love, folks."

The crowd clapped.

"We gather once more in the presence of pure intimacy. I'm non-denominational, but if there is a God, he'd want the two of you to be together."

I tossed him an amused glance. Lisa's hands were shaking. I caressed the top of one with my thumb, silently telling her she was okay. She squeezed my hand back in response.

"Now, do you Jack Tiberius Reynolds—"

The crowd of people laughed. Without taking my eyes off the beautiful creature in front of me, I said, "Yeah, my parents watched a lot of *Star Trek*."

Lisa let out another laugh/sob.

"Do you Jack Reynolds take Lisa James to be your wife?"

"You're damn right I do."

He turned to Lisa. "Do you Lisa James take Jack Reynolds to be your husband?"

She swallowed hard to hold back her tears and nodded her head vigorously. "I do."

In that moment, I realized she was all mine. I couldn't believe I'd snagged a woman like her. I was a lucky son of a bitch. Even Silas thought so. Because I could see him against the far wall, clapping.

"Now, please...kiss your bride, Jack."

Before I could lean in, Lisa grabbed me and pressed her lips against me. Her hair smelled like coconuts, but she tasted like strawberries.

"Ladies and gentlemen, Mr. and Mrs. Reynolds!"

*   *   *

"Are you happy?"

Lisa looked up at me with her beautiful blue eyes. Ms. Huntington had been kind enough to take care of Rex and Alex while we were given the second biggest room in the mansion for the night. Raychel and Gregg got the biggest. And thank God it wasn't next to ours.

"I can't even put it into words."

"Oh? That's a first." I sat next to her on the large bed and brushed a strand of hair out of her face. My hand trailed to the back of her neck.

"I know." She smiled. "Who could have guessed this horrible plague would have brought you to me?"

I allowed my hand to follow the curve of her spine. "Well, I could've been a little more proactive and met the best friend of the woman who'd been living across from me for two years."

She sighed. "I was a different person then."

"No you weren't. You just hadn't come out of your intellectual shell."

She straightened when I tickled the small of her back. "We've come such a long way." Her voice faded into a somber tone. "We've lost homes and family. We've lost friends…"

Her words caught in my chest. I'd married her without telling her the darkest secret in my life. I was a murderer and she didn't even know. And as she looked at me that night with her eyes full of love and hope, I felt like I'd failed. I leaned over and put my head in my hands.

"Jack? What is it?" She placed a gentle hand on my back.

There were tears behind my eyes, so I rubbed my face to keep them at bay. I had to tell her. But I couldn't look at her while I did.

"I did a bad thing."

I could see her cock her head to the side in my peripheral vision. "What do you mean?"

"My…my friend Silas. The one I told you about that…died before this whole thing started… I told you one of those things got him, but…"

"You did."

I snapped up to look at her. There was no judgement in her face at all. She was calm and collected like always. Unfortunately, that made me well up and I couldn't stop the tears this time.

"I fucking murdered him."

Her hand touched the back of my head. She ran her fingers through my hair. "Tell me what happened."

"He was... I was downstairs sleeping on the couch because I was watching the news...waiting for them to come into our neighborhood. He...he came stumbling down the hallway and groaning like he was a fucking Biter. He even had foam coming from his mouth.

"I slept with the shotgun in my lap in case of something like that and I...I didn't even think twice. I just cocked it and blew a fucking hole right through him. Fuck, the look he gave me before he went... It was a Goddamn prank!"

We sat in silence for a moment. My breath came in ragged gasps and hitches. I felt stupid for crying.

"Well, that was an idiotic decision for him to make. Did he always prank you like that?"

I rubbed my eyes. "We joked all the time, but he never did something like that before."

"Well, it's not your fault. You know that."

I looked into her eyes. My brain was a fog of confusion, sorrow and anger. My heart was pumping so hard I thought she could hear it too.

"He shouldn't have done that."

I couldn't bear it any longer. I grabbed her and held her tight. She understood. I didn't think I could ask for more, but she understood me completely. Even when I didn't understand me.

"There's more."

"Go ahead."

"Ever since then, I've...been seeing him. He comes to me and talks to me. He's got this huge hole in his chest and he keeps decomposing every time he comes around. I'm going fucking nuts, aren't I?"

Lisa sat back. "No." She said it with such nonchalance that it startled me. "That's just your guilt. It's manifesting in a way your brain can handle it. It's perfectly natural. Now that you told me, you probably won't see him again."

"You think?"

She shrugged. "Most likely. It was just guilt."

I cleared a few stray tears from my eyes. "Wedding nights are supposed to be about lingerie and bubble baths...not confessions."

Lisa studied the pattern of the comforter on the bed. "Well, as long as we're confessing."

At first, concern rose into my chest. Was something wrong with her? Was she sick? Had someone died? And then I thought about the chef kid and got a little angry.

"What do you mean?" I kept my tone low and quiet.

"I want to tell you what happened to Sylvia outside the casino in Las Vegas."

Shaking the bad thoughts out of my head, I almost laughed. "Go on."

Lisa took a deep breath. I couldn't read her face. "They ate her."

And I waited. She seemed to be staring into space a bit, so I let her take time to collect her thoughts. But I wasn't willing to give more than thirty seconds.

"And?"

Her gazed snapped to me, brows furrowed. "What's that?"

"What happened?"

"I told you. They ate her."

I paused. "But...how? How did it start? How did it make you feel?"

She cocked her head to one side. "Well, they tore her throat out so she couldn't scream. That's about all I recall. Of course I was frightened. Then a bit angry. But I've dealt with it."

"Oh-kay." I kicked off my shoes and fell back onto the bed.

"What is it?"

"What would happen if I get eaten?"

That line creased into her forehead. "Well, I should hope that doesn't happen."

"Yeah, but if it does. How would you feel?"

"Devastated, of course." She answered so quickly that I had to believe her. Even though her tone was flat, I knew it was true. I felt a smile spread across my face.

322

December 26

Monday morning approached with both an excitement and dread. I didn't want to venture back out into the diseased world for fear of death, but I knew I had to get that sample over to the doctor. If there was a doctor.

Jack and I had set an alarm for six a.m. so we could travel in daylight. But my brain wouldn't shut off during the night. I somehow managed a few hours of sleep, but woke just before the alarm.

As I lied there thinking about all the possibilities that could arise during the journey, I felt a bit frightened. But I wasn't frightened for myself. I was frightened for Jack.

I turned my head to watch him sleep. He looked peaceful. With the need to make him feel safe, I cuddled next to him as close as I could.

He responded by – almost instinctually – wrapping his arm around my waist and pulling me into a hug. Then he snuggled into my hair. I thought I'd woken him, but his breathing remained steady and deep until the alarm sounded.

"Five more minutes…" Jack mumbled.

"We better get going if we want to make it before dark."

"But I'm tired from all the sex."

"I never believed I'd hear you say that. Ever. Is your libido dropping already?" I teased him with a poke.

"All right, all right. I'm up." He nearly whined the words, but there was a hint of annoyance in them as he pushed himself up onto both hands. But before he could even get out of the covers, he fell onto his back and put one arm over his eyes.

"I'm coming… Get the kids ready?"

Something about what he'd said struck me in the chest. It was a warming feeling as if we'd established a family all of a sudden.

"Sure."

*   *   *

Saying goodbye to everyone – as difficult as it was – felt liberating to an extent. It felt as though we were off on a journey. In a way, we were. Jack and I were married. My last name was different. We were starting a life together.

Raychel promised that she and Gregg would come visit whenever it was possible. After all her travels, she wanted a place to call home. And I didn't blame her.

We'd taken an old work truck left behind by a previous visitor. With all of our belongings, it was barely enough room to fit the four of us. It was snug, but comfortable. And the diseased victims had found somewhere else to go. They were no longer littering the grass outside the mansion.

We picked the fastest route of six hours and drove as fast as possible without frightening Rex, but he still needed a break halfway.

We stopped at an abandoned home just off the highway. We were right in the middle of the Rocky Mountains so the views were breathtaking. The white house stood atop a small hill with a large desk wrapped around the back. From there, we could see bison roaming about, snacking on grass in a valley a few miles away.

I touched a few Halloween decorations still hung in the windows. Suddenly, I felt frozen in time. Halloween, Thanksgiving and Christmas had passed and I hadn't even given it a second thought. Not even when writing the dates down in this very journal.

A cloud passed over the sun, shrouding the house in a dark quiet. I found myself wondering where the occupants were – if they were dead or diseased.

"Wow…" Jack's words came to me from the living room. He was in front of the media player, holding a disc in his hand. "Blink 182."

"What's that?" I approached him.

"Blink 182." He showed the disc to me. "Haven't heard them in years. Wonder if their all still alive."

We were quiet for a few moments before Rex and Alex scrambled into the room shouting nonsense.

"Whoa, whoa, whoa!" Jack held up both hands, the CD wedged between the thumb and forefinger of his right. "One at a time."

"One time! One!" Rex bounced up and down, clearly unaware of how to express what was so exciting.

"Good. Lexi?"

She began pointing out the sliding glass door while spewing excited words. "There's a big buffalo outside! It's hurt!"

Jack and I glanced at each other before turning and heading for the door. Outside, the world was quiet. A peaceful breeze shifted the leaves in each tree with a subtle whisper.

Beyond the large wrap-around deck, a dog began to bark. Then, it came around the side where we were, rearing up on its hind legs.

"What is it, boy?" Jack approached the mutt slowly. It continued barking for a few more seconds, then ran off in the opposite direction. We followed without a discussion.

The barking hit a crescendo as we rounded the corner of the house to see a large bison lying on its side. The breathing seemed labored, but it seemed to still be fighting off the dog whenever it came too near.

I stopped first in front of everyone, holding out my arms to signal they shouldn't get too close. I used caution when approaching the beast. It eyed me with suspicion, so I slowed my pace even more, holding out my hands to show I had nothing in them.

"What, uh...what do we...?" Jack's sentence emerged in broken pieces before I shushed him.

Near the bison's front right haunch was a wound infested with maggots eating away at the necrotic flesh. From where I stood, it looked like a bite mark.

"Someone get me gloves." I didn't wait for an answer before stroking the coarse fur of the animal. The bison closed its eyes when it noticed I wasn't posing any threat.

Upon closer inspection of the wound, I determined all I could do was clean it and hope for the best. When Jack came back with the gloves, I asked him to find rubbing alcohol as well. He disappeared again, so I began my analysis.

I made sure the clear as many of the maggots from the wound as I could. The bison grunted and flinched several times, but I made sure to run my hand along its haunch, calming it.

"So what's the diagnosis, doc?"

I stood, facing the animal. "It's been bitten." I turned back to Jack. "*Weeks* ago. By a human."

Jack's face screwed up. "How do you know it was a human?"

I held up my hand, unfurling my fingers so he could see what I'd found inside the poor bison's wound.

"That...that's a..."

"A bicuspid."

Jack's tongue made a quick pass over his top teeth before he shuddered. "Goddamn."

"Indeed." I took the rubbing alcohol from him and turned back to the animal. "The stranger aspect of this whole epidemic seems that humans can't infect animals with this particular strain of rabies."

"Meaning?"

I finished dressing the wound. "I have no idea. That's why we need to keep going."

It was time to get back on the road.

The only information I had about Braycart was that it was in a little town in Colorado. I had no idea where in the town it was, but Jack insisted we'd know when we saw it. And he was right.

The entire town was surrounded by a large brick wall that must have stretched up about ten feet. Someone had hand-painted the word Braycart across the stone. As we drove quietly down the highway leading to the town, we noticed abandoned cars gathering in strange spots. The most unsettling thing was that the only diseased within a mile of the city were all dead.

"Haven't seen that before." Jack couldn't keep his eyes off some of the bodies littering the road. "I'm pretty sure everywhere else has a Biter clean-up crew."

"Like the Ghostbusters?" Alex chimed in.

"Precisely."

The gates of the city loomed ahead of us. They were made of what looked like steel. I could see faint shapes of people on top of the wall. They had very large guns.

Jack rolled down his window as the gates opened. A man with armor crisscrossing his chest walked out.

"Do you know where you are?" He asked, ducking his head and checking us all out.

"Yes. Rumor has it you have a doctor here."

I let Jack do the talking.

"Yup. Dr. Holmes. Someone been bitten? We have rules. No one who's been bitten is allowed inside."

"No, none of us have been bitten. But I have something the doctor may find very interesting." I leaned over Jack to speak to the man.

After a moment's pause, he seemed to lighten up. "You folks need a place to stay?"

"Yes."

"Welcome to Braycart." He stepped aside and waved to someone on top of the wall. The gates opened fully and another man ushered our truck through.

The city was breathtaking. I had expected a desolate and run down dump of a place, but the sidewalks were neatly paved and the homes were cookie-cutter. The man who'd let us in gave us directions to the lab, and on the way there, we passed a grocery store looked to be well stocked and a working gas station.

The lab looked more or less like a hospital. And it seemed to double as one as there were people with broken limbs emerging past us. A woman at the front desk informed us that she'd been told to let us see the doctor and instructed us to go to the fifth floor.

Rex struggled a bit on the elevator. He was getting hungry. But after bouncing him a few times, Jack was able to quiet him.

The elevator let us off on a quiet floor with glass doors on both sides of the hallway. Beyond them, we could see white-jacketed workers bent over steel tables littered with samples. None of us had talked since we'd been let in, but we hadn't noticed until I spoke.

"I guess we wait here." There were benches lining a wall across from an office with Dr. Holmes etched into its window. We sat and I held what was left of Gregg's leg tightly in my lap. I'd made sure to wrap it so no one could take a guess what it was.

Finally, the door to the doctor's office opened. An older man with white hair and a beard to match stepped out.

"You must be Dr. James." His voice was gruff with a hint of an English accent.

I stood. "Actually it's Dr. Reynolds now. It's lovely to meet you." We shook hands as I introduced him to Jack, Alex and Rex.

"You have a lovely family, Doctor. I hear you have something you'd like me to see?"

"Yes." I handed him the wrapped leg. "I removed a limb from someone who'd been bitten. This is the limb."

Behind his spectacles, the doctor's eyes widened. "May I?"

"Absolutely."

330

He walked back into his office and we followed, sitting in a few cold metal chairs across from his polished desk.

He unwrapped the package carefully while we stayed silent. After studying the leg for a few moments, he looked up at me.

"This is very important, Dr. Reynolds."

"Yes, I know."

"Did you have proper medical equipment for this job?"

"No. I had a paring knife, dental suction, a flame torch and a binder clip."

"These incisions are superb."

"Thank you."

He stopped studying the leg and gave me a hard stare. "Did the man survive?"

"Yes."

Dr. Holmes sat back in his chair. The leather stretched under him. "I'd like to study this specimen further. I'll give it to my assistants to dissect. Thank you very much."

He stood to show us out, but the wheels began turning in my head. "Just a moment." I stood as he rounded his desk. "I would like to supervise the dissection."

Dr. Holmes's eyebrows pulled together and he frowned. "I'm afraid I can't allow that. This facility is not authorized to the public."

"But, we—"

"I must insist that you leave now. If you have any questions, please speak to the information assistant at the front gates."

With that, he ushered us out of his office and into the dark hallway. I was fuming. My heart was hammering in my chest and I could feel blood creeping into my cheeks. Jack laid a gentle hand on my shoulder.

"Maybe we should go talk to the information assistant."

December 26

I knew Lisa was pissed, but I didn't know how pissed until we got out into the open. She hadn't said a word the entire way out, but once we stepped onto the sidewalk, she let loose.

"That was *my* discovery."

"I know."

"If they mess it up, I swear on all that is good and Holy..."

"Yeah."

"I will take them to court and he'll lose his license."

I refrained from mentioning the fact that courts and licenses no longer held much weight, because she looked like she'd bite my head off if I differed from her opinion. She continued to rant under her breath from the moment we got in the car until we stopped in front of a little strip mall. The word *Information* was scrawled in all capital letters above a glass door.

I turned to her. "You okay?"

"No."

We were all silent until Alex spoke. "What do we do now?"

Lisa sighed through her nose. "Maybe we should just go back to Huntington House."

"Well...we're here. Let's just see what they can do for us."

We stepped out of the car. I was almost worried Lisa wasn't going to budge, but she eventually unbuckled her seatbelt to join us. Inside, the office was warm, cozy and inviting. The walls were painted a dull blue as if trying to shelter people from the outside world. A woman sat at a desk in the front.

"Can I help you?"

I looked at Lisa, but she was still pissed off. "Yeah, we just got here and have no idea what we're doing." I figured I'd be honest.

"I knew what I was doing..." Lisa said under her breath.

The woman at the front desk glanced at her, then back to me. "No problem. We invite all kinds of people to our city. I'll just have one of our reps ask you a few questions and you can get settled."

I wanted to ask, "Get settled with what," but before I could, the woman jumped out of her seat and scurried down a narrow hallway. Lisa took Rex from me. I hesitated, but she gave me a look assuring she was capable. Well, it was more of an I'll-murder-you-if-you-so-much-as-say-something look, so...

"Hello!" A chipper dark-haired woman came down the hallway and greeted us. She introduced herself as Margaret and invited us back to her desk down the narrow hallway. I still had no idea what was going on.

"Does that work?" I asked, nodding toward the computer monitor on the woman's desk.

She smiled. "For Solitaire." No one laughed. "It's more for record keeping than anything else. Has anyone told you what we do?"

"Not a word."

"Okee dokee." She folded her hands together. "Braycart was established with one thing in mind – a cure. Dr. Holmes is a very intelligent man who was able to section off what used to be the hospital of a small town here and create a laboratory. We've had all kinds of doctors come from all around to try and help. We've gotten close, but no dice yet.

"After the construction of the lab, the doctor decided to build up some walls to keep out the infected."

"I call them Biters." I was trying to lighten the mood, but Lisa was still sour at the mention of the doctor's name.

Margaret smiled. "Dr. Holmes was able to secure a HAM radio and he set about telling everyone he could to come to Braycart. Now, how it works is that we take your skills and assign you a job. In turn, this job denotes what type of housing you receive. Lower levels such as secretaries or trash collection will be granted apartment homes and higher-level jobs will be granted higher level housing."

"Makes sense. Right, Lisa?" I elbowed her gently.

She cleared her throat. "Yes."

"Great! So, let me start off with a series of questions. Are you two married?"

"Yes."

"Are these your children?"

Two Men and a Lift Auto Garage

"We Auto Know"

"Well...kinda. This is Rex," I said gesturing to him. "And this is Alex. She's our—"

"They adopted me." Alex finished my sentence for me with a smile. I tossed her a thumb's up.

"Wonderful. I love when people can help out wherever they can. You sound like great parents. What did you do before the outbreak?"

"I was a mechanic for seventeen years," I said.

Margaret perked up. "Oh. Wonderful! We've been needing another one. People come from all around to get repairs since this is really the only place for thousands of miles. Our system is wonderful, too. Our mechanic repairs the vehicle and we either trade something for it, or gain a new citizen. Can you start immediately?"

I raised an eyebrow. "Yes?"

"Great! And how about you, Mrs. Reynolds?"

Lisa scooted to the edge of her seat and took a deep breath. "I graduated summa cum laude from John's Hopkins University with a bachelor's degree in Anatomy, and three associate's degrees – one in chemistry, one in biology and another in physics. I scored a fifty-two on my MCAT while studying certifications in narcotics, microbiology, veterinary sciences and psychology. I received a Doctor of Medicine in Anatomy when I was twenty-five. After working alongside some of the best doctors in California, I scored a 270 on my USMLE. By the time I was twenty-eight, I had completed my residency at Tehachapi hospital and was attending there up until two

337

months ago. We just returned from delivering a key piece of information that can possibly lead to a cure, but I was kicked out of Dr. Holmes's office."

Yeah...Lisa helped me write that out.

Margaret's smiled faded the slightest bit. "I'm sorry to hear that. Dr. Holmes takes his work very seriously. Unfortunately if he didn't invite you for a job in the hospital or lab, we'll have to find you some other work to do. Do you like gardening?"

"I'd rather be unemployed."

The plastic smile faded even more. "If you insist, but your housing will be minimal."

"Uh...how minimal?" I leaned forward.

"We'd put you in an apartment."

And they weren't kidding. The apartment they'd put us in was one bedroom, about 600 square feet and old as hell. Lisa was even angrier than before. I didn't mind the apartment, but she'd gone from living in a very nice house in Tehachapi to a tiny apartment in the middle of Colorado. What was worse was that there was only one bed – which Rex and Alex had to share. We got the sofa. Or rather Lisa got the sofa and I got the floor.

"This is no way for a newly married couple to live."

I reached up to hold Lisa's hand. She sighed and rolled onto her stomach so she could look at me.

"I know. I'm sorry."

"I think we should go back to Huntington."

I was quiet. There were no words that came to me in the form of a response. I wanted to make her happy more than anything, but...

"You want that job." She already knew.

"I've been dreaming about cars for months now."

She reached down and touched my face. "I'll go back to the lab tomorrow and wait there. I'll wait all day if I have to."

I smiled. "Atta girl."

*   *   *

My thoughts of worry about Lisa melted almost instantly when I arrived at work the next day. The garage was perfect. The concrete floor was dirty and grimy, the shelves were lined with crap and nothing was labeled. As I drew in a deep breath, smelling the exhaust and grease, I felt good. Great, in fact.

"Ah, shit, dude. You my replacement?" A large and intimidating blond woman approached me. And by large, I meant she was buff. Her voice was commanding as it bounced off the walls.

"That'd be me. Jack Reynolds." I held out my hand for her to shake. She took it and practically yanked it out of my shoulder socket.

After eyeing me for a moment, she squinted. "Reynolds, huh? Anyone ever tell you—"

"All the time. Where should I start?" I started to walk toward one of three cars in the shop, but she held out a strong arm and stopped me.

"Whoa, there, cowboy. I don't know nothing about you. You're too pretty. Can you even fix cars?"

I gave a condescending chuckle. "Can I fix cars...?"

She stood back, folding her arms. "All right. How would you fix a hard cold start?"

"Depends," I said. "Chokes may need cleaning or I might need to replace the spring."

She sucked her teeth. "Okay, that was an easy one. Replace an engine."

"Really?"

"Show me, movie boy."

I rolled my eyes. "Mark the bolts and remove the hood. Disconnect the ground cable on your battery. Drain the coolant and disconnect the hoses. Loosen tension or alternator pullies and remove all the belts. Then take out the radiator. Disconnect the intake and fuel lines. Gotta make sure the A/C and steering hoses stay connected when you unbolt the pump. Take out the exhaust manifolds and all connects to the transmission – unless you have a four-wheel drive. Because then you have to break it out with the engine. Jack up the—"

"I got it, I got it. You're good. Now help me figure out why this bad boy is knocking." She walked over to a 1975 blue Camaro in amazing condition. I could hardly contain my excitement as I looked under the hood.

"How's it breathing?"

"Fine. Dyno shows the right horsepower and all that shit. But it just fires wrong. Can't even describe it."

340

"How many cars have you turned on in here today?"

"Just this one."

I nodded, removing myself from under the hood and rounding the back of the car. The woman asked me what I was doing, but I didn't answer straight away. Upon opening the gas cap, I took a whiff.

"It's knocking because this dude put diesel in the fucking tank."

"No shit." The woman came around and put a hand on her hip. "You know I've been working on this thing for three days and you just solved it in five seconds by smellin' it."

I shrugged. "What do ya know?"

"Okay, familiarize yourself with the garage and then we'll fix more shit."

Before I knew it, five o'clock rolled around. I was so involved in what I was doing that I didn't even notice Lisa waiting for me at the front desk. Instead, my new intimidating friend Kelli yelled it at me from across the garage.

"Hey, Foxtrot. How'd it go with the doc?"

She sighed. "He wouldn't see me." Her features had gone from stressed to anxious. I could tell she was worried about something. "I sat there all day, but he never came into his office. They wouldn't let me roam around because the whole damn lab is off limits."

"Sheesh. Maybe you should go on a hunger strike."

One corner of her mouth curved into a smile. "I might."

Two Men and a Lift Auto Garage

"We Auto Know"

"Well, if you do, wait one more day, okay? I have a surprise for you tonight and it involves dinner."

December 26

 "So, the deal is that there's a watch rotation. All men in the city have to be a lookout once each month unless physically unable," Jack explained as we hiked up a long winding staircase inside what looked like a tower.

 "Okay."

 "My turn isn't for another week, but Kelli took me around at lunch today and I thought this would be the perfect spot for my surprise."

 "And what would this surprise be?" The night air felt great on my warm skin as we exited a doorway at the top of the stairs.

 "Surprises are no fun unless they're surprises." Jack tossed me a smile.

 Looking around, I noticed we were on top of the city wall. It twisted around the entire town, meeting the side of the hospital. It divided Braycart in two and we were smack in the middle. Jack took my hand and led me to a secluded corner of the wall. There were trees on both sides. Then, he spread out a blanket and we sat down to eat.

 "So, tell me about your day."

 I tossed my head back to look at the stars. "There isn't much to tell. I just sat around waiting. Alex and Rex made friends at school, though."

 "Oh, yeah?"

 I looked back at my husband. It felt so odd referring to him as such. But looking at him while he was watching me with such interest made my heart flutter.

 "Yes. They seem to be having fun."

"Good." Jack moved closer to me. I could smell his unique scent. It put me into a sort of numb happiness. I felt his fingertips brush my left arm. "I have something for you."

"What is it?" My breath caught in my throat as he kissed me.

"Look." He leaned back while holding onto my left hand. Then he brought my gaze to my own fingers where there was now a beautiful diamond ring sparkling at me.

Feelings welled up inside me. "Oh my God. It's stunning."

"You think so?" Jack was smiling.

"Absolutely." I kissed him. "Where did you get it?"

"We have a whole bin of items we trade for fixing cars. I found this and knew I wanted you to have it right away. I even used an engraving pen on the inside. It has our initials."

"I love it. I love you."

"Do you love me enough to have sex right here under the stars?"

I paused. "As long as no one's around."

"I'll take that as a yes."

*   *   *

Jack had finally lifted my spirits and I felt like a teenager as we walked back to our apartment where Alex was watching Rex. He held my hand and made me laugh. It was an important few moments for me. And then I saw the woman standing outside our complex. When she saw us, she approached me.

"Are you Lisa Reynolds?" She was pretty with light brown hair and green eyes. And while she was hugging herself – suggesting she was either anxious or cold – she held somewhat of an independence about her.

"Yes."

"Thank God. I've been waiting here for an hour. My name is Catherine Holmes. I'm Dr. Holmes's wife."

"I'll take these inside." Jack excused himself and left.

I turned back to Catherine. She seemed so much younger than Dr. Holmes. But the more important thing on my mind that moment was why she was at our home.

"Mrs. Reynolds, it took me a whole day to find you."

"What can I help you with?"

"Well, in short, my husband is an idiot." She gave me a weak smile. "You were the one who brought in the leg, right?"

"Yes."

She looked around briefly, then jumped on me with a tight hug. My muscles wouldn't respond fast enough to push her away, so I allowed it to happen. When she pulled back, she apologized.

"My husband understands how big of a break this is, but he's being an idiot about how to deal with it. He kept raving about the doctor who'd cut it off saying it was expertly done."

"But he didn't hire me." I felt the anger bubbling back up inside me.

Catherine looked at the ground. "Malcolm is very private. He means well, but he needs to realize that we're in it together. These are my children too."

I wasn't sure what she meant, but her tone suggested not to touch on the subject. "Is there a reason why you came here so late?"

She looked me straight in the eye. "I'm offering you a job at Malcolm's lab. I'm under the assumption that you have

346

some information that could help us and I'm not going to let that go to waste."

My anger faded completely. I almost felt as though a weight had been lifted form my shoulders.

"He's brought so many doctors here, but you came here yourself. I took that as a sign."

"Won't your husband be upset?"

She screwed up her face. "Not if he knows what's good for him. Besides, I'm right and he's wrong."

I could tell I was going to like Catherine Holmes. I invited her inside for some tea. She agreed with reluctance, letting me know she couldn't stay long.

"Oh, my God. Your husband *totally* looks like Ryan Reynolds." Catherine whispered the words to me across the tiny kitchen table while Jack made tea.

My synapses lit up. "*That's* what his name was!"

"Whose what name is who?" Jack came back to the table, sliding out a chair and sitting backward on it.

I could see blood creep into Catherine's cheeks which made me smile on the inside. "Oh, um… I was just telling Lisa that you look exactly like—"

"Ryan Reynolds? Yeah. I'm told that about eighty seven times a day."

Our visitor looked my way as if she wasn't sure whether or not he was joking.

"Okay, okay. It's more like eighty eight times a day, but who's counting?"

"Oh!" Catherine's surprise was followed by a bout of giggling. "I'm sorry… It's been such a long time since I've heard a joke. Malcolm and our two children are so somber all the time."

"So what did you do before the outbreak?" I asked.

Catherine glanced down at the table. "I was a model."

"Oh, really?" Jack seemed interested. "Have we seen you in anything?"

Catherine shook her head. "It was mostly magazine covers and such. But after I had my kids I had to stop."

We were silent for a moment until the tea kettle began to whistle. It startled Catherine who jumped a little. When Jack walked away, she leaned toward me, lowering her voice. "Just promise me that no matter what my husband says tomorrow that you stand up for yourself."

I nodded. "Absolutely."

December 27

The next morning, I waited patiently for Dr. Holmes to come into his office. When the door opened and he saw me, he gave a heavy sigh.

"Hello, Dr. Reynolds."

"Good morning, Dr. Holmes." I almost couldn't hide the tinge of superiority in my voice.

"I suppose I was wrong about you. My wife...informed me of your credentials, so I suppose I owe you a chance at this."

"Yes, you do."

"However..." He took off his spectacles and looked down his nose at me. "You have to do one thing for me."

"What is that?"

"Find me a cure."

I nodded. "I'll do my best."

"We shall begin with a tour of my facility."

"With all due respect, sir, I'd like to look at the dissected specimen I brought in."

Dr. Holmes waved a hand in the air as we entered the hallway.

"Later. Someone with your credentials doesn't need to be bothered with busy work." Dr. Holmes walked me down the hallway while explaining that the facility doubled as the town's hospital. The first three floors I could explore and work on cases as I saw fit as long as it didn't interfere with finding a cure. He informed me that I had complete access to the entire lab and hospital for whatever I needed.

"I must warn you that I believe having a personal life outside of work is what is going to help us. I don't want half-asleep employees. Therefore, you are required to only work

350

eight to ten hour shifts. But you must go home promptly at six." He looked me directly in the eye.

We stopped outside a door that read, "Authorized Staff Only" in large bold letters. It piqued my curiosity.

"What's in here?" I reached out to touch the card reader, but he grabbed my wrist.

"You do not have access to this room."

I sized him up for a moment. "With all due respect, Dr. Holmes, if I'm going to be working to find a cure, I'll need—"

"Yes. And you have access to the entire lab. Except this room."

I didn't argue further as I was eager to get to my specimen. The tour lasted longer than I would have liked, but I stuck to it. When we were finally back on the lab floor, he could see I was becoming anxious.

"All right, Dr. Reynolds, let's take a look at your specimen."

We entered the lab where the associates in white coats stopped what they were doing to watch us. I felt as though they knew who I was.

"Please bring out the slides of the leg."

At Dr. Holmes's words, one of the assistants scampered over to a locked cabinet, used his card reader to open the doors and took out a box of slides. My fingers felt itchy. I snatched the box as soon as it was handed it me and found the closest microscope.

The slides were unlabeled which irritated me, but I picked one out of the box without a word and slid it into the teeth of the scope. My heart beat like a jackhammer as I looked into eye piece.

And saw nothing.

I shut my eyes tight for a moment as if to clear my head and looked again. And again I saw nothing. Clearing my throat for fear of berating the poor assistants, I fished in the box for another slide. And found another slide of nothing but skin.

At that point, I became frantic. I plunged my hands into the box and slipped slide after slide into the scope's teeth, but each time, only flesh was visible.

"What is it, Dr. Reynolds?"

I'd had no idea Dr. Homles was still in the room when I slammed a fist down on the metal table.

"These slides are useless." I looked up at the assistants. "Where's the saphenous nerve? Where's the popliteal vein? There's nothing here but flesh."

No one said anything.

"Where's the leg?"

"It was destroyed," one of the assistants said.

"What was that?" I could feel the stress and anxiety rise up into my chest again.

"Protocol is that any and all specimens containing the disease are to be destroyed once dissected." Dr. Holmes approached the microscope.

I shook my head as if that would cause everything I'd heard to make any kind of sense. "I should have been the one to dissect the leg. I should have been here to oversee the slides. I can't do anything with what I have and now we're back to square one!"

January 1

It was a completely innocent night. My turn to be watch came up and I was excited to make new friends. What I wasn't expecting was to get handed an AK-47 and sent up to the top of the wall. That gun wasn't going to hit shit. The guy I was watching with agreed.

"Paul, let me ask you something, Paul." I pulled at the Kevlar vest they'd put me in.

Paul laughed. "Yeah, go for it."

"You *really* think this shit's gonna kill one of those Biters if they attack us?"

"You sayin' I'm a bad shot?"

"Nah, man. I'm saying these things suck. They spread. Sure, you can get a bigger target range, but your probability of hitting something is like, one in a fucking million."

Paul was quiet for a second. "Man…I don't know what the fuck you just said, but it sounded smart."

I felt a smile on my face. "I don't hear that nearly often enough."

The two of us sat back on a bench facing away from the open world. It was a rickety bench with one broken foot, but it was nice to get a load off.

"Your wife wear the pants in the family?"

I snorted. "We both wear the pants, man. Makes for an interesting living situation."

"She nag a lot?" Paul picked at a stray thread on his shirt sleeve.

"Nah." I leaned back and looked up at the stars. "She's amazing. Super smart. Super hot. And super wild in bed."

"That's what I'm talkin' about." Paul lifted a hand to give me a high five. I stared at him.

"That's my wife you're talking about, dude."

He lowered his arm. "Sorry, man."

I laughed and gave him a well-deserved high five. "Just kidding."

We sat for a few moments in silence. If we weren't on watch, I was positive we could have shared a beer. A light wind picked up. Someone at the top of a nearby tower shined a light at us.

"Your turn," I said.

Paul rolled his eyes. "It's just a security check."

"I know. But I don't feel like gettin' up."

Groaning, Paul stood and stretched his arms above his head. Then, he flipped me a thumbs up and walked toward the tower. I relished a bit of quiet while enjoying the cold wind. The bench creaked beneath me.

Once again, I tilted my head back to look at the stars. As I began to relax, I studied the constellations. It was amazing that even though the entire world had changed, the universe stayed exactly the same. We were just a speck of dust in an ever-expanding dark void.

Something suddenly didn't feel right. I felt like I was losing equilibrium. The stars weren't the same. They were falling. No. I was falling.

Two Men and a Lift Auto Garage

"We Auto Know"

The bench had tilted too far back. It couldn't handle my weight and I went tumbling right over the wall into the open world.

*   *   *

I had no idea how long it had been since I fell. I woke up to clouds covering most of the sky. My only light source was dampened by weather. I lifted an arm. Branches and twigs stuck to my sleeve. I'd landed in some bushes. Itchy bushes.

"Ugh." I groaned to myself as I stood to brush dirt off me. Luckily there were no Biters around. I stooped to pick up my gun. Swinging it over my shoulder, I took a good look at the area surrounding the town.

Grass and trees littered a small hillside. I could see down to where there probably used to be a small town. I imagined lights twinkling as people would be sitting down to dinner.

But I had no time to muse. I had to get back inside so I could continue the watch. I was halfway between the barbed wire defense and the wall when I heard someone call out. But it wasn't from inside the city or up by the watch tower. It was from outside.

I stopped in my tracks to listen. For a while, I heard nothing. Not even crickets. But then, I heard it again. A weak voice was calling for help. I looked around for some sign of a human being, but saw nothing.

Venturing closer to the barbed wire, I strained to listen once more. The voice came again, on my right. To my surprise, a woman was tangled in the wire. Some of her clothes were

356

shredded, but I couldn't see much as she was wearing darker colors. But her white skin contrasted with the black night. When she moved her hand, I rushed over.

"Don't worry! I'm coming! Hold on!" I ran over to the woman with the gun I'd been given bouncing against my back. Her choked cries became clearer as I neared. But when I got to her, she'd stopped. She was still. I bent forward to feel her pulse and immediately pulled away. She was ice cold. Had been dead for a while. A large chunk of flesh was missing from her left calf. She'd been bitten. And it looked as though it had happened ages ago.

Then whose voice had I heard?

I didn't have much time to think it over because a long sorrowful howl caught my attention. I squinted into the darkness, but all I could see was the faint light coming from the town gates.

And then a Biter appeared out of nowhere, coming out of the light and into the shadows toward me. It was fast. It was on me sooner than I could react.

"Oh, shit!" I fell backward trying to grab my gun and landed on my ass. Bringing the gun forward, I didn't have time for a cool catchphrase, so I just pulled the trigger.

And got nothing.

"Oh, fuck's sake! Seriously?"

The Biter was closing in. When he lunged at me, I swung the butt of the rifle into its head. A crack told me I'd made

contact and the thing fell to the ground in a convulsion. Shaking my head, I stood to see what the hell was wrong with the gun.

I checked it over. It seemed fine until I reached the magazine. The damn thing was stuck in place. My brain went straight to whatever-mode and I started toward the gates again.

Another howl caught my attention. But this time it was behind me. Right behind me. I swung around in time to see a Biter jump from a nearby tree onto my side of the barbed wire. Okay. It was time to fix the gun. While backing away, I pounded the magazine with my palm. Nothing. I tried the trigger again. Still jammed. I shook the damn thing, but that didn't work.

"*Help.*"

I stopped dead. The Biter had slowed down and was actually *grinning* at me. Those garbled scratchy words had come from it.

"*Help.*" The foam-tipped smile grew wider somehow. Then it made a half-bark, half-heaving sound. It was laughing at me while its throat convulsed from muscle spasms. It had somehow tricked me into thinking the dead woman needed help.

"Well, fuck." Without another moment's hesitation, I threw the AK-47 at the monster and turned tail to run. I heard the gun hit the thing, but it only slowed it down. I was almost at the gates when I felt its finger wrap around my wrist.

It appeared that someone had noticed my absence as there were watchers yelling for me at the top of the wall. They

were already getting ready to open the gates. I yelled at them to go faster, but the damn Biter sank its teeth into my shirt sleeve.

"Oh, come on!" I turned and kicked the thing in its stomach. At least I had steel-toed boots. It let go of me, ripping a chunk of fabric out of my nice new shirt, and fell on its ass just as the doors opened behind me.

I rushed the fuck inside as three other guys shut the gates behind me. I could hear the thing outside screaming and clawing at the metal. A gunshot rang through the air and all went silent.

*   *   *

"Watch the alcohol, man. That stings." I swiped at the nurse assistant's hand as she dabbed a cotton ball on the scratches running up and down my arms.

"Sir, you're lucky they let you back in. You were bitten."

"Bitten?!" Lisa's voice echoed down the hallway. When she saw me, she ran. I stood to receive her and she almost pushed me over. "You've been bitten?!"

I pushed her away lightly and showed her the hole in my sleeve. "Didn't break the skin."

She fell to her knees before me. "Thank God."

I went down and took her face in my hands, tilting her chin up until our gazes were level.

"I'm sorry," I said.

"Don't ever do that to me again."

Two Men and a Lift Auto Garage

"We Auto Know"

I laughed. "Don't worry. I'm a liability so they removed me from the watch permanently. Me and the bench."

January 7

After a bit of trial and error, we'd finally settled into a routine. Lisa would get up in the morning, get the kids fed and ready for school, then I'd get up and take them to school and go to the garage. It was refreshing to work again because it took my mind off the evils in the outside world. The town felt incredibly safe.

There was always plenty to eat and do once the city had upgraded our living arrangements from apartment to four bedroom house. Lisa kept busy most of the days and I'd usually be home before her. So I'd pick up the kids after school, bring them home and made sure they ate. I never would have thought playing house would feel so satisfying.

Unfortunately, the lab assistants had taken the leg and cut it into a thousand tiny pieces, destroying what Lisa had reviewed. The purpose was to make slides and see how the virus reacted to certain things, but they'd cut the wrong pieces and destroyed the rest. Now they had started at square one.

But at least we were happy. Stressed, but happy. Lisa and I didn't even argue about how to raise the kids. It was as if we fell into an instant rhythm.

One particular night, Lisa came home explaining Dr. Holmes' wife had had some sort of breakdown and was hospitalized. Therefore, the lab was shut down until further notice. I could tell it bothered her as she'd flit around the house trying to find things to clean. And she could not cook to save her life.

362

Two Men and a Lift Auto Garage

"We Auto Know"

The second week she'd been home by herself, she'd surprised me by picking up the kids and making dinner. I still have no idea what the hell she made. She said it was meatloaf, but it tasted like a yak that had been hit by a bus carrying twenty-five sweaty weight-lifters.

"Thanks..."

Alex giggled. "That sucks, Aunt Lisa."

"Well, my son seems to enjoy it." She eyed me while Rex shoveled food into his mouth with glee.

"Uh oh. I'm in trouble."

"Oooh." Alex's gaze darted between us.

"What should I do to make it up to her?"

Alex looked skyward and thought for a moment. "Dance with her."

"All right." I stood up and put out a hand. But Lisa just stared at it. I wiggled my fingers, but she just sat there.

"I don't know how you can have the energy to dance after not eating."

"Oh, my gosh!" I bent down and picked her up in my arms. She yelped. "I am so insensitive! Will you ever forgive me?" I twirled her in a circle as she gripped my arms.

"Put me down and I'll think about it."

Alex laughed. Rex joined in.

"I'll put you down when you promise to forgive me."

"I'm starting to feel queasy."

363

I laughed as I stopped dancing in circles. Her grip on me lightened. I took a good look at her face in the waning light of the day streaming through the windows.

"You're stunning." I kissed her. "But you can't cook."

Her eyes rolled toward the ceiling. "All right. I won't cook anymore."

"Rejoice!" I said as I set her down. The kids were still amused.

"In that case..." Lisa sat back down. "What on Earth am I going to do tomorrow? There are absolutely no new cases at the hospital."

"Maybe we should have a party." Alex suggested.

"For whom?"

"It's my birthday tomorrow, remember, Aunt Lisa?"

Lisa's hands flew to her cheeks. "Oh, no. I forgot, I'm sorry, honey."

"It's not your birthday tomorrow." I teased Alex. "It's mine."

A smile lit up her face. "We share a birthday?"

"I guess. How old are you going to be, twenty-five?"

She giggled. "Thirteen. Are you turning fifty?"

"Oh..." I clutched a hand to my heart. "That hurt."

*   *   *

"Hey, Reynolds!"

I looked up from the brake pads of a twenty-ten Toyota to see Kelli motioning me over to the front. "Yeah?"

"That little hot cookie is back for her Subaru. You better come deal with this one."

As I wiped my hands on a dirty rag, I chuckled to myself. Kelli sounded almost exactly like Silas. Sure, there was a faint sadness about the thought, but I pushed it away.

In the front of the shop was the young blond woman from the day before. She was fiddling with something in her hands. If it weren't for the outbreak, I would have assumed it was a phone.

"The Subaru's ready to go." I grabbed the keys from the front counter as she turned to face me.

"Oh, hey. Thanks." She flashed me a bright smile. "How much do I owe you?"

"We don't take money here. Got anything to trade?"

She lifted one shoulder in a shrug. "Sure." Her hand reached out to touch my arm. "I can do anything you'd like."

I couldn't help but laugh. "We don't trade sexual favors."

"Speak for yourself, MacGyver!" Kelli called from the back.

The girl smiled again. "What do you know. How about it?"

"Sorry. I'm married. Happily."

The girl scoffed. "It's the end of the world. How much can vows mean?"

"A lot."

Two Men and a Lift Auto Garage

"We Auto Know"

"Whatever." She picked up her keys and walked out of the shop. "I'll bring some clothes back."

"Nice doing business with you!" I still held a smile on my face. As the girl exited, Lisa walked by her. They stared each other down for a moment, but it was quickly over. "Hey, you."

"Hello. I felt bad that I didn't know it was your birthday so I thought I'd drop by."

I leaned on the front counter. "Oh, you made it up to me plenty this morning." Could've sworn I saw her cheeks redden just a little when I winked.

"What did that young woman want?"

"Which?" I stood straight.

"The one who just left."

I smirked. "To trade sex for car repairs. Can you believe that? Kids these days…"

"Yes. I can believe it. The party is all set up."

The change in conversation made me chuckle. "Already? We haven't been here long enough to make friends."

Lisa looked around the shop briefly. "Our lovely neighbor Barbara saw me tying a balloon to the fence and just insisted she take over the party. I swear the woman insinuated that I couldn't do it on my own."

"Now, honey…" I walked toward her with my arms outstretched. "Don't take this the wrong way, but…"

"But what?" She put both hands on her hips, effectively stopping me in my tracks.

"Well, I imagine you trying to find gray and white birthday invitations that just say 'it is your birthday.'"

She shrugged, her features softening. "I suppose that would be the most efficient way to propose a party. But that doesn't sound very exciting."

"Well, there you go."

"Hey! MacGyver, where'd you go? We got this POS to finish!" Kelli's voice boomed from the back.

"MacGyver?" One of Lisa's eyebrows rose.

"I fixed a bumper with duct tape and gum this morning."

"I don't understand the reference."

January 8

A series of loud bangs on the door stirred me out of a deep sleep around three in the morning.

Jack shot up in bed. "Yes, I want fries, you motherfucker!" After a few seconds of silence, he looked at the clock and groaned. "God...I miss fast food..."

The bangs came again. "Someone's at the door." I threw the covers off and stepped onto the soft carpet. Still bleary, Jack followed me out the door to the stairs. He continued mumbling something about French fries.

The door was practically rattling on its hinges as the banging continued. And then a voice came through. "Dr. Reynolds! Please, open the door."

I sighed. "It's Dr. Holmes."

"Christ..." Even though Jack was in nothing but a shirt and boxers, he sat down at the kitchen table while I opened the door for our dear doctor friend.

Dr. Holmes seemed flustered. His white hair was a mess with wisps of it matted to the sides of his head with sweat. He'd forgotten his spectacles somewhere and his blue eyes were wild. He pushed his way past me into the kitchen.

"I've decided to let you into the room."

I could feel the furrow in my brow. "I'm sorry?"

The doctor spun in a small circle, acknowledging Jack on the way with a nod. "You need to see what's in the restricted room."

"Dr. Holmes, it's three in the morning."

"It's important. Very very important."

I looked to Jack who simply nodded and waved me to go. Then he stood up to return to bed. "Nice to see ya, doc."

369

*   *   *

"As usual, my wife was right."

I look back at Dr. Holmes as we drove through the small town toward the lab. "I'm not sure what you mean."

"Do you know why she collapsed?" He made a sharp turn into the parking lot of the hospital. I held onto the armrest.

"No, I don't."

"Because of the leg." When we pulled to a stop, he looked me in the eyes. "She was very sure we'd found a breakthrough and I pissed it away."

"With all due respect, Dr. Holmes—"

"Oh, I wish you'd stop saying that. You don't respect me at all."

I was a bit taken aback, but that faded quickly. "While that may be true, I believe in second chances." We got out of the car and headed into the hospital. "But all of this would have been avoided if you'd given me the opportunity to study the specimen myself."

He waved a hand as we boarded the elevator. "Yes, yes, I know. It's all my fault and I should bugger off. I take responsibility for it. But understand, Dr. Reynolds..." He pushed closer to me as if someone else would overhear our conversation. "That leg may not be our only chance for a breakthrough."

The wheels in my mind began turning. "Something in that room is going to help us."

"It certainly may." We hopped off the lift on the fifth floor. After rounding the corner and coming to a stop outside the restricted door, Dr. Holmes gave me one last look. "Don't say I never warned you."

Skepticism rose inside me as the door to a dark room squeaked open. I couldn't see anything. And my hunch was that either Dr. Holmes was keeping something he shouldn't have been in there — like infected blood — or he actually had nothing.

But then the light flickered on. And in the steel cage at the center of the room, a very ill woman rose up and began to scream.

"Oh, my God..." I approached the cage with caution. The girl was young — she couldn't have been more than twenty. Her limbs jerked with uncontrollable spasms as she moved, jumping at the cage. She was trying to bite me. Dried foam dusted her chin.

"I just couldn't do it myself."

I spun around to look at Dr. Holmes. "What is this?"

"*She* is my daughter."

"My God..." I circled the cage while she watched me. She had an IV in one arm that was fastened to her with duct tape. "What are you giving her?"

Dr. Holmes approached the IV machine. "Some steroids and anti-inflammatories. It seems to have slowed the disease some."

"Some?" I cocked my head. "When was she bitten?"

"Six months ago."

My synapses fired at an alarming rate. "But that would mean..."

"Yes. My daughter is patient zero."

I was stunned into silence. None of the victims I'd treated at my hospital lasted longer than fourteen days. A few of them died before the incubation period had even transformed into symptoms.

"Does she have a chart I can see?" I held out my hand while still staring at the girl before me.

"Yes." Dr. Holmes shuffled around a bit and handed it to me.

I stopped reading after her symptoms. "Lord... She's pregnant?"

Dr. Holmes sighed. "Not anymore. We hoped the stem cells would repair damage, but instead the fetus aborted itself."

Scanning the chart for a second time, I looked for the pertinent information I already had, but it wasn't listed anywhere.

"Dr. Holmes, did your daughter suffer from insomnia?"

He paused. "Yes. How did you know?"

"Did you ever take her to a doctor to get diagnosed?"

"Well, no. she was seeing a therapist for nightmares due to a traumatic incident earlier the prior year, so we assumed it was that causing the sleeplessness. Why do you ask?"

I snatched a syringe from the desk nearby. "How do you subdue her?"

*   *   *

Seeing a victim up close so far into the disease was upsetting to say the least. It broke my heart to think Dr. Holmes had to watch his daughter delve into insanity with no cure. I reached for one of the fuzzy heads of the tranquilizer darts he'd punctured her with.

"Leave those." He put a hand on mine while looking me in the eye. "We learn things the hard way here sometimes."

I nodded. Searching her body, there were few signs of the disease present while she was unconscious. Her skin was slightly gray, but even the bite wound on her thigh wasn't necrotic. It was an open wound that hadn't healed, but it seemed that the doctor took good care of her. My heart skipped a beat in my chest.

I checked her eyes. Her pupils were heavily dilated. I felt as though I was an archeologist finding a rare artifact. No one had been able to study a living rabies victim so late in the stages.

"Her teeth are quite clean."

"I brush them when I can."

I looked up at him. "What's her name?"

His eyes became misted. "Victoria," he said quietly.

Taking a deep breath, I picked up a syringe and slid it into the vein inside her arm. There was a slight twitch which caused me to jump, but then her body settled.

"Tell me, Dr. Reynolds... What is the point of this?" There was a mild amount of hurt in Dr. Holmes's voice.

"I have a hunch that your daughter has Fatal Familial Insomnia. Are you familiar with that?"

"No."

I explained the disease and the theory I had while I collected the blood sample and helped the doctor put Victoria back in the steel cage.

"So I'll do some genetic tests and see if any of the prion proteins are folded. If they are, then we at least have our breakthrough and can go from there."

"How would we treat something like that?" His eyes pleaded with me.

I inhaled. "I don't know. But you've been doing *something* right if you've kept her alive this long."

He nodded. "We nearly lost her early on, but found that steroids combined with anti-inflammatory drugs slows the progress."

It took until eight in the morning and three phone calls to Jack to get the results of the tests. And my theory was correct. We had our breakthrough.

February 5

As days faded into weeks and we became even more comfortable in our environment, I could feel the hope emanating from Lisa. She was like a different person – finally doing what she loved and making a difference for the whole world. I was so sure that she'd find what she needed that when she came home one day stating happily that she'd combined two compounds that she was eighty percent sure would help clear up the advances stages of the disease, that I offered to take her out.

But she seemed nervous. "I really should check on my samples. There could be some movement."

I pulled her toward the door. "It's been, like, eight minutes."

"Twelve."

"Same thing. Let's go." I was finally able to get her through the door in a nice dress. And when we sat down to eat, I noticed she'd cleaned her ring. It sparkled in the pale light of the nice restaurant.

"So tell me what you found."

Her eyes lit up when I asked. "Okay. I dug my way through a lot of books and papers. Without Internet, medicine is very difficult to study. But I found that in 2013, a drug called tafamidis was shown to unfold proteins in the Thalamus. So that at least helps us treat the TSE. Remember when I told you about the TSE's?"

Two Men and a Lift Auto Garage

"We Auto Know"

I thought back to the day in the library at Huntington house. "How could I forget? You were wild." I touched her hand as she smiled. Our food arrived. She continued while we ate.

"So, I thought if we could unfold the proteins, that would give us access to at least treat the rabies virus. Obviously the vaccine won't treat the disease once symptoms show, but I have a hunch that using neurogliaform cells to target the specific neurons affected and shutting them down may be able to kill the virus. Then we can resuscitate those neurons with shock therapy."

After we shared a decadent dessert, I took her out to dance at a nearby bar. And even when I twirled her around the floor, she kept talking about the project. Even at home in bed, she couldn't stop going on and on.

"Can I read you my paper on Tourette's?"

"Say what?" I sat up on my elbows. The sheets tugged slightly away from her hips.

"You said I could read you my Tourette's paper after sex."

I screwed up my face. "Wasn't that like, eight years ago?"

She was quiet, her features blank.

"Can...you even find it?"

"Jack Reynolds, are you telling me no?" While her features were serious, there was a slight teasing tone in her voice.

"What? No!"

377

Shaking her head, she swung her legs over the side of the bed. "I suppose I should check on my specimen."

"Whoa, whoa, wait!" I caught her waist and pulled her back in to me. "Read it to me. I'm interested."

February 6

The next morning, I was eager to see what had become of my specimens. While the likelihood of anything significant happening overnight was small, I still held high hopes for it. A miracle, maybe. I managed to go into the lab relatively early. Only one other lab assistant was there aside form myself.

I turned on the lights as we entered at the same time. After setting down my things, I all but ran over to the cabinet to retrieve my work. I just couldn't wait to get everything out on the table under the microscope. I stuck a slide in and peered through the viewer.

And saw nothing.

I checked three more times, alternating the slides out. But there was still nothing. Had my sample been tampered with?

"Julie."

"Yes, Dr. Reynolds?" The other lab assistant approached me.

"Where are my specimens from yesterday?"

She paused, reading the label on the dish. "Those are them."

I took a deep breath, trying to assume that she knew how to read. "No, these are not mine." I lifted them to show her the labeled tape on the outer edge of the dish. In turn, she picked it out of my hand and turned it to face me.

"Three thirty-three?" I shook my head. "No. That can't be right. Someone switched the labels."

"What is it, Dr. Reynolds?"

I began to scramble, rustling through scattered papers and other arbitrary dishes of samples.

"This isn't my sample because there is no trace of the virus in—" I immediately stopped what I was doing and looked straight at the assistant. "Call Dr. Holmes now. I've found a cure."

*   *   *

While the lab assistants scrambled to combine the ingredients I'd discovered to have wiped out the virus, Dr. Holmes and I worked on his daughter's blood transfusion. It was a tedious process and we had to constantly ensure Victoria was sedated enough. By the end of the operation, half the day was already over.

While she was resting, I pulled a vial of blood and inspected it under the microscope. Absolutely no trace of the virus was visible. We'd done it.

"Before we contact anyone in the government, we'll need to test the vaccine," Dr. Holmes said.

"Of course."

"We must follow all protocols in order for this to be successful. You understand?"

"Yes."

"Can you please check on my daughter? I'm going to bring Catherine in right now."

"Absolutely."

As I walked down the hallway to the quarantine room, lab assistants applauded me. It felt odd to be congratulated for something that was entirely necessary, but I didn't want to spoil their good moods.

As I opened the door to Victoria's room, I prayed to myself that she would be stable. And what I saw was more than any of us could have asked for. She was sitting up in bed with her eyes open, sipping water.

"How are you feeling?" I tried to keep my excitement in check.

"Who are you? Where am I?"

"Try to relax." I took a seat in the chair across from her bed. "My name is Dr. Reynolds. You're in a town called Braycart, Colorado. About six months ago, you were bitten by a rabid animal."

"Holy shit... *Six months*?"

"Yes." I nodded. "The virus spread and became an epidemic. The entire world has been affected."

"I started the zombie apocalypse? That's kind of cool and a bummer at the same time."

"Well, as you can tell, we've been able to bring you out. Are you feeling all right?" I moved to check her vitals.

"Oh, yeah. A little hungry."

"Great. Your heart sounds greats and your blood pressure seems steady."

"Where's my dad?" Her voice grew soft.

"He's just gone to retrieve your mother and he'll return shortly."

"Oh."

"I can get you something to eat. What would you like?"

"Ugh, anything." She rolled her eyes to the ceiling. "I'm starving."

I managed a smile. "All right then."

"Dr. Reynolds."

I turned. "Yes?"

"What's going to happen to the world?"

After a moment of silence, I said, "We're going to save it."

*   *   *

Even though Jack knew the good news, I dreaded going home that night. I had a decision to make and it wasn't a simple one. As I walked through the door, I could hardly contain the sting of tears when the smell of a flavorful meal hit me.

"Welcome home, hero." Jack was at the stove with a spatula. I stayed in the doorway until he turned around. "You ready for...? What's the matter?"

He must have seen the serious look on my face because I could feel it. "Jack."

"Hey, you got amazing news today. You aren't happy?"

I took a deep breath. "Jack. We need to talk."

"What's up? Did something happen? Did the girl relapse?"

I shook my head. "No."

He wiped his hands on a dish towel, but stayed at the stove. "What is it?"

"The only way to make sure the vaccine gets out is with animal testing then human trials."

"Okay."

"But animal testing can take decades."

Jack's face went blank. "Lisa..."

"We have to skip straight to human trials."

There was a silence between us that stretched out too long. "Please tell me you didn't..."

My trained etiquette wouldn't allow my gaze to fall to the floor. All I could say was, "I had to."

"What do you mean, you had to?" Jack's voice dropped to a low tenor – a sure sign he wasn't happy. "You didn't have to do anything. You've done plenty already. Now tell me you didn't inject yourself with an experimental drug that could kill you!"

"I'm sorry."

Jack put his hands to his face. "Oh, my God, Lisa. Are you...are you fucking serious?" His voice began to rise. "You're telling me that you're totally okay with abandoning your family for an experiment?! Did you stop for one second to think about your own son? How I'm going to have to take care of him now? How am I going to tell him his own mother would rather sacrifice herself to her job?"

"I did think of you." I kept my voice low and calm, but Jack let out an exasperated laugh.

"At what point? Before or after you slid the needle into your arm?"

"Jack, please."

"No, Lisa. Seriously. What were you thinking?"

"I was thinking about you!" I couldn't hold my tone down any longer. "I was thinking of you and Alex and Rex! I was thinking of all the people who've lost loved ones to this completely preventable disease. I was thinking about how I could fix everything with a small sacrifice."

"Small?! How is this a small sacrifice?"

"The needs of the many over the needs of the few."

Jack's eyes narrowed at me. "You'd rather break our hearts than let someone else volunteer."

"No. I'd rather sacrifice myself than bring this upon any more people."

He rubbed his hands over his face. "That was really...really stupid." Emotion flooded his voice as his entire body deflated. "I don't know if I can take care of two kids on my own."

"Jack. I'm confident this will work."

He sniffed. "Your confidence usually gets me through a lot. But right now...it's not much to bank on."

I tilted my head to one side and approached him, laying a hand on his arm. "Will you come be with me while I'm quarantined?"

His eyes squeezed shut as a sigh escaped him. "How could I not?" His voice was soft. "Let's go."

February 5

It took everything I had to keep it together while the kids were with us. When we arrived at the lab, Dr. Holmes and three other assistants were waiting. I tried not to glare at the doctor, but it was difficult.

They prepped her by putting her in a gown and showing her to the quarantine room. It was a tiled area with a bed and bathroom. A large window filled the wall for viewing purposes.

Lisa stopped to say farewell to us. Alex kept as strong as she could while hugging her aunt. But Rex was busy playing with his toy cars on a nearby bench. She bent to speak to him.

"Rex, sweetie? Mommy is going to be gone for a while, okay? You won't see me for a few days."

"A few days." He repeated her statement without giving her eye contact.

"I love you, baby boy." She attempted to give him a kiss on the head, but he leaned away. I felt awkward, but it was just another day in the life of the two of them. She stood as though it didn't faze her. But as she walked away, Rex looked up and called to her.

"Love you, momma. Miss you, momma."

Lisa smiled then turned to me. I swallowed hard as her gaze bore into mine. The woman I loved more than I thought possible was leaving. She might come back or she might die. I had no idea. We had to wait three agonizing days to find out.

"I guess I'm...not allowed to kiss you, right?" I asked, touching the side of her face.

She shook her head. "I'm fine while in the incuba—"

"Good." I interrupted her by pulling her entire body into mine for a long kiss. It was one I wasn't going to let her forget. All my emotions flooded out of me and into her. I wanted her to feel how much she meant to us.

"Come back to us." I whispered the words as I pressed my forehead against hers.

"I will."

The door closed in my face. I moved to the glass window. She pressed a hand against it and I did the same on the opposite side. My chest felt hollow as if my heart had followed her in there. I had a bad feeling.

"Oh." I turned to find the bag she'd brought with her. After rifling through it, I brought out a book and handed it to Dr. Holmes. "Her journal. She likes to write it in and document everything. Will you make sure she gets it?"

He nodded. "Of course."

*   *   *

The next day, I pulled the kids out of school and called in sick to work. It was useless, though since the entire town knew what was going on. I felt like an experiment myself. Everyone was watching us and trying to give their support. But I didn't want it. I wanted my life back. It got to the point where I was wallowing in so much self-pity that Alex made me go to the lab to see Lisa.

At first, they told me she needed to rest, but I told them that was bullshit, so they let me watch her on a grainy monitor.

She seemed okay – she mostly walked around aimlessly or laid in the bed.

"You wife's a very brave woman." Dr. Holmes stood next to me.

I sighed. "Yeah. We're not so much. Honestly, Doc, I don't know how you let her do this."

"Me?" He looked at me as though I'd called him a terrible name. "I told her not to mess with it. I told her we had to follow protocol. She did this of her own accord."

We were silent for a moment, watching Lisa fiddle with the tray of food she'd been given.

"As a matter of plain fact, I was on my way back here to do exactly what she'd done."

I looked at the doctor. "You should learn to drive faster."

He hummed a half-agreement. "I understand you're frustration. You may see her for a moment, but I'm afraid we need a controlled test area."

*　　*　　*

A loud clang echoed through the garage followed by a loud curse from me.

"MacGuyver, that is the third time you've dropped that wrench in twenty minutes and it's getting on my fucking nerves. What the hell is wrong with you?" Kelli stood over me like the Great Wall of China.

She screwed up her face. "The fuck did you just say to me?"

Oops. Guess I'd said it out loud.

"And why the hell are you back here? This car just needs an oil change!"

I waved her off and trudged toward the front of the car. Alex must have heard the commotion as she'd left Rex with his book and came over to help.

"And just what do you think you're doing, little lady?" Kelli's angry toned turned down to a stern motherly scolding.

"Uncle Jack taught me how to change oil. I can help."

"Is that so?" Kelli looked at me.

"Yup. Better believe it." I patted the girl on her head.

My boss eyed me. "Have you...have you been drinking, movie boy?"

"Me?" The wrench slipped out of my hand again. "I'm gonna change my last name to Daniels."

I thought it was funny. But she didn't. So, I spent the next thirty-six hours either sitting by the phone waiting for that fateful call or wallowing in self-indulgence. Kelli even took the kids to stay with her until, in her words, I got my shit together.

I hated to tell her that "my shit" left when Lisa injected herself with a deadly virus. Then I got called selfish. Then I got slapped. I think. I can't really remember. I do remember my face hurting pretty badly once I got back to the house. But that could have been because I tripped on the sidewalk or something.

My entire body was starting to feel itchy. I had to do something. So I left the house and walked until the lab came

into view. Then I marched straight up to the fifth floor and into the viewing room. There, I watched the most beautiful woman I'd ever met throw things at the glass window inside the quarantine room.

And I immediately sobered up.

"What the hell is going on?" I burst into Dr. Holmes's office.

He stood. "Mr. Reynolds. Please calm down."

"Don't tell me to fucking calm down! My wife is rabid, isn't she? Isn't she?!"

Dr. Holmes put up his hands. "Relax. She's fine. She's just a bit irritated at being cooped up. She's still eating and drinking fine. There are no signs of the virus. Not even a fever."

That quelled my anger enough to sit in a chair next to his desk.

"Would you like a cup of coffee?"

"No." I spotted the journal sitting on the corner of his desk where I'd left it. "Wait...why haven't you given this to her?"

He looked at it, pondering its existence. "Well...I didn't quite see the point."

I stood up again. "You didn't? And why not? No, no, wait. Don't tell me. Because you don't think she'll make it out of there."

The doctor cleared his throat. "Mr. Reynolds..."

"Stop treating me like I'm a baby who needs a bottle."

He straightened. "If you insist. With our track record of mishaps in this lab, I truly give the situation about a twenty-five percent chance of succeeding."

"Oh, Jesus Christ." I gripped the side of his desk.

"Until your wife came along. With her track record, I'd say there's an eighty percent chance."

I pushed my hair back with both hands while groaning. "You should probably have led with that, doc."

"I'm sorry."

"Don't they teach you bedside manners in medical school?"

"Well, I actually wasn't a doctor before the outbreak. I—"

While holding a hand to my chest, I held the other in front of me. "Please, doc. No more revelations. I don't think my heart could take it. I also don't think your face could."

"Duly noted." Dr. Holmes put both hands behind his back. "Now then, Mr. Reynolds, you've got...twelve more hours. Would you mind terribly...?"

I rolled my eyes. "Yeah, sure..." I turned to leave right as his office door slammed open. One of the lab assistants stormed in.

"Dr. Holmes! Dr. Reynolds has lost consciousness!"

I didn't even hesitate. I didn't even ask. I just followed them all down the corridor. There was no way in hell I was going to let my wife die.

February 8

My stomach was churning. I felt ill. Fog filled my brain. Everything was dark. I couldn't escape. I supposed it was how I went. Nothingness.

But slowly, my surroundings came to me. The faint beeping of a heart monitor. The hum of fluorescent lighting. When I opened my eyes, white replaced the black. I could hardly move. Grogginess filled my senses.

I rolled my head to the left. Sunlight streamed through a tall window. A vase of orange flowers sat on the bedside table. Then I noticed the shackle. It was taught around my left wrist. I still wasn't out of the water.

I struggled a bit against it to get comfortable. That was when I woke Jack. He'd been asleep against the bed, bent over in a chair. When he saw me, he jumped up and gave me seven kisses.

"Jesus...I'm so glad you're okay."

"How long have I been out?"

He glanced at the leather bands. "About ten hours. They want to keep you restrained for a few more."

I nodded. "Sounds about right."

Jack slid a hand underneath mine. "I was so scared."

I squeezed. "Everything will be okay."

The door opened to Dr. Holmes holding a clip board. When his gaze met mine, his eyes widened in what I assumed was surprise.

"Ah, you're up."

"How are my vitals?"

Dr. Holmes chuckled. "My dear, you have no trace of the virus in you. I've already attempted contact with what's left of

394

the government and the CDC. I'm hoping to receive notice of their cooperation any day now."

Excitement bubbled into my chest. "That's fantastic. Can we undo these things, please?" I lifted my hands as far off the bed as I could. Jack and Dr. Holmes helped me out of them.

"There is one more thing."

Jack and I both froze.

While checking his chart, the doctor scratched at his chin. "We found elevated levels of human chorionic gonadotropin in your blood. Do what you wish with that information. I'll leave the two of you alone to discuss it."

As soon as the door closed, Jack looked at me with concern written all over his face. I could tell he was scared to death that something was wrong.

"What does that mean? Are you sick?" He seemed to search me all over for signs of something.

"No."

He stopped and sat on his heels. "What's going on?"

"Jack. HCG is a hormone your body makes when it's pregnant."

He opened his mouth to say something, but quickly closed it once again. We were silent for a few seconds, just reveling in the hum of those lights.

"What...are you talking about right now?"

"I'm pregnant."

"Holy...shit."

"I'm open to discussion."

"Discussion of what, Foxtrot? If this means I'm gonna be a daddy, then I'm all for it!"

*　　*　　*

A few days later when the CDC finally arrived, there were only three men left in the entire organization. After a few talks, it was established that only those just bitten would be given the cure as the others were too far gone.

The vaccine would be distributed as denoted by birth month. The schedule allowed survivors to be done in just three short months, this giving enough time for the current infected victims to die off.

Jack, Rex and Alex were the first to receive the vaccine. The others I administered to almost every person in the town. The three months passed as if it were days. And even though there were discussions of what we'd do once let free, we never really settled on a definite plan. But the day those doors opened were bliss.

May 17

Now what do we do? No idea. The four of us are just having fun running around in the grass for a while. The sun is shining and a light breeze is stirring. To be honest, there's nowhere else I'd rather be. Lisa says the same.

I found a nice spot to sit. Looks like it used to be a fountain. It's empty now and crumbling with weeds sticking out of its cracks. I can see Lisa at the gates still. She's just ironing out a few details I guess.

She's done now. And coming toward me. God, she's beautiful. Even more so now that we're free. She sits next to me and I give her just a little kiss. It's little because there's more to come. We have our lives ahead of us now. And she agrees this is a life now.

Rex and Alex are running around after each other. Rex already has grass stains on his knees. Lisa says something about how she'll have to wash them again.

And she laughs. It's such a heart-warming sound. She laughs because she realizes it's a ridiculous statement. It's ridiculous because now we can be normal again.

I watch her. Her hair is moved in wisps by the wind. Her face is serious — hands folded in her lap and watching something that doesn't really seem to be there.

"What are you thinking?" I ask.

She looks at me with a smile. "About how amazing this all is. The grass, the trees. I feel like I've taken nature for granted."

The kids laugh in the background.

I put my arm around Lisa as I write. "Hey. We're a family now. And ever growing."

She touches her slightly rounded stomach. "Another baby. I honestly never thought it would happen."

"Yeah," I say, "it's a miracle."

She looks at me with that skeptical raised eyebrow. "I don't believe in miracles."

I laugh. "Of course you don't. You never studied religion in college."

She turns back to look at the kids. "No. I didn't."

"Light! Light!"

We turn back to watch as Rex and Alex seem to be looking at

399

[END SUMMARY]

Page intentionally left blank.

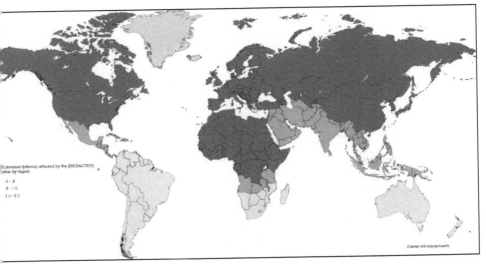

Figure 1.1 – Map of epidemic: estimated damage 5.5 billion

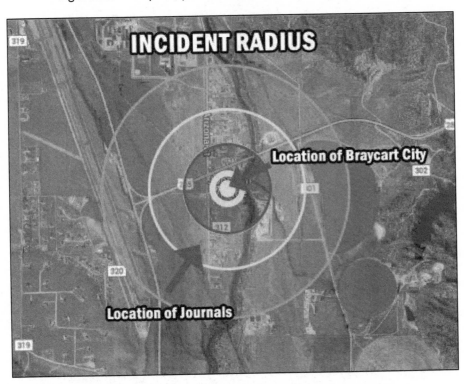

Figure 1.2 Radius of incident near Braycart City

Figure 2.1 Image of Braycart City – inside wall

Figure 2.2 Image of Braycart City following incident.

MISSING

LISA JAMES

AGE: 31 YEARS OLD
SEX: FEMALE
HEIGHT: 5 FEET 5 INCHES
WEIGHT: 125 LBS
HAIR: BLACK
EYES: BLUE

MISSING FROM:
TEHACHEPI, CALIFORNIA

DATE MISSING:
AUGUST 15TH

IF YOU KNOW OF HER WHEREABOUTS OR HAVE ANY INFORMATION, PLEASE CALL SOLEDAD POLICE

Figure 3.1 Missing poster for Lisa James

Figure 3.2 Missing poster for Jack Reynolds

Made in the USA
Charleston, SC
05 June 2016